Estelle Ryan

The Sirani Connection

The Sirani Connection

A Genevieve Lenard Novel

By Estelle Ryan

First published 2019

Chapter ONE

"PHILLIP? WHAT'S WRONG?" The concern in Vinnie's voice jerked me out of studying the data on Francine's computer. I straightened from where I was leaning over the infamous hacker's shoulder and turned to Vinnie, our investigative team's self-assigned protector and my best male friend. A deep frown pulled his brow down as he stared towards the elevator. I followed his gaze and inhaled sharply.

Phillip Rousseau, owner of the high-end insurance company in the building adjacent to ours, shuddered when the elevator door closed behind him. He shook his head as if to clear it and walked towards me. He ignored Vinnie repeating his question, as well as Manfred Millard, the only law enforcement official in our team, shoving his chair back as he jumped to his feet.

In the nearly thirteen years I'd known Phillip, there had been only four times that I'd seen him this distressed. Today was the fifth.

He'd offered me employment when everyone else had balked at my non-neurotypical bluntness and lack of social skills. It had taken many years before I had allowed myself to accept his uncomplicated affection.

Because I'd come to view him in a paternal role in my

life, the severe disquietude I now observed on his face immediately brought the blackness of a shutdown to my peripheral vision. I forced myself to focus on reading his nonverbal cues. Engaging my mind intellectually often aided in preventing a shutdown.

His *orbicularis oculi* and *orbicularis oris* muscles lowered and brought his brows together. His upper eyelids were raised and tightened, his lips a thin line. Confusion, anger and fear.

He stopped in front of me and allowed me to study him for a while longer. I swallowed and blinked a few times. "What happened?"

"I'm not sure."

"Truth." There was no denying the honesty in his immediate answer, his open hands lifting as he shrugged.

"Enough." Manny walked to the round table in our open-space team room and pointed at it. "Sit down so we can talk." He shook his finger when no one moved. "Now!"

Manny's rudeness jerked Phillip out of the internal processing I was witnessing on his face. He took a staggered breath, pulled his shoulders back and nodded at me. "I'm rattled, but I'm well, Genevieve."

I shook my head. "Clearly your definition of 'well' is not congruent to mine."

The soft smile relaxed his facial muscles. "Likely." He turned towards the round table when Manny knocked loudly on it. "Shall we?"

Only when Francine got up from her chair next to me

did I remember her presence. A few minutes ago, I'd reprimanded her for yet again hacking into a foreign government's database in our search for an Iranian fugitive. I'd been rather disappointed in her, even though I hadn't been surprised. Now I found myself grateful for her steady presence beside me.

She pushed me with her shoulder. "Come on, girlfriend. Let's hear what this is all about."

I nodded once and joined the men at the table. Vinnie had moved to the small kitchen on the far side of the team room. He was putting his homemade oat cookies on a plate while waiting for the coffee machine to fill another mug with the steaming beverage.

No sooner had I taken my usual seat at the table than Colin sat down next to me and took my hand. It had taken me many years before I'd grown accustomed to being part of a team. More than that, being part of this group of friends.

But it was Colin's unconditional acceptance of me that grounded me on a daily basis. He squeezed my hand lightly, but didn't say anything. He'd told me numerous times that he knew I was capable of handling any situation challenging my autistic mind. He only wanted to remind me that he was there whenever I needed him. I'd come to depend on that predictable reassurance more and more each day.

"Well?" Manny slumped in his chair and jerked his chin at Phillip. "What is this thing that has you so rattled?"

"I received an email this morning." Phillip smiled when

Francine jumped up to grab her tablet. She returned to the table already tapping and swiping, no doubt accessing his email as she did all of ours. Privacy was a very loose concept to Francine, especially when it pertained to our safety. Phillip sighed. "At first I thought it was yet another spam email and was about to delete it when I decided to open it."

"Never a good idea." Francine looked up from her tablet. "How many times do I need to tell all of you to never open an email if you don't know who sent it?"

"And how many times must we tell you that Phillip can't ignore potential clients?" Vinnie put a laden tray in the centre of the table. "You bore me with your repetition, Franny."

Francine's eyes widened, then she looked at me and grinned widely. "See what he did there?"

It took me eight seconds of staring at Francine's expectant face to understand their humour. I sighed. Vinnie was teasing Francine with a phrase I often used. The difference was that I never verbalised this in jest.

I turned away from Francine, whose smile was widening. As much as I valued these people in my life, it was most tedious when they constantly went off topic. I leaned towards Phillip. "Who sent the email?"

"I don't know." The corners of his mouth turned down as he turned to Francine. "Can you forward it to everyone? I didn't think to do that. I just came here immediately."

Francine tapped her tablet screen twice. "Done."

Different notification sounds filled the team room. I

shifted to get up, but Colin's hand tightened around mine. "I have my phone. You can read it here."

I would've preferred to use my own phone or tablet, but both were in my soundproof viewing room. Colin was already holding his phone for me to look at the email Francine had sent.

"Will someone read this out loud?" Vinnie shrugged and took a cookie from the plate. "I'm too lazy to get up now."

"It's not a written email. It's an audio file." Francine put her tablet on the table, crossed her arms and stared at Phillip. "Opening an email from an unknown source is one thing, but opening an attachment? Seriously, Phillip. It could've been riddled with malware."

Manny straightened. "Is it?"

"No." Francine's long silver earrings jangled as she shook her head. "That was the first thing I checked." She looked back at Phillip. "You're lucky."

"I don't know so much about that." Phillip pointed at her tablet. "I have no idea who these people are. There are two voices and I've never heard them before. At least, they're not voices I remember ever hearing."

"And the email address is not helpful either." Colin pointed at the anonymous-looking numbered address.

"What the bleeding blazes?" Manny tapped his smartphone screen, his top lip curled. "7833X2-on@TPZ.com?" He looked at Francine. "Isn't this the type of address you people use?"

Francine blinked in mock innocence. "What people?"

She smiled when Manny's lips thinned. "Hackers use addresses that won't identify them, but so do CS bots."

"English, woman."

"Some large corporations have an automated customer service system that answers questions." Phillip smiled at Francine's impressed expression. "I had someone offer such a system to me, but I prefer to be old-school and have business queries answered by a real person."

Francine's smile disappeared. "You should never open attachments."

Again they were digressing. I leaned forward. "Can you trace this email address?"

Francine tapped her tablet screen. "It doesn't have tracking data." She looked at Manny. "In your Queen's English, you can usually right-click on an email's header and look at the original data, which will give you the IP address of the sender. Put that into an IP tracker and voilà! You know in which city, even on which street the sender lives."

Manny fell back into his chair. "Every time I hear this, I consider going back to pen, paper and postage stamps."

"Aw, that's so romantic." Francine fluttered her eyelashes. "But way too slow for this chick." She looked at me. "I'll see how far back I can trace this email."

I nodded. "Play the recording."

"Okey-dokey." Francine tapped her tablet screen twice and sat back.

"Police arrested Tomas Broz last night." The male voice sounded young, but I wasn't good at gleaning much information from auditory input only. I needed nonverbal cues to fully interpret neurotypical communication. My skills at interpreting words and tone of voice were limited, my expertise in nonverbal communication a learned skill, not a natural talent. I folded my hands on my lap and stared at them while I listened for any clues I might catch. The young man chuckled. "Can you believe the idiot had an Elisabetta Sirani hanging on his wall? His wall!"

"Stop." Manny sliced his hand through the air and the young man's chuckles were cut off when Francine tapped her tablet screen. Manny turned to Colin. "Who is Tomas Bronze and who is this Elizabeth?"

"How interesting that you assume I would know."

"Frey!"

Colin smiled. "Strangely enough, I do know who they're talking about. Tomas Broz? I'm surprised to hear that he's been stealing again. He's been out of the game for a while."

Colin had built a reputation as one of the top art thieves in the world. Interpol had relied on his skill and status in the art crime world for many years to help them in operations that were most often legally dubious. With our investigations into art and other crimes the president of France sent our way, Colin's knowledge and insight into this criminal field had proven invaluable more than once. He looked up at the ceiling for two seconds. "The last time I heard anything about Tomas was"—Colin's eyebrows rose and he smiled—"when the *Venus and Cupid* by Elisabetta Sirani was stolen in Berlin three years ago."

"Is this Eliza Siri worth anything?" Manny asked.

Colin gave Manny an irritated glare and turned to Phillip. "As far as I remember this painting was valued at a hundred thousand euros, right?"

"It was sold at auction for one hundred and thirty-seven thousand, five hundred US dollars to be exact." Phillip narrowed his eyes. "The owners wanted Rousseau & Rousseau to insure this piece, but I… I had a bad feeling about the deal, so I declined."

"Hmm." Colin leaned back and stared at the ceiling. "Elisabetta Sirani has become trendier recently. There are not many female artists who have had such an impact on how the world perceives women who paint and sculpt. She founded an academy for other female artists in an era that was very male-dominated. Male artists like Rembrandt, Vermeer, Rubens and Caravaggio monopolized attention and funding. Female artists didn't always find their way as easily. With recent awareness of the disproportionate lack of women in senior management positions and the rife discrimination against and, sadly, abuse of women, she became iconic to women in the art industry.

"This has brought a lot of attention to her works—masterpieces which were bought by nobility, royalty and the wealthiest of that time. This painting specifically is an amazing example of her later works. The sweet and intimate scene of the *Venus and Cupid* shows Sirani's mature style and also what placed her works in such high demand. And with price tags to match the interest and quality."

"Is this what has you so worried?" Manny asked Phillip. "That you almost insured that painting?"

"No." Phillip looked at Francine's tablet. "There is a lot more on that recording."

Manny nodded at Francine and she tapped her tablet screen.

The young man's chuckle ended. "They found this idiot in Prague. Apparently the painting will be given back to the family this week."

Manny grunted, but shook his head when Francine went to pause the recording.

"At last, we get a break." The female voice which replied had a husky quality to it, her diction sounding refined, educated. "I should just go to Prague and speak to this thief. I'm sure I'll find out more and hopefully get closer."

"Shall I book a ticket for you?"

"Book two tickets. You're going with me."

"I am?" The excitement in his voice was unmistakable. He cleared his throat in an attempt to sound unaffected. "I am. I will book those tickets now." It was silent for two seconds. "Um… what about the other thing?"

A loud sigh sounded. "I haven't decided yet."

"Just set up a meeting and talk to him." The young man's voice was gentle and sounded sympathetic.

The woman snorted. "And say what? No. I'm not going to email Phillip Rousseau…"

Her sentence was cut off so abruptly that we sat in stunned silence for three seconds.

"Where's the rest of it?" Manny's glare snapped from

Francine's tablet to Phillip. "What did she want to email you about?"

"I don't know." Phillip pulled at his collar. "I listened to the recording three times before I came here. I also checked if I had any other emails from this address. This is the only email and the only recording I've received."

"He's right." Francine was working on her tablet, shaking her head. "There's nothing else here. Just this recording and it ends on one mother of a cliffhanger."

"There was no mention of cli…" My shoulders drooped. It was not often my friends used euphemisms, metaphors and other easy-to-misinterpret expressions when I was around, because I took it literally almost without fail.

Francine smiled and winked at me.

"Why on God's green earth would you receive this odd recording?" Manny's scowl deepened.

"Ooh! Let me answer that." Francine waved her hand in the air, her eyes wide with excitement. When Manny sighed and raised one eyebrow, she lowered her hand and leaned forward conspiratorially. "AI."

Chapter TWO

MANNY UTTERED AN ANNOYED sound after two seconds. "If you're trying to piss me off, it's working. Talk."

"You ol' charmer, you." Francine held up both hands, laughing. "Okay, okay. I'm talking about artificial intelligence. A few months ago, someone received an email from a work contact that contained a recording of a private conversation similar to this."

"I read about that." Colin narrowed his eyes. "Wasn't this Alexa or Siri or one of the AI systems that registered words in that conversation as commands and then sent the recording?"

"That's exactly what I'm referring to."

"Now in my Queen's English." Manny was no troglodyte. This was his way of gaining more information. I had considered this method to be ineffective, but on this he had proven me wrong countless times.

Francine smiled at him. "There are many artificial intelligence systems available on the market nowadays. Systems that can run an entire home so you can enjoy all your smart home features, systems that function when activated by certain command words to record dictation or order food from your favourite restaurant or shoes from your preferred online shop."

"You think this is what happened?" Phillip pulled at his cuffs. "Her AI system emailed me when she said that she was not going to 'email Phillip Rousseau'?"

Francine nodded. "I'll bet all my earrings that this is exactly what happened."

"And you are sure you don't recognise the voices of these people?" Manny asked.

Phillip took a moment to consider his answer. "I can honestly say I don't. If I've ever spoken to them before, I don't remember her accent. I would like to think that I would've remembered her unique voice and the eloquent confidence I hear..." He shook his head. "I don't remember her."

"She didn't sound very confident about emailing you." Just because I hadn't heard it didn't mean it wasn't there. I wanted to understand.

"Hmm... no, I don't think it's a lack of confidence. She sounded unsure, nervous even." Phillip thought about this some more. "Confident about the theft, but nervous about me."

I leaned back. "That is a lot to surmise from those few sentences."

"I agree with Doc. It will be better if we can find out who she is and what she wants with you."

I tilted my head and carefully catalogued Phillip's nonverbal cues, ignoring the conversation flowing around me. He was rubbing the nape of his neck, his breathing was irregular, shallow and he adjusted his cuffs much more than usual.

"This see—" I nodded apologetically to Francine when I realised I'd interrupted her. She smiled back and rolled her hand in a gesture to continue. I turned back to Phillip. "This seems to be a mere mention of your name. Yet you are extraordinarily distressed. Why?"

Phillip dusted both his sleeves as if to remove specks of lint. He didn't often employ any form of self-soothing. His lips tightened. "There is something in her voice. I know you want something definitive, but I can't give it to you. It's a feeling. I hear something and it worries me."

"I hear that too." Francine shrugged when I looked at her. "That woman sounds nervous and excited and relieved all rolled into one sexy phone voice."

My *levator labii superioris* muscle lifted my top lip in disgust at the last part of her sentence. It took considerable effort to focus on what was relevant. I hadn't heard any of these emotions they were talking about. Interpreting someone's tone of voice was not my strength. I decided to keep my focus on my expert skills—nonverbal communication.

I trusted Francine's intuition when it came to understanding emotions. She'd proven time and again that she understood much more than what people were saying with their words alone. "You attributed emotions to this woman's statements. Nervous, excited and relieved. Not angry? Scared?"

She was shaking her head before I even finished my question. "Oh, definitely not angry. Not scared, not in the we-are-all-going-to-die kind of way. Rather nervous, like she's going for a job interview she really, really wants."

"Is she?" Manny asked Phillip. "Are you recruiting? Interviews with applicants?"

"No, I'm not hiring new people." Phillip took his phone and swiped the screen a few times. "But talking about interviews—" He tapped his phone screen, then shook his head. "I don't have any interviews with magazines or anyone booked for the next month. So it can't be a journalist."

"It might be that she needs your help as an insurer," Colin said. "It might be as simple as that. Occam's razor and all that. Maybe she bought a forgery or she lost a piece of art and needs professional assistance."

"Nah." Francine wrinkled her nose. "I tell you now, it's not that simple. This feels personal."

Phillip didn't have to say it. I could clearly see he agreed with Francine. I'd known him long enough to assume his reluctance to confirm her suspicions was borne from always acting logically after considering the facts. Yet he never discounted his own intuition about people.

Neither did I. His accuracy in reading people and situations had proven to be unerring.

"Well, you can feel as much as you want." Manny lifted his hand to stop Francine when she inhaled to speak. "Hunches won't help us legally and you know this. We need cold, hard intel."

"Of course we do." Francine lifted her tablet and shook it. "I'm already on it. I'll have Husky Voice's name and favourite ice cream for you before you get annoyed again."

"You're annoying me already."

I sighed. "Can we discuss the part of the conversation that sounds like they are investigating something?"

"We can't assume that they are investigating the Sirani theft just because they are talking about Broz." Colin looked at the ceiling for two seconds, then looked at me. "What do you think?"

"I don't know yet." I didn't. I also wasn't going to speculate.

"Huh." Vinnie tapped his chin. "Yo, Frannie. You might want to narrow your search for private inve—"

"Already on it." Francine rolled her eyes, then looked towards the elevator as it pinged and opened.

"Tiny punk!" Vinnie got up and walked towards the twenty-three-month-old child running out of the elevator into our team room. So young, yet his nonverbal cues were unmistakable as his eyes widened and his smile lifted his cheeks. He ran to Vinnie, his arms raised.

Vinnie caught him and lifted him high in the air. The result—squealing giggles. I smiled.

For a man who'd started a criminal career in his teenage years and had built a continent-wide reputation for callous criminal behaviour by the time he'd turned thirty, Vinnie showed none of that ruthlessness as he swung Eric into the air again.

"Well, hello to me too." Nikki struggled into the team room, raising her shoulder awkwardly to keep the sling of her canvas bag from slipping down her arm, her hands clutching bulging shopping bags. The responsibilities of motherhood and of her art restoration job had not made her any more organised or less messy. The bun on top of her head was a perfect example, half of her hair no longer contained by it.

She walked to the round table and put all the bags on it with a rustle and a loud sigh. She shook an angry finger at the plate with two remaining cookies. "Don't tell me you've eaten and now you don't want Chinese."

"No worries, punk." Vinnie walked to the table, with Eric on his hip. "I made sure everyone only got two cookies. Think of them as appetisers."

"Humph." She opened one of the three brown paper bags with familiar logos on them. "Lunch is served. The rest of this stuff is all for that little goblin."

"Not little for much longer." Colin smiled at Eric. "He's getting bigger by the day."

Eric noticed me and immediately started wriggling in Vinnie's grip, his arms reaching towards me. Vinnie laughed and put Eric down. "Go on, tiny punk. Run free!"

Eric ignored everyone's chuckles, only focused on running around the table to where I was pushing my chair out. Nikki often joked that Eric never walked, he only ran at full speed. It certainly looked like that as he made his way to me, his hands outstretched and his face lifted in a genuine smile.

A quick inspection of his hands revealed no grubbiness. I was relieved that I wouldn't have to worry about a major transfer of germs. I caught him as he threw himself against my legs. He grabbed my thighs and lifted his foot to get leverage to pull himself onto my lap. "Dohgee. Up. Dohgee."

"I love that he calls you that." Francine laughed as I picked Eric up and settled him on my lap to face the others. Nikki had moved into the flat I shared with Colin five years ago when she'd still been a minor and her father had been killed while we'd investigated a case that involved him and his illegal activities. Since the first day, she'd called me 'Doc G'. Eric had only recently started speaking his first words, so it had not been surprising that he couldn't separate sounds. The closest he got to my name sounded far too similar to 'dodgy'. For now I allowed it.

Eric didn't like the position on my lap and turned around to look at me. He stared into my face for a long time, gripping my shirt with both hands. He studied me with an intensity that made me smile and he reacted immediately. His face lifted in a happy, toothy smile. After a few moments, he wriggled around to face the others.

Francine gave Nikki a quick hug and helped her unpack the many takeaway boxes.

"I haven't seen you in ages." Nikki turned to me, her smile soft as she looked at Eric. But then her eyes narrowed as she looked around the table. "Something tells me I interrupted a serious discussion." She straightened, her open palm pressed against her chest. "Did you find Shahab?"

"No." I wished we had. It had been eleven months since we'd met Shahab Hatami and discovered that he had been importing heroin into Europe for over nine years. Not only that, he'd also been involved in the smuggling of Near Eastern antiquities—a crime that his police unit had been investigating.

It had been a shock to his unit leader to discover that one of their own had been involved in these crimes as well as the brutal murders we'd been investigating. Even worse, Shahab had been smuggling drugs and art while enforcing the law with highly trained officers. For years, he'd been the team member everyone had relied on. Not only for his tactical skills, but also his more advanced IT skills.

"We're stuck." Francine pushed the Chinese food my way and opened a box that I assumed contained her most recent favourite—duck chop suey. "We know more than we did ten months ago, but not much."

"We have three more victims than we did a year ago, but that fu"—Vinnie looked at Eric—"bad man tortured and killed those people soon after our case last year."

"He tortured only two." I despised incorrect reporting. "One he executed."

"That was his lawyer, right?" Nikki asked.

"Hmm." Manny nodded. "Didn't think he would do that to his own lawyer. But he's not been active since. And those later victims and crime scenes didn't give us anything extra to go on." He exhaled angrily. "All in a bloody nutshell. Dammit. We need to find that man."

Phillip nodded. "I agree. Finding Shahab and stopping him from torturing and killing more people takes priority. This email can wait."

Nikki sat down and looked at Phillip, then at me. "What email?"

"Franny reckons Phillip received an email sent by an AI," Vinnie said.

"By accident, I might add." Francine glanced at her tablet. "I'm pretty sure they didn't actually want Phillip to hear that conversation."

"Oh, come on!" Nikki grabbed chopsticks and shook them at Francine. "You're killing me with your hints. Give me the low-down. Uh. That is if I'm allowed to know."

Phillip reassured her there was nothing classified about this email and asked Francine to play it again. After wiping her hands, Francine tapped her tablet screen. I absently stroked Eric's denim-covered legs and listened even more attentively to hear any inflection or intonation that might confirm what Phillip and Francine had heard in the woman's voice. I didn't hear that.

What I did hear was an accent close to mine. An accent shaped by living in different countries where English was not the first language. Now living in France, I spoke French fluently, but the times I did communicate in English, I'd learned to temper my accent to make my pronunciation clearer, easier for people to understand. But this observation was too speculative to share with the others.

"Ooh! Elisabetta Sirani!" Nikki looked at Colin when the recording ended. "How cool is that?" An immediate frown followed her enthusiastic outburst. She turned to Phillip. "I suppose you've been over this, but do you kn—" Her shoulders slumped when Phillip shook his head. "Thought so."

Francine put her tablet next to her takeaway box and picked up her chopsticks. "I'm running a search, but have very little to go on."

"Huh." Nikki looked at Colin. "What do you make of the art angle?"

"Nothing more than what is being said." Colin smiled. "I've only told them the basics about Sirani. Want to tell them more?"

"Ooh, yes!" Nikki straightened. "She's part of the 27 Club, also called the Forever 27 Club."

"Nikki." Colin shook his head.

"I was not being disrespectful. She died when she was twenty-seven like many other very famous people." She counted on her fingers. "Jimi Hendrix, Kurt Cobain, Janis Joplin, Amy Winehouse."

"These were all musicians," Francine said.

"There are more. Jean-Michel Basquiat was a famous neo-impressionist and graffiti artist, but yeah, most of the club members are musicians." She smiled at Manny's frown. "More about the artist, gotcha. She was born in Bologna in 1638. Her father was a painter like her and also an art merchant.

"Her father wasn't keen on training her at first, but then he taught her the way of Bolognese painting. When her father could no longer work because of gout, she started running the family workshop and landed up supporting her whole family, three siblings and all."

"She was prolific," Colin said. "She produced over two hundred paintings, a few etchings and hundreds of drawings."

"And she was one of the few female artists of that time to depict male nudity in her *Ten Thousand Crucified Martyrs*." Nikki sat back in her chair and sighed dramatically. "She's like only my favourite Italian Baroque artist."

"I thought it was Caravaggio." I closed my eyes, then sighed and stared at Nikki. "Stating that someone is your favourite implies there is only one favourite. Be accurate and say she is one of many."

"Aah." Nikki's expression softened. "I really miss you, Doc G. The last two weeks have been too busy. Pink and I will come over for dinner tonight." She winked at Eric sitting quietly on my lap. "We'll even bring him too."

Nikki and Pink shared an apartment two floors below the apartment I shared with Colin, Vinnie and his partner Roxy. Pink was given this an inane moniker, yet he was a very capable young man who was part of the top GIPN team here in Strasbourg. Similar to the SWAT teams in the US and the SCO19 teams in the UK, GIPN had become an integral part of our investigations in recent years. After six years of working together on numerous cases, I'd come to consider the team leader, Daniel Cassel, a close friend.

My eyes were drawn to Manny when he shifted in his chair. He scratched his stubbled jaw and looked at Nikki. "Don't stay too long. Doc has to pack."

"I do?" Panic pushed down on me. Any change in my

carefully planned schedule caused me great anxiety. My hands tightened on Eric and he turned around to look at me. I forced myself to relax.

Manny nodded as if confirming a decision. "Yes. We're going to Prague."

Manny's expression was unusual. I studied his non-verbal cues.

"Ooh, goodie! Prague." Francine clapped her hands, but then stilled. "What about Shahab?"

"We're not getting anywhere with him at the moment." Manny's tone hardened in frustration. "Five weeks and we haven't unearthed any new intel. We can take two days to find out what this bloody robot email is all about."

Phillip pulled his shoulders back and lifted his chin. "No. This email sent to me is definitely not a priority. Finding a terrorist is much more important than this."

"Nothing is more important than family." Vinnie pushed his empty meal box away and lowered his chin as he looked at Phillip. "You're family and that's all there is to this."

Phillip swallowed as colour slowly crept up his neck. He nodded once at Vinnie. "Thank you."

"Let's not forget about the art thief and the stolen Sirani," Francine said. "This is right up our alley."

She was right. Our team worked directly under the supervision of the president of France. He only assigned a few cases to us, giving us discretion to investigate select cases. Most of these involved art crimes to some extent, some of these leading us to more sinister crimes.

My eyes widened and I turned to Manny to confirm my sudden suspicion. "The president has already spoken to you about this case."

"What? Dude!" Vinnie lifted his chin and peered at Manny through narrowed eyes. "Why didn't you say something earlier?"

"Don't 'dude' me." Manny shifted in his seat. "The president received a phone call from Prague asking if we could take a look at this case. It sounds like they have a suspicion that there is more behind Broz's theft."

"You're a sneaky bastard, Millard." Colin crossed his arms. "Why didn't you take this case on?"

Manny shrugged. "We're looking for Shahab and I know Doc doesn't like travelling. And they already have the painting and the thief."

"All this is true." I pointed at Manny's face. "But this is not the reason you didn't take the case."

"Oh, my God!" Francine burst out laughing. "Oh, this is priceless. Oh, oh."

"Franny!" Vinnie was smiling, his frown one of curiosity.

Francine took a breath and giggled. "Manny had a… well, let's just call it a"—she raised both hands to make air quotes—"'situation' in Prague a few years ago."

"Enough of that for now." Manny slapped one hand on the table and straightened. "I'll tell the president we're taking the case."

"Ah, man!" Nikki sighed dramatically. "This sucks big time. Prague. I wish I could go."

"Says the chick who just returned from two weeks in

Rome for work." Francine's emphasis on the last words indicated her doubt that Nikki had indeed been in Rome for work.

I knew Nikki had worked ten hours a day while there. She'd only managed to sightsee the day before she'd returned.

"Hah! I knew you were jealous." Nikki laughed. "Okay, I feel a bit better now for having to stay in boring ol' Strasbourg without you guys."

"When are we leaving?" Francine tapped a manicured nail on her lips. "I will need at least two hours to pack."

"Let me liaise with Prague and speak to Daniel." Manny looked at Phillip. "Most likely, we will leave in the morning."

Only when Colin put his hand over mine did I realise I was gripping the arm of my chair. His smile was gentle. "We'll drive if you want. It's only a six-hour drive."

Immediately relief flooded my mind. I had no fear of flying. It was sharing an enclosed space with too many other people and their countless germs that brought intense panic at the mere thought of entering a plane.

That and the sudden change to my routine. The only unchanging constant was Colin's presence and the space he gave me to decide how to handle changes.

"Road trip!" Vinnie's hands fisted in a celebratory manner. "Hey, can I choose the music?"

Eric mimicked Vinnie by throwing his small fists in the air and babbling. Everyone laughed. I didn't.

I didn't want to change my routine.

Chapter THREE

I WALKED FROM THE hotel bathroom into our room for the third time, fighting hard against the panic pushing down on my brain. We'd arrived thirty minutes ago after six hours and forty-seven minutes on the road.

We had left Strasbourg twelve minutes past four this morning. Twelve minutes late. I'd been most annoyed at Roxy for pulling Vinnie back into their bedroom. He'd joined us in the living room fifteen minutes later, his cheeks slightly reddened and a genuine smile lifting his cheeks. I'd been vexed.

The journey itself had been uneventful. Vinnie had slept most of the way, declaring us boring. Colin and I had debated the sense of Daylight Saving Time for two and a half hours before we'd found acceptable middle ground on the topic. I still maintained it was counter-productive, since it had been proven that the human circadian clock never adjusted to the time change, which resulted in a drastic decrease in productivity and quality of life and an increase in susceptibility to illness due to fatigue.

Our hotel was in the historic part of Prague between Kinsky Garden and the Vltava River. To the north of us was the breathtaking St Nicholas' Church and north of that the majestic Prague Castle. The famous Charles Bridge was a twelve-minute walk from our hotel. I didn't know if we would have time to visit the fourteenth-century structure or any of the other historical and architectural marvels.

I looked around our room and considered the elegant décor. When I'd asked Francine how she'd met the owner's son, she'd changed the topic to talk about the many benefits of all of us living on the luxurious eleventh floor. The hotel had designed this floor with team conferences in mind. There were seven rooms, all leading to a central living area and small kitchen.

Francine had claimed the largest room for her and Manny. Her reasoning was that she deserved it after getting us such a great discount. It was only five percent. I didn't care. The room Colin and I stayed in was more than spacious enough. It was the cleanliness that had me walking back into the bathroom.

I leaned over to study the chrome towel rails, looking for fingerprints or any other hint that this space had not been meticulously cleaned.

"Anything?" Colin walked into the bathroom and lifted a towel. "Hmm. Tielle towels. I'm impressed. I checked the sheets and agree with Francine's boasting that they have at least a thousand thread count."

"Oh, cut it out, you two." Francine walked into our room and stopped outside the bathroom. "This place is fabulous. Dawid told me his dad sent in the team with steam cleaners and God knows what else to make sure there's not a speck of dust anywhere."

I straightened and frowned. "That would be impossible. Only in a vacuum would one be able to…" I sighed. "It's clean."

Francine's smile crinkled the corners of her eyes. "As my conscience."

"Okay, now you went too far." Colin chuckled and waved his hands at her. "Shoo. Let's go to the living room."

"That's why I'm here." She turned and walked through our room. "Manny the Moaner wants us together before Daniel brings his buddy here."

"Why is Manny moaning now?" Colin asked as he held out his hand towards me. I looked around the bathroom one more time, but knew I wouldn't find anything untoward. I took his hand and followed him out the room.

Vinnie was rummaging through the cupboards in the small kitchen. He looked over his shoulder and snorted. "Manny the Moaner. Good one, Franny."

"He wants to sleep next to the window." She lifted one shoulder. "I want that side."

"Why? Don't you always sleep on the right-hand side of the bed?"

"She does." Manny was sitting on one of the three dark blue sofas, his top lip curled. "But now all of a sudden, the side closest to the window has better internet reception. As if I would believe such nonsense."

"It's not nonsense. You saw that I had more bars on my

phone when I was standing by the window." Francine didn't even attempt to conceal her deception. I'd seen this far too many times. She was teasing Manny. More than usual.

After years of watching their interaction, I'd learned that Francine did this when something had upset Manny. For a moment, I considered asking whether it was related to this case, but decided against it. If it were pertinent, Manny would tell us. Most likely, Manny had been annoyed by slow service at the airport. Another reason I preferred travelling by car.

Francine sat next to Manny as Colin and I settled on one of the other sofas. Vinnie closed the fridge door, joined us and sided with Francine, escalating the argument. Their bickering always seemed to ground them, to be a form of focus. Academically, I understood the psychology behind that. Personally? This strategy made no sense.

I was growing bored with their quibbling and was about to reprimand them when the door to the suite opened.

Daniel Cassel walked in, followed by a dark-haired man. This had to be Daniel's friend here in Prague. Manny had informed us last night after his call to Daniel that he would be joining us to liaise with his counterparts here in Prague, especially his friend, who held an important position in law enforcement.

Colin's muscle tension increased and Manny slumped deeper in the sofa, his scowl deepening as they both stared at the stranger.

"Guys, this is Ivan Kemr." Daniel stood to the side and

waved his guest forward. "Ivan, this is Colonel Manfred Millard, Francine, Vinnie, Doctor Genevieve Lenard and Colin."

Colin got up and shook the newcomer's hand. "Pleased to meet you. How do you fit into this investigation?"

"Oh, sorry." Daniel huffed a laugh. "Ivan used to lead an URNA team here. Like our GIPN teams."

"Until this happened." Ivan lifted his left hand and nodded towards it. Scar tissue covered most of the back of his hand. His fingers were slightly crooked and looked stiff. I wondered if the damage to his vocal cords that made his voice sound like a harsh whisper was related to this injury. Such damage occurred when someone screamed for an extended period. His smile was genuine when he lowered his hand. "Now I'm a detective and the art theft case is mine."

Even though he was of average height, his posture made him appear taller. In this sense he was similar to Daniel and his team. The training these men and women received kept their bodies in peak condition, enabling them to respond to situations that would tax the average person's physical condition. It was clear Ivan had maintained his fitness level despite it no longer being essential for his job performance.

"Ivan is being modest," Daniel said. "He's one of the top detectives and runs a specialised unit."

"Specialising in what?" Manny's scrutiny could easily be construed as hostile. He was evaluating Ivan.

"Well, we fall under the NCOZ—the National Centre

against Organised Crime." Ivan rubbed the scar on his hand. "Our unit does a bit of everything though. We generally take on cases that are out of the norm."

"What does that mean?" Manny's eyes narrowed.

Ivan looked at Manny for a long moment, then nodded as if he'd come to a conclusion. "We're kind of doing what you guys are doing."

"Ivan and I have been friends for twelve years." Daniel pointed at the third sofa and waited until Ivan sat before he joined him. "We met when we worked a joint operation many moons ago."

"Both of us were still seconds in command." Ivan's English was accented, but he exhibited no discomfort communicating. He nodded at Daniel. "Now you have your own team."

"And you have two." Daniel punched him lightly on the shoulder and smiled at us. "Ivan's second team is three teenage boys and an amazing wife."

"Yeah, three boys who are eating me into bankruptcy, but you are right about the amazing wife. I have no idea why she puts up with me."

"She knows how to manage her men." Daniel grinned. "Ivan's oldest son is passionate about rap music."

"And he wants everyone to listen to it with him." Ivan shook his head. "So my wife decided the only way to allow him to have his own taste in music and not cause war in our house is to soundproof his room. Guess what I did last summer?"

"He did an amazing job. He soundproofed three rooms

for the boys." Daniel stretched his legs out in front of him, crossing his ankles. A position revealing a feeling of safety. He trusted Ivan. "The two youngest offered to share a room so I can have one of theirs. I hear myself breathe when I sleep."

"Breathe or snore?" Francine laughed when Daniel's smile dropped and he mock-glared at her.

Ivan wasn't listening to Daniel and Francine as they joked about sleep disturbances. He studied me for three seconds, then turned to Manny. "I know about some of the work you've done. Your investigations are always quiet, but you've done a lot of good. How much do you know about this case?"

Manny looked at me even before Ivan finished talking. "Doc?"

I was familiar with his expression and his question. "Ask Daniel."

"I'm asking you."

"I've seen no deception. Daniel clearly trusts him. Enough to sleep in his house."

"Genevieve is right. You can trust Ivan." Daniel sat up and leaned forward. "I do."

"Hmph." Manny gave a curt nod and looked at Ivan. "What did Daniel tell you?"

Ivan's gaze didn't falter as he looked at Manny. "He only told me that you've taken an interest in a case in my jurisdiction that involves Tomas Broz."

I leaned forward and stared at Ivan.

A rueful smile lifted the corners of his mouth. "Okay,

full disclosure. I asked for you guys to come and help us. This is an important case and Tomas Broz is proving to be quite uncooperative. I thought we could do with your expertise."

"You have such authority?" Manny asked.

Ivan lifted one shoulder in a half shrug. "I'll ask for forgiveness later."

"Why would you ask us here if you have the thief and the painting?"

Ivan rubbed the scar on his hand. "There's something off about the case. I want to make sure we're not missing anything."

I didn't observe outright deception, yet Ivan's micro-expressions made me pay even closer attention. He was withholding information from us, but his hesitation made me wary. People like Ivan—in law enforcement—were naturally reluctant to trust. I wanted to confront him about whatever he was not sharing with us, but decided against it. I first wanted to see how much he was going to share without interference or encouragement. Or threats, if Manny were to become vexed.

Manny stared at Ivan, then nodded. "Daniel, tell Ivan about the email."

I was pleased with Daniel's concise briefing. He added details to create context, but didn't waste time with anything that was not germane. This briefing also afforded me the opportunity to further study Ivan and establish a baseline for his nonverbal cues.

Ivan leaned forward, resting his elbows on his knees.

"Can you tell me more about the email? Have you been able to trace its origins?"

"Yes, Franny." Vinnie raised both eyebrows as he looked at Francine. "Do we know that woman's favourite ice cream yet?"

Francine flicked her long brown hair over her shoulder and sighed. "No. I haven't been able to pinpoint her location."

"Bloody hell." Manny turned and scowled at her. "What have you been doing on your computers the whole night then?"

"Tracing the email and narrowing searches." A small smile lifted the corners of her mouth. "I'm impressed with the security this chick has. I mean, it's much more sophisticated than most large companies'."

"PIs would have strong internet security," Colin said.

"Absolutely." Francine sighed again. "Look, I chased that email the whole night. I lost count how many countries it bounced through, but eventually I got to Germany."

"City?" Manny asked.

She shook her head. "Only Germany. Sorry. But that helped me narrow my search for PIs in Germany. There is no law that regulates internal or private investigations. As far as I could find, there are a lot of investigators without any reference or registration of any kind—not even as a business."

"A dead end." Ivan nodded. "It looks like PIs in Germany are the same as here. Most of them try to stay completely off the radar."

"Why?" Daniel asked.

"To protect their clientele, right?" Colin smiled when Ivan nodded. Then his smile dimmed when Ivan's eyes narrowed and he studied Colin closer.

"Dude." Vinnie slapped his hands on his knees and smiled when he pulled Ivan's attention away from Colin. "Maybe you have some ideas how we can find PIs who don't want to be found."

"Here, sure. But I have no jurisdiction in Germany." He looked at Francine. "Do you?"

"I have what I need." Her confident yet ambiguous answer convinced Ivan. Not me. I knew her deception cues.

Manny grunted. "Just keep looking."

"And don't dismiss other possibilities." Often people became so focused on their ideas that they stopped looking for alternative answers. "She might not be a private investigator at all."

"Preach, sista." Francine winked at me, then pointed at her tablet. "I have a few more ideas I'm running here."

Ivan leaned forward to look at Francine's tablet. "When you have time, I would like to hear how you decide what kind of searches to run."

"It might be best if you don't." Manny lowered his chin and stared at Francine. "Keep it clean."

"Sir, yes, sir!"

It was interesting to watch Ivan's curiosity grow. What interested me even more was the contradictory emotions that flashed over his face.

"Why are you confused and disappointed?" I pushed

back into the sofa when everyone's heads turned to me, their expressions varying from shocked to angry.

"What is she talking about?" Manny shook his index finger towards me, but his glare was solely for Ivan.

It didn't intimidate him. Instead, he smiled as he looked at me. "Your reputation does you no justice. Your astute observations are both impressive and quite… well, they're quite scary."

"Answer her!" Manny's voice boomed through the room.

Ivan's eyes moved to the ceiling for a moment before he turned his attention to Manny. "Daniel contacted me last night, so obviously you guys didn't know about this, but when you arrived this morning, I was sure you would—"

"Bloody hell!" Manny glared at Daniel. "Make him speak."

Ivan's smile was apologetic. "I'm sorry for not getting to the point immediately. We found a homicide victim."

Francine jolted upright and started swiping and tapping her tablet screen.

"Go on." Daniel twisted on the sofa to face Ivan.

Ivan looked at Manny. "A jogger found a body in Kosire-Motol Park this morning."

"Why would you think we would be interested in your homicide?" Manny asked.

Ivan rubbed the scar on his hand and rolled his shoulders, not succeeding in loosening the tightness still visible. "It's the second body we've found in the last three days."

An unwelcome tightness formed around my chest, constricting until it felt like I couldn't breathe. "Are their deaths connected?"

"Obviously, the forensic team as well as the medical examiner still have to do their jobs, but I'm one hundred percent sure they're connected."

"There's more." I could see it clearly on his face.

Ivan inhaled deeply and nodded. "There were a few specific things about the placement of their bodies that caught my attention. Especially when we found the second victim this morning. So I entered it into our database."

"And found nothing." It was becoming increasingly easy to read his facial expressions.

He nodded again. "So I put it into Interpol's database. I wish I'd checked after we found the first victim. But I only went to Interpol's database this morning. We might have been able to prevent there being a second victim."

This was fascinating. Why would Ivan tell the truth about checking Interpol's database, but lie about the day he did it? I filed it away for future reference.

"Oh, my God!" Francine bounced on the sofa, her eyes wide as her fingers flew over her tablet screen.

"For the love of all that is holy." Manny rubbed his hands hard over his face. "What now?"

"There's enough evidence to make me think that the victims have something to do with the murders you had in Strasbourg last year. And your suspect Shahab Hatami." Ivan jerked back and blinked a few times at the expletives that exploded from Manny and Vinnie.

"That motherfucker is here?" Vinnie jumped up from the sofa and walked to the kitchenette and back. The scar running down the left of his face stood out against the red anger in his cheeks.

"What evidence?" I shuddered at the memory of the horrors of those murders. The three young people who had been murdered by Shahab Hatami had been viciously tortured before their bodies had been disposed of in public parks. His other victim had been left in her home where she'd died.

A sense of failure pushed at me. I had wanted to stop Shahab before any more people died.

"Broken fingers." Ivan closed his eyes for a moment, then exhaled heavily. "Taken to a second location. Signs of torture over a period of days. Also, this morning's victim was found just off a path in a popular hiking spot. Like in Strasbourg, the dumping site is a public place that will ensure discovery, but not too crowded that he would be caught red-handed."

"Bloody hell." Manny sank back in the sofa. "That sounds like Shahab's work."

"Is the crime scene—" I stopped when Ivan nodded.

"I locked everything down when I made the connection this morning, knowing you were here."

Manny swore, then got up and snapped his fingers in my direction. "Move it, Doc. We've got a crime scene to go to."

Chapter FOUR

COLIN FOLLOWED IVAN'S dark blue SUV into a tree-lined road. The narrow road curved to the right and we slowed down. Ivan turned left into a private road and we followed him through an open gate, tennis courts on our right. The road ended with only forest ahead and Colin parked behind Ivan. I had spent the entire twenty-seven-minute trip mentally writing Mozart's Flute Concerto No.1 in G major to aid me in ignoring the argument in the back seat.

"If Franny's side of the bed has a better connection, I want that room. The internet in my room is barely enough for a good video call with my Roxy."

"Oh, for the love of all the saints." Manny shoved open the door and got out.

Vinnie leaned over Francine towards the opened door and inhaled to continue the argument that had been going on for most of the drive here, but didn't get the opportunity. Manny slammed the door so hard that Colin's SUV rocked.

Vinnie sat back and huffed. "Well, that was rude."

Francine snorted and hopped over to the door Manny had slammed and also exited the car, Vinnie getting out with a chuckle.

Colin squeezed my knee. "Good to go?"

I cleared my throat. "Yes."

"Okay, then." His smile was soft. "Let's do this."

We got out the SUV and Vinnie uttered a content sound when he stretched his neck first to the left, then to the right. "Man, it's pretty out here."

The weather was surprisingly warm for this time of the season. The thermistor in the SUV had measured the temperature at nineteen degrees. Thermistors were notoriously inaccurate, and standing outside, the real temperature felt closer to fifteen or sixteen degrees. Still pleasant though.

Francine and Manny were standing with Daniel and Ivan. We joined them and looked at the greenery in front of us. "Tell me about the park."

Ivan looked at the forest, his smile genuine and proud. "This is one of the few surviving examples of Prague's Baroque era. There is a maze of paths that a lot of people refer to as Alice in Wonderland paths. This park is a favourite for people who want to be close to nature, but don't have the time or means to leave the city."

He must've noticed my impatience, because he started talking faster, his smile fading. "There are a few statues, but what we are going to now is the Poustevna Hermitage. It's small and the history is not important now, but this is our crime scene. I got a call a few minutes ago to tell me the medical examiner finished his work here. We can go to the scene. The ME will do a full forensic autopsy as soon as the body is in the morgue."

"The victim?"

"He was tortured. Badly. The ME's preliminary finding is that this man died from exsanguination. He was dead when he was dumped here."

It was well-hidden, but it was there. I didn't like speculating, but I was convinced Ivan knew I could see he was hiding something from us. He glanced at me every time he caught himself touching his neck, crossing his arms or covering his mouth when he answered. I gave myself more time to observe before I would challenge him with this deception.

"Blood loss. So there is a primary crime scene somewhere drenched in blood." Manny pushed his fists in his trouser pockets. "Holy hell."

"Do you have a name yet?" Francine's hand hovered over her tablet screen.

Ivan nodded. "Jan Novotný. His fingerprints were in our database because of his work."

"What did he do?" Vinnie asked.

"He was a scientist working for Prokop Industries. As soon as we're done here, I'll find out what exactly he did that required his fingerprints to be on file."

"Hmm." Francine raised one eyebrow, scrolling and tapping on her tablet screen. "Ol' Jan seems like a boring old fuddy-duddy. No social media, his bio on the company website talks about his passion for his work and how he inspires his colleagues and the whole department." Her top lip curled. "He has a comb-over."

"What's a comb-over?" Ivan frowned.

"Something not relevant to the case." I stared unblinking at Francine. "What else do you have that is relevant?"

"Oh, a bad hairstyle is always relevant, girlfriend." She winked at me. "But I'll keep my opinions to myself. For now." She turned her attention back to her tablet. "Doctor Jan was a guest lecturer at quite a few universities. University of Zurich, Karolinska Institute in Sweden, Université de Lyon." Her head jerked up. "Hey, you also lectured there. Maybe your paths crossed?"

I didn't have to think hard. "I never met a Czech scientist when I guest-lectured in Lyon."

"Damn." Her mouth twisted as she looked back at her tablet. "Hmm. He was researching a cure for opioid addiction. Not treatment for addiction. A cure. Interesting. And he's currently on a sabbatical. He also gave a TED talk about genomics."

"If he worked with narcotics, it would explain his fingerprints being on file." Ivan tilted his head. "What is this genomics?"

"It's a field of science, an interdisciplinary field that deals with the structure, evolution and editing of genomes. And genomes are complete sets of DNA, including all of its genes. Genetics is the study of individual genes. Genomics focuses on the collective quantification… of… genes." Vinnie slowed down and stopped when he noticed everyone's wide eyes and Manny's slack jaw. "What?"

"Dude!" Francine punched him on his shoulder. "You just totally geeked out on us."

Vinnie shrugged, colour rising from his neck to his

cheeks. "Rox and I talk."

"Ya think?" Francine snorted. "The two of you are like gossiping teenage girls."

I didn't know what gossiping teenagers would be like—male or female. As a child, I had never had friends and to this day had no patience for idle talk. But if Francine was implying that Vinnie and his romantic partner, Doctor Roxanne Ferreira, talked a lot, she was correct.

It had taken me some time to get used to the chaotic characteristics of the highly regarded international specialist in infectious diseases. Roxy would leave a wake of dirty dishes and disorder behind when she made a simple cup of tea. In private, she was an organisational disaster, but professionally, she was one of the best in her field.

Manny looked at me. "Why would Shahab need a Geronimo scientist, Doc?"

"Genomics." I sighed. "And you know better than to ask me to speculate. I have far too little data to extrapolate anything worthy of a conclusion."

Manny gestured impatiently towards the forest. "Then we might as well go and get more data." He looked at Ivan. "Take us to the crime scene."

Ivan nodded. "Sure. But I don't want to take too many people. We're trying to preserve the scene as much as possible."

Manny pointed at me. "You. The rest can stay."

"Do you need me, love?" Colin lifted my hand and covered it with both of his. I hadn't realised how tight my hold was until he flexed his hand a bit.

I relaxed my hand and thought about his question. "I don't know."

Ivan looked from me to Daniel to Colin and back to me. "Colin can stay close just in case."

Clearly Daniel had briefed him and for this I was grateful.

"Thank you." Colin's smile was sincere as he looked at Ivan. "I'll stay out of the way if I'm not needed."

"Vin and I will hang back and keep Daniel from breaking the law." Francine didn't look up from her tablet as she delivered this outrageous statement. It took a lot of effort not to remind her that Daniel was one of the most conscientious people she would ever meet. I clenched my teeth and followed Manny and Ivan.

They were walking towards the forest, Manny asking Ivan about the number of people who had already trampled all over the crime scene. I watched as Ivan's muscle tension increased. He turned his head to look at Manny, the downturned corners of his mouth telling.

His thought process was visible in his micro-expressions and I saw the moment he relaxed. A sardonic smile replaced his anger. "Is being insulting your way of establishing dominance?"

Manny's eyes widened briefly before he came to a stop. He turned around to face us and shook his finger at Colin. "Stop laughing, Frey."

We caught up to them and Colin grinned. "You're becoming too easy to read, Millard."

"Oh, bugger off." Manny rubbed his hand over his face

and looked at Ivan. "I apologise for being condescending. I didn't mean to imply that your people don't know how to process a crime scene."

"No worries." Ivan's smile was genuine. "Daniel warned me that you might come over a bit strong." He shrugged. "And I'm used to power struggles."

"What does that mean?" I held up my finger before anyone could answer. "I know what a power struggle is. I would like to know why you are used to it."

Ivan shrugged again. Then he rubbed the scar on his hand. "It took a long while before the other detectives considered me more than just a first-responding, gun-toting, superhero wannabe."

"That must've been rough," Colin said.

Ivan nodded, then pointed his chin towards the footpath. "It took more than a dozen investigations of crime scenes like this before they would accept that I actually had an intellect."

"The way Daniel talks, it sounds like you are highly respected in your department."

"It was hard work." Ivan started walking along the footpath and we followed. "Putting my head down and just doing the work, ignoring the noise around me. Nobody wanted to partner up with me. The first two years, I worked alone. Then I got all the rookies."

"Let me guess." Manny pushed his hands in his pockets. "Now they all want to partner up with you."

The corners of Ivan's eyes crinkled, his cheeks lifting in a genuine smile. "Yeah. But I've grown to enjoy working with the rookies. They're so eager to learn and they always bring fresh eyes to a case. They often look for things that aren't there and ask obvious questions."

"And often those are the things and the questions seasoned detectives overlook because they think they know better." Manny huffed, then pointed at me. "She's the one asking all the annoying questions. Keeps me on my toes."

Manny's tone and the part of his face I could see informed me that his intention was contradicting the insulting meaning of his words. I was about to confront him with his lack of clear communication when Ivan stopped and turned around to face Colin. "You can wait here for us." He pointed at a grouping of trees ten metres ahead of us. "The crime scene is over there." He looked at me. "Anytime you need him, just say and we'll call out."

I nodded and let go of Colin's hand. He took my hand again and pulled me closer to him. "I'm here, love."

"I know. I see you."

He smiled and kissed my temple. "Yes, you do."

By now I knew that there was a double meaning in his assertion. A few years ago, he'd explained to me that I understood him in a way no one else did. I saw who he really was.

I had disagreed with him then and I still did. Our friends also 'saw' Colin. But I wasn't going to rehash that argument now. Instead, I nodded and left him standing in the pathway and walked towards the copse of trees.

Ivan and Manny were five metres ahead of me. They

turned to the right when they passed the shrub on the other side of the trees. My mind rebelled against witnessing Shahab's brutality yet again. I inhaled and exhaled while counting to ten. Only then did I step around the copse of trees to find Manny and Ivan waiting for me.

Ivan was standing in a manner to prevent me from seeing behind him. His brow lowered in concern. "This is one of the most brutal crime scenes I've been to."

"I've seen Shahab's victims before." And sometimes had flashbacks that had twice brought on shutdowns. I forced Mozart's flute concerto back into my mind and pushed my fisted hands in my jacket pockets. "I'm ready."

Manny stared at me for two seconds, then grunted and walked further off the wide footpath. With trepidation I waited for Ivan to step aside so I could see the crime scene.

To our left was a building that looked like ruins, but I assumed was the hermitage Ivan had talked about. It was a small unassuming building with three arches in the front and stonework on the sides. I forced myself to look away from it to the right of the building where Ivan's and Manny's attention was focused.

It was as bad as I had expected. Not even four metres from where we were standing, a body was lying under the low-hanging branches of a shrub. Or it could be a tree. I had never developed a sufficient interest in flora to be able to identify the plant where Shahab had left his latest victim.

My feet felt heavy as I walked closer, my breathing laboured. Shahab had made no effort to hide the man in his fifties who was staring at the bottom of the lowest branches with unseeing eyes. The beard covering his jaw was unkempt, dried blood turning his gray hair into a matted rust colour.

Manny was on his haunches, studying Doctor Jan Novotný's face. I stopped next to him, a shudder racing down my spine. Looking at the scientist's left hand was like stepping back into Neuhof forest outside of Strasbourg.

A year ago, Shahab had brutally tortured Jace, a young non-verbal autistic man, then dumped him in Neuhof forest to bleed out. The fingers Manny and I were looking at now were as bent out of position, swollen and clearly broken as Jace's had been. This man had suffered unspeakable pain at the hands of Shahab Hatami.

A dead leaf left over from winter floated from the tree above and came to rest on Doctor Novotný's torso. I didn't even want to think about the bruising and internal bleeding the medical examiner would find during the autopsy.

My attention shifted to Doctor Novotný's right hand. Immediate darkness pushed into my peripheral vision, threatening to take me to a safer place, void of this level of violence.

I couldn't speak and it took great effort to unfist my hand so I could point a shaky finger to draw Manny's attention to the hand half hidden from our view. It took four seconds before he glanced at me, frowned, then turned to see what was causing me such distress.

"Holy bloody fuck." His expletive was a mere whisper,

but conveyed the emotions I was feeling. Revulsion and shock. Manny stood up and stepped into my personal space. "Doc, I'm going to touch you now and turn you away from this."

I shook my head. I didn't want him to stand this close and I didn't want him to touch me. But my brain couldn't get the message to my vocal cords to communicate this. So I just continued shaking my head. And couldn't stop.

"Frey!" Manny scowled at me before swearing yet again. "Bugger this."

He grabbed both my shoulders and turned me to face the direction we had come from. Seeing Colin rush towards me loosened something inside me and I gulped in a deep breath.

"I'm here." Colin pushed Manny's hands off my shoulders and glared at him. "You should know better."

"Bugger off, Frey." Manny stepped away.

I knew the moment Colin saw Doctor Novotný's right hand. His body stiffened, his gasp audible. He took a controlled breath. "Okay, let's get you away from this."

Again I shook my head. Colin waited.

I focused on Colin's warm hands resting on my shoulders and mentally turned up the volume of the Adagio of the flute concerto. I only needed eight seconds. "Shahab's behaviour has escalated."

"Understatement of the year, Doc." Manny walked away from us, then swung around and came back. "Never mind what I said. Just tell me what you're thinking."

I didn't need to look at Doctor Novotný's hand. The

image of the reattached fingers was burned into my memory. "The swelling and discolouration leads me to think that Shahab cut off and crudely sewed back Doctor Novotný's fingers while he was alive. I can't see whether the fingers were completely severed before they were reattached, but the pain must have been excruciating."

"Shahab would want that," Colin said quietly.

"Why is this so significant?" Ivan walked closer and stood next to Manny.

"He didn't cut off his other victims' fingers and sew them back." Manny rubbed both hands over his face. "This… this… I don't know."

Colin stared at me. "Do you need to see more or shall we go?"

"I want complete photographic records of this crime scene and the body." Manny waved us forward with both hands. "If Doc doesn't want to go, I do."

We walked in silence back to the SUV. Ivan stopped briefly to instruct an officer, then joined us while Manny gave Vinnie and Francine a quick summary of what we'd found.

"Motherfucker!" Vinnie walked away and slapped the roof of Colin's SUV hard enough to make the vehicle rock. He turned back and shook his index finger at me. "We're finding him, Jen-girl. This will stop."

I looked at Francine, then at Ivan. "I need to know as much as possible about Jan Novotný. More than just his online biography. There was a reason Shahab tortured him so extensively. Previously, he tortured his victims to get information from them. This time? I don't want to speculate—"

"But you're thinking that he developed a liking for this," Manny said.

"No." I frowned at him. "Although that is very likely given what we know about Shahab. To finish my thought you so rudely interrupted, I wonder if the importance of the information is related to the level of torture."

"So the stuff Jan Novotný knew was more important to Shahab than the intel he wanted in Strasbourg?" Manny scratched his stubbled jaw. "Hmm."

"I also wonder how a scientist fits in with Shahab's previous patterns. If we look at victimology, he doesn't match the young people Shahab targeted in Strasbourg." I thought about this some more. "Was Doctor Novotný a new entity in Shahab's plans or was Shahab already active in Prague when we encountered him? Is this also connected to Shahab's drug trafficking? Is this related at all or something completely different?" I raised one hand, palm out. "Don't try to answer with speculation. My questions are rhetorical."

"I'll get you everything our people can find on Novotný." Ivan rubbed the scar on his hand. I didn't need to see this telling habit to know he was thinking hard. He looked at me. "Do you think Shahab might be connected to the art thief and the Sirani?"

I jerked back. "The little evidence we have so far does not connect these two whatsoever."

"It's connected." Vinnie crossed his arms. "I'll bet my

left nut the stolen art and Shahab are connected."

"That's just gross, Vinster." Francine sniffed. "But I do agree. I don't believe this is just coincidence."

Manny walked to the SUV, opened the door and turned back to us. "Well, don't just stand there. Let's go find out from that *Venus* thief what the hell connection he has to Shahab."

Chapter FIVE

"WHY DO THAT TO his fingers? That's just sick, man." The disgust in Vinnie's voice brought back the horror I'd experienced when I'd seen Doctor Novotný's hand. I reached for the antibacterial gel in my handbag and vigorously rubbed it on my hands for the fourth time since we'd entered the SUV. We'd only been on the road for ten minutes.

"It prolongs the pain, Vin." Colin's quiet answer stopped Vinnie's grumbling. "I'm willing to bet the ME will find Novotný's torture had been stretched over days, even weeks."

"Damn. Sorry, dude." Vinnie sighed deeply. "Man, this sucks."

"I'm okay, Vin." Colin had suffered six months of tremendous torture at the hands of Russian criminals six years ago. He cleared his throat. "This finger thing takes torture to a new and crazy psychological level. But the pain—"

"Bloody hell! Enough, Frey. This is making me sick to my stomach." The slight tremor in Manny's voice indicated anger more intense than usual. "We need to find and stop this bastard."

No one responded.

The rest of our journey following Ivan's SUV to the police station was in morbid silence. I spent the time mentally writing the last movement of Mozart's flute concerto while pondering the significant differences in victimology when I compared Jan Novotný to Shahab's other victims in Strasbourg.

I allowed myself less than a minute to question the validity of our assumption that this was indeed the work of Shahab Hatami. But there were simply too many factors lining up to his previous crimes to dismiss it. So I moved back to analysing victimology.

The first victim in Strasbourg we'd found had been Jace—Jason Connelly, a young autistic man whose death had disturbed us all greatly. Another victim, Adèle Martin, had died from a pre-existing heart condition soon after Shahab had started torturing her, her heart unable to handle the strain.

The deaths of Camille Vastine and Martin Gayot had not been that fast. Shahab had broken every bone in Martin's face and stabbed Camille in the chest before he'd dumped them in another forest on the outskirts of Strasbourg.

Jace, Camille and Martin had been members of the same geocaching club. Adèle had been a successful drug dealer whose connection to the others had been accidental, but had led to all their deaths. The lawyer had been executed and the other two victims had been low-level drug dealers who had tried to steal from Shahab.

Unlike those victims, Doctor Jan Novotný was an internationally renowned scientist and much older than any of the victims we knew about. What made him different? Important enough to warrant extended torture?

Colin parked next to Ivan and turned around to face the back. "Hey, sexy. You okay?"

"Hmm?" Francine sounded distracted. I pulled down the visor and aimed the mirror so I could see her behind me. She blinked a few times, then smiled at Colin. "You think I'm sexy?"

"I don't think it, I know it." Colin's smile was genuine, but also filled with concern. "You're quiet."

"I'm wading through tons of boring academic shit." She looked at me in the mirror. "You should be reading this. You or Roxy. You guys will make more sense of all Doctor Jan's genomics mutant evolutionary revolutionary uprising."

"There is no such thing." I closed my eyes when she smiled. "You knew that."

"That's just about the only thing I know." She turned to Vinnie. "We need your chica here."

"She's busy."

"Well, ain't we all?"

Manny swore under his breath, pushed open the door and got out. Then turned back and leaned into the interior of the SUV. He glared at Francine. "Stop faffing about and get us real intel."

I winced when he slammed the door. Francine snorted. "I'm staying here for now. My trusty tablet and I will get you the data Mister Moody is moaning and groaning about."

I stared at her in the mirror. Colin would not have asked about her wellbeing if he hadn't had reason. Her gaze was unfocused, her breathing shallow and she swallowed compulsively as if something was stuck in her throat. I turned around and pointed at her face. "Why are you scared?"

She blinked. "I don't know. Really, girlfriend. I've seen some awful stuff before, but for some reason Shahab is pushing my fear buttons. I'm really terrified of this man and what he's doing to people."

I didn't experience the fear Francine was exhibiting, but Shahab's level of ruthless cruelty was equal to only a select few criminals. What concerned me more was his motivation. We didn't know what drove him to torture his victims and what his end goal was. I considered my response until I knew it to be true. "We will do everything in our power to find and stop Shahab."

"I know." Her answer was as serious as mine. She took a shaky breath, then winked at me. "Go and find out if Tommy the thief will get us closer to Shahab."

I nodded and opened my door to find Colin already waiting for me. His smile was gentle. "Vin will keep Francine company. And I'll keep you company."

I was glad Vinnie was staying with Francine. Her fear was not familiar and I found it distressing. Anything that negatively affected the people I cared for deeply troubled me.

I shook my head as if I could physically remove the distracting thoughts and followed Ivan, Daniel and Manny to the seven-story building. It took up the whole block and, in contrast to the more historic-looking buildings across the street, the architecture was uninspiring. Square and painted a dark beige, its only interesting feature was the architectural sculptures flanking the glass doors leading into the building.

Ivan held the door open for us to enter. The interior was clean, although not modern. The walls appeared to have been recently painted—the light cream paint still without scuffmarks or handprints. Despite all this, the smell of unwashed bodies, smoke and scents I didn't want to identify reminded me of the few other police stations I'd been to. The five people sitting on the plastic chairs bore similar nonverbal cues to the people in those police stations as well. Two of the three men sat with their legs spread wide, their faces drawn in disrespectful expressions, their disinterest practiced. The other man sat with his head in both hands, his shoulders slumped. Defeated.

Two women sat as far away from the three men as they could, their bodies turned away. One was comforting the other, her eyes roving the reception area as if looking for possible danger.

Manny and Daniel were with Ivan, talking to the officer behind a large wooden reception counter. Manny stated our credentials, his tone impatient.

My eyes were drawn to one of the three doors leading to the area behind the reception desk. A petite woman closed the door behind her as she exited the restricted area and walked towards the front entrance.

She wore a draped knitted beige cardigan over a white

shirt half-tucked into khaki-olive trousers. A large leopard-print scarf covered her neck and a khaki bandana held back her long messy braid hanging halfway down her back. I noticed her outfit because Francine had taken it upon herself to educate me about hipster fashion. Francine would approve of this woman's flat double-buckled boots. That and her natural beauty.

But there was more that drew my attention. I thought back to the moment she had closed the door and turned to the exit. She had noticed me. No, she hadn't only noticed me. She had recognised me.

I frowned and watched her as she walked away from us. Her back was straight, her posture confident. Yet her arms were held too tightly to her torso. People did that when they didn't want to be noticed. This nonverbal cue was often seen in shoplifters as they moved through the store they had robbed.

My frown intensified when she straightened her shoulders and pushed the glass doors open. She was tense. Nervous. Was it because of the reason for her visit to the police station or because she had recognised me? The widening of her eyes had been unmistakable before she had hastily turned away from me.

I'd investigated crimes for long enough to adhere to the paranoia that was currently pushing at me. I closed my eyes and recalled her face when she'd looked at me. Her darker colouring made me suspect that she came from a mixed-race union, the stark contrast of her light blue eyes framed with long lashes confirming that. Her cheekbones were prominent and her nose straight. That symmetrical perfection brought the question of whether she'd had cosmetic surgery.

But she did carry herself with an unselfconsciousness not found in women who were overly concerned with their looks. If her full, deep red lips had not gone from slightly agape to thin, Francine would've called her the perfect model for lipsticks.

"Jenny, love?" Colin squeezed my forearm, his tone the one he used when he'd been unsuccessful in getting my attention. "What's wrong?"

I opened my eyes in time to see the woman cross the street and disappear out of sight. "I don't think anything is wrong."

"Sure?"

I thought about this. I might not have outstanding social skills, but I remembered the people I'd interacted with. And I knew that I'd not met that woman before. She might have recognised me from an article I'd written or a guest lecture I'd given. There was no logical reason to worry. Yet. "Yes, I'm sure."

"Millard is ready." He nodded towards the reception area where Manny stood with his hands pushed in his trouser pockets, his lips thin in annoyance. "He's been ready for a while."

Manny widened his eyes and nodded to the door the woman had used. "Whenever you two feel like joining us."

"Oh, my." Colin grabbed his chest in contrived shock.

"You want me to come as well?"

"Shut up, Frey." Manny followed us as we walked through the door. "You know that I want you in there with your illegal art knowledge."

"Illegal?" Ivan stopped and looked from Manny to Colin to Daniel.

Daniel shook his head. "Colin is an expert in art history and crimes."

Manny snorted and Ivan's eyes narrowed. "Dan?"

"We're on the up and up, Ivan." Daniel put his hand on Ivan's shoulder. "You won't face any fallout from this."

"Famous last words." Ivan exhaled loudly and continued walking down the long corridor.

I wondered about these famous words, but decided to dismiss this nonsensical phrase. A familiar ringtone sounded and Manny took his phone from his jacket pocket. He glanced at the screen and swiped it. "Phillip?"

I could only hear the slight fluctuations in Phillip's voice, but wasn't able to distinguish any words. Manny made a few agreeing sounds before he disconnected the call.

"So?" Colin asked when Manny didn't say anything.

"Phillip will join us later at the hotel. He arrived in Prague, but has gone to a colleague to find out if they know anything about the Sirani and Tomas Broz."

Daniel raised his hand and smiled at Ivan. "Before you even ask, Phillip knows how to ask without asking. We will not jeopardise your case."

"You don't trust us." I narrowed my eyes when Ivan turned to me. "No, it's something else."

"I trust you because I know and trust Daniel." He glanced towards the ceiling, then looked at us. "Look, my job is on the line here. I was the one who suggested getting in outside help when Broz was captured. I had and still have a feeling that something is off about him and the Sirani theft. But my boss outright refused."

"Oh, Ivan." Daniel made a soft sound of sympathy. "You went over your boss' head?"

Ivan nodded. "The police chief was my team leader when I first joined URNA. He knows me. He also knows my reputation. I never let go of a case if I suspect something is off and I've been right every single time. So he pushed it through. He's the one who made contact with your president."

"If I were your boss, I would also be pissed," Manny said.

"That's why I'm trying to keep everything as quiet and by-the-book as possible. On the way here, I had to convince my boss again that having you here is a good idea. That you guys are the best for this job and will make us look good. He wants to close the case because we have the painting and the thief. It's only because of the police chief and my success rate that he's allowing this."

"And you're thinking you might be collateral damage if something goes south." Manny lifted his palm towards me when I inhaled and shook his head. "Don't bother, Doc. This is just childish political stuff." He looked back at Ivan. "We don't do politics, we don't do games. The only thing we're interested in is solving our case and putting an evil bastard away."

Ivan's facial muscles relaxed. "Good. That's my agenda as well."

"Then let's do this."

Ivan pointed at a door down the corridor. "Tomas Broz is in there. We've had our best guys interview him, but he's not giving us anything."

"You've spoken to him." I saw this on his face.

"Yes." He winced. "I'm not too bad when it comes to getting the truth from someone, but this guy is not budging. My feeling is that he is scared of someone or something."

"Don't worry." Manny slumped. "Doc will get intel from him."

I looked at the door Ivan had pointed out. "I need the interview to be recorded. I will need that recording as well as any other recordings you have of him."

Ivan opened the door closest to us and waved us inside. "This is the observation room." He stepped in after us and pointed at the five monitors on a long, curved desk. Three monitors were at the bottom, two on top. "Every interview or even casual conversation in these rooms is recorded here. We observe the interviews here as well."

"Good." Studying Tomas Broz's behaviour with the other policemen would give me more data to use in analysing him.

"Is that him?" Manny pointed at the top two monitors. One camera was placed in front of an elegantly dressed man in his early thirties to give us a full view of his face.

The second was in the corner of the room, giving us a view of the left side of his face. It was placed in such a manner that I was able to see most of his body above and below the table. I approved.

"That's Tomas Broz." Ivan sat down on the only chair in the room, facing the monitors.

"Holy hell." Manny stepped closer and shook his index finger at the monitor. "His watch is worth more than my car."

Colin snorted. "Nikki's pink rubber watch is worth more than your car. You didn't quite make your point, but I agree. This man has money and he likes to show it off."

"He also likes to flirt." Ivan shook his head. "We had one female detective in there and Broz used his good looks like a weapon."

I tilted my head and studied Tomas Broz. He was indeed good-looking. My frame of reference came purely from conversations with Francine. She would sit with a fashion magazine and list all the features needed for a man to become a supermodel.

Tomas Broz had all of those. High cheekbones, strong jawline, soft lips that were not too feminine, green eyes and laughter lines that made him look approachable. His modern hairstyle and expensive outfit would have Francine in raptures. Even his day-old beard appeared to be a style choice and not because of a lack of shaving equipment in jail.

"And?" Colin looked from the monitor to Ivan. "Did his flirting work?"

"It had the opposite effect. Our detective took great offence that a man would think she would so easily be swayed." Ivan looked from Colin to Manny. "But Broz is smart. He knew it would shorten that interview. And he's also smart in an intellectual way. So far he's spoken to our investigators in three languages. Fluently. He's laughing at us."

"He's not laughing." I focused on Tomas Broz's eyes. His upper eyelids were raised, but the lower lids tense and drawn up. "He's scared."

Ivan looked back at the monitors. "Yeah, I got that feeling when I spoke to him. His blustering is just to hide his fear."

Colin stiffened next to me. Manny was staring at him. Colin stared back. "The last time you looked at me like that, I landed up in handcuffs."

"Excuse me?" Ivan straightened in his chair.

Manny waved his hand half-heartedly at both men. "I'm thinking about the interview."

"I recommend only two people interviewing Tomas, but since I didn't get much from him doing it this way, feel free to do it in your own way." Ivan took a deep breath and held it for three seconds while he visibly tried to relax. "Just don't talk about your own criminal histories. I don't need that stress."

"Wuss." Manny turned his back on Ivan and looked at Colin. "Frey? You in?"

"What? You want me to go in there with you?" The shock on Colin's face was real. Almost comedic.

"No, you daft bugger. You and Doc." Manny turned to me. "Doc?"

I thought about it. "Colin can build rapport with him about art and I will observe."

"Then that's how we'll do it."

Ivan looked at me. "If you don't mind me asking, why would you rather have Colin speak to him?"

"Look at Tomas Broz's nonverbal communication." I turned to the monitors. "It's clear."

"Um, not really." Ivan smiled. "Indulge me?"

I took a moment to think how to explain in layman's terms. Being with the team had given me practice. "See the position of his head, his tall posture even though he's sitting down? He's making a point to convey his confidence. His raised top lip and the way he's raised his chin and is looking down at his surroundings shows his disdain for being here. Displaying his linguistic skills was most likely to amuse himself, but also to intimidate. He will need someone who can meet him on his level."

"Colin." Ivan nodded. "Makes sense."

"Just don't let this get to your fat head." Manny pushed his hands in his trouser pockets when Colin smiled at him. "Go in there and do your bloody job."

"Your trust in me is touching, Millard." Colin pretended to wipe a tear from his cheek. "Touching."

"Get lost, Frey."

I ignored them and turned back to study the monitors. When I'd seen enough, I looked up to find Colin standing at the door, waiting for me. I blinked a few times and walked to him.

"Doc." Manny waited until I stopped and looked at him. "I want to know who he worked for. Who he was going to sell the painting to. *If* he was going to sell that painting. Why the bleeding hell he had it on his own wall. And if he has any connection to Shahab."

I nodded and joined Colin. Fifteen seconds later we entered the interview room.

Tomas Broz sighed when he saw us. "More of you? Really?"

"M-mister Broz, m-my name is John D-dryden." Colin's stutter and strong Irish accent took me aback. I wished he'd warned me. I always hated when he took on the name of a seventeenth-century British poet as an alias. It was distracting.

But it caught Tomas' attention. His eyes widened as recognition set in. "*The* John Dryden? As in the hermit art critic feared by many?"

"Indeed." Colin walked to the chairs opposite Tomas, his gait different as if he had problems with his left knee. He lowered himself slowly onto the chair, his movements ageing him at least ten years. His slightly rounded shoulders and the now-constant grimace on his face completed the ageing.

Tomas straightened in his seat, his eyes not moving from Colin. I sat in the other seat across from Tomas, content with not being noticed. That gave me more freedom to observe and learn.

"It truly is a great honour to meet you, sir." He took a

deep breath, a clear attempt to gather himself. Then he tilted his head. "Aren't you on a self-imposed lockdown in Sweden?"

"I was." Colin's reluctance to answer conveyed both his annoyance at being forced out of his pretend lockdown as well as his unwillingness to engage in personal revelations.

Tomas leaned back in his chair, his eyes narrowed. "Hmm. So it begs the question how the authorities managed to get you here."

Colin waved his one hand weakly. "D-doesn't m-matter. What m-matters is that you were caught."

It was fleeting, but I saw it. People only jutted their tongues—sticking out their tongues, usually slightly clutched between the teeth—when they were caught in a faux pas or felt like they were getting away with something. Interesting.

Tomas sighed deeply, his discontent almost convincing. "I forgot the cardinal rule."

"D-don't become comfortable."

His smile was genuine. "You understand."

"No, I d-don't." Colin's *depressor anguli oris* muscles turned the corners of his mouth down. "You've been in this business for nineteen years. Oh, come on. D-don't look surprised. I know all about you, son."

"No one knows anything about me."

Colin raised one eyebrow and lifted a shaking hand to count on his fingers. "Born into an extremely wealthy family, you were a spoiled brat who had everything he wanted. Yet you couldn't keep your hands off other people's valuables. The first item you stole was a tennis bracelet worth around thirty-seven thousand euros."

Tomas' eyes widened fractionally, his lips parting for a second before he controlled his features.

Colin continued. "The embarrassing detail in that bit of history is that you took it from your girlfriend's m-mother. And you were only fourteen. Nineteen years later, your name has been associated with numerous high-end jewellery and art heists and you've only been caught once. Two days ago. Why?"

Tomas sat quietly for a long time. His expression went from controlled to panicked to calculating and back to panicked. "How do you know this about me?"

"Not important." Colin leaned forward, wincing as if in pain. "Who commissioned the theft of the Elisabetta Sirani?"

"I took it for myself."

Colin uttered a derisive sound. "Hmm. I d-don't know if I believe you. Not if I take into account your reputation for m-moving stolen m-masterpieces as fast as possible. M-mind you, if I had that Sirani, I would also want to look at it every day. The d-dynamic and colourful composition, that painting is both intimate and full of playful joy. How can you not look at that and marvel?"

"And be reminded of the high cost of that acquisition." Tomas' words came out as an anguished whisper, the fear evident in his thin lips and his brows raised and drawn together.

"The high cost?" Colin stared at Tomas for a few seconds.

"Let me guess. You d-didn't know who commissioned the theft of the painting. Not until you already had it. Then you realised how d-deep you were in and d-decided to d-disappear off the planet."

I bumped Colin's leg with my knee. Tomas' reaction had confirmed everything Colin had said. Colin nodded. "Who's your d-dealer?"

Tomas' internal debate took mere seconds before he exhaled, relief stamped on his face. "I've been working with Ant for years. Many years. Hell, if I have to be accurate, it started… yes, I did my first job for him the year before I went to university. I was still in school.

"He proved to be incredibly reliable. His commissions were carefully selected. Not only did he exclusively do business with people who would not betray him, he also chose works that would never be traced back to him, his clients or me. As far as I'm concerned, he's the best in his field."

I saw the recognition on Colin's face and wasn't surprised. He knew anyone of worth in the art industry. Whether artists, legitimate dealers or thieves and their fences, Colin knew them. I didn't.

"D-did he know who he was d-doing business with when he agreed to the acquisition of the Sirani?"

Tomas huffed a humourless laugh. "Honestly, I don't know. But he was the one who hinted at who was to receive the painting. I did more homework and when I confronted him, he said nothing. That has always been his 'yes' when he didn't want to commit to a verbal answer."

I narrowed my eyes. He was not being completely deceptive, but also not completely truthful.

"Who was the client?"

Tomas' inhale was sharp, his fear real. "No. Just no. Look, I love being able to talk to a living legend like you and would tell you everything I know, but not that. No. That... No. And tell them"—he pointed at the door—"that I'm done talking. They can send in Van Gogh for all I care. No number of sexy female detectives will get me to talk."

"Sexy female d-detectives?" Colin's smile was conspiratorial. "I'm sure you wouldn't m-mind speaking to another one, right? Even if you d-don't tell her anything."

Tomas' facial muscles relaxed slightly, one corner of his mouth lifting. "Yeah, man. That last woman they sent in here was much hotter than the first one. Cute little thing."

I narrowed my eyes. Ivan had told us only one female detective had been in here. I wondered if my suspicion was correct. "Are you talking about the detective with the bandana and leopard-print scarf? The one with the beige cardigan?"

Tomas looked at me as if seeing me for the first time. He crossed his arms. "Yes, that's the one. She tried really hard and I almost told her what I told you. I mean, it was hard to resist those pretty blue eyes and sexy voice." Tomas looked back at Colin. "But she didn't have my respect. So I only gave her some tourist tips. This is a beautiful city to sightsee."

"Hmm." Colin looked at Tomas for a few seconds then pushed himself up with a pained groan. "We won't take up any m-more of your time, M-mister Broz. I d-do wish you luck. You're going to need it if you're going to get through this legal m-mess you landed yourself in."

Chapter SIX

MANNY WAS WAITING for us in the hallway. His fists were resting on his hips, his lips a thin line. He glared at me while waiting until Colin closed the interview room door behind him. "Care to tell us who the hell this detective is, missy?"

"Detective Maxová is blond and never wears bandanas or leopard print." Ivan stood next to Daniel, his frown pulling his eyebrows low over his eyes.

"I don't know who she is."

"Oh, you better give me more than that, Doc."

I sighed. "I saw her while you were registering us. She came out of the restricted area and left the building."

"But you noticed her." Colin leaned against the wall. "Was she the reason you zoned out?"

"I thought I saw something."

"How many times must I tell you that you must say something when you see something, Doc?" Manny's jaw clenched, his nostrils flaring as he took a few deep breaths. "Bloody hell. Who else is involved in this mess?"

Colin looked at Ivan. "She must be on your security footage."

Ivan nodded and turned back to the observation room.

"I'll also download the footage of the other interviews with Broz for you."

We followed Ivan into the room. Manny mumbled his displeasure under his breath. "Frey, I assume you know who this bloody Ant is. By the gods, if you don't know and you didn't ask for his full—"

"Take a breath, Millard. Antonin Korn is a well-respected art dealer here in Prague."

My eyebrows rose. I'd investigated eleven of Antonin Korn's clients when I had been working for Phillip's insurance company. He'd sent them to Rousseau & Rousseau to insure their newly acquired artworks. Phillip had insisted on a thorough investigation into the clients as well as the art before he'd agreed to as little as a first appointment. I had never asked Phillip why Antonin Korn's clients had required this extra scrutiny.

"Well-respected my arse." Manny's *buccinator* muscles pulled his lips into a sneer. "No one is well-respected if he's a criminal."

"He's not a convicted criminal," Colin said. "There have been rumours for decades and he's been investigated a few times, but no one could ever find anything on him."

"Um, guys?" Ivan scratched his head, leaning back in the chair facing the computer console. "We have a problem."

"What now?" Manny walked closer to the computers.

"It seems like all the footage of Broz's interviews has been wiped."

"How the holy blazes did that happen?"

"I'll get our IT people on it." Ivan's jaw tightened. "If it's truly gone, it means that somebody has been in our system."

He took out his smartphone and spoke in rapid Czech to someone. For a moment he paused and held up a finger towards us. Then his eyes narrowed, his forehead creased and he leaned back. He listened quietly for eight seconds then ended the call. "Fuck."

"That definitely doesn't sound good." Daniel looked pointedly at Ivan's phone.

"It isn't." Ivan shook his head. "IT says they can't see any unauthorised access to the system, but they can see that files have been deleted. Not only deleted, the person also overwrote those files. We've lost everything related to Tomas Broz. Even your interview."

Manny's shoulders slumped. "Are your people good? We've got people who might be able to get the footage back. I've been told that nothing is truly deleted."

"We have brilliant IT specialists here. I know that if something is deleted, there is still a chance of recovering it. But if someone overwrites the file numerous times, then deletes it?" Ivan shook his head. "No, I doubt they'll be able to recover it. I also asked about footage of the reception area when I was signing you guys in, but that has also been deleted."

"We need to find out who the bleeding hell that woman is, what she was doing here and what her connection is to Shahab." Manny turned towards the door. "And we need to visit this well-respected art dealer."

"Give me a minute." Ivan turned back to the computers. "I'll get my team to start on this woman's ID and get clearance for visiting Antonin Korn. I'll meet you by the cars."

Manny responded with a curt nod and marched down the hallway. Ten minutes later we were driving through Prague. The architecture in this city was spellbinding enough to give me a reprieve from the overload of information bombarding my mind.

Prague was one of the few European capital cities that had not been rebuilt during the eighteenth or nineteenth centuries. All the different eras were represented in the majestic buildings. It was not the Gothic, Renaissance or Baroque eras that enchanted me. It was the magnificent buildings hailing from the Romanesque era that drew my eye each time we passed one. The thick walls, large towers, round arches and symmetrical designs appealed to my autistic mind.

Colin had given Vinnie and Francine an update on our findings. Manny sat quietly in the back, his head tilted back and his eyes closed. His scowl contrasted his relaxed posture. Francine was working on her laptop, Colin and Vinnie talking about the luxury cars on the road with us.

This time of the day, traffic allowed us to reach the gallery without delay. It was on the outskirts of the Old Town, the paved street lined with large Classicist buildings that made the street feel even narrower than it was. The cream buildings were in stark contrast to the clear blue sky. This city was truly beautiful.

The gallery sat between a boutique with tall mannequins wearing evening gowns in the shop window and a cigar salon. The window display of the art gallery was an elegant reproduction of a library, three paintings hanging on the walls between bookshelves and two sculptures on the antique side table next to a leather wingback chair. It looked exclusive. Unlike the neighbouring shops, there were no lights on inside the gallery. A large sign hung above the door, 'Korn's Art' engraved in decorative letters.

Colin parked his SUV next to a police vehicle that looked like it could belong to URNA—Czech's SWAT teams. We got out just as Ivan parked next to us. He also got out and nodded towards the URNA vehicle. "They were fast."

Vinnie was studying the five men dressed in dark gray camouflage uniforms, their bulletproof vests similar to the ones I'd seen from Daniel's team—laden with tools, weapons and pockets. "Why did you get an URNA team out here?"

"Precaution." Ivan touched his neck, then smiled. I didn't pay attention to his genuine smile. It was his first, unchecked nonverbal reaction that had caught my attention. He took a step towards the men next to the URNA vehicle. "Let me introduce you to my previous team."

I barely paid attention to the introductions. Instead I watched Ivan. That slight gesture had brought back to my mind his quickly controlled hesitation at Jan Novotný's crime scene, his earlier reaction in our hotel room as well as his telling micro-expressions in the police station. What was he hiding?

The URNA team came out of the gallery while I mentally recalled every non-verbal cue that had caught my attention from Ivan. I hadn't even seen the team enter the gallery.

"All clear." The leader looked disappointed as he shrugged and looked at Manny, then at Ivan. "Nothing here for us to do."

Manny was glaring at the gallery door. "What do you mean it's all clear? There's no one inside?"

"Nobody," the URNA leader answered. "The door is unlocked, but none of the computers are turned on, no lights are on."

"Huh." Manny pushed his hands in his trouser pockets. "Well, let's go inside then."

Ivan went in first and located the light switches. When the strategic lighting came on, the gallery transformed from a dark space to a beautiful display of artwork. Unlike many other galleries I'd been to, this one was divided into five sections—each designed to look like a room in a house. The living room section had a large fireplace, a landscape painting in a heavy frame above the mantelpiece.

Colin's eyes widened in pleasure and he walked to the bedroom section. Above the bed were sketches of nude women. He shook his head in awe. "These are Henri Matisse drawings."

"I don't care." Manny walked towards the back of the gallery. "Where's the office?"

"In here." Ivan pointed to the door that looked like it led to a garden from the dining room section.

I left Colin to admire the art and followed Manny and Francine into the back room. It was a well-organised space, for which I was grateful. I never understood how people could function, not to mention be productive, in a chaotic and cluttered environment.

Antonin Korn had lined his office walls with dark wooden filing cabinets and cupboards. Ivan had opened the filing cabinet behind the desk, Daniel was looking through a cupboard next to it and Manny was going through the desk drawers.

Francine stood with her hands on her hips. "Where are the computers?"

"Looks like this guy did everything old-school style." Daniel stood to the side and pointed at the open cupboard. Rows upon rows of ring binders, labels on the back of each one, the large print stating the date and content.

"No way." Francine's jaw was slack. "That's just… barbaric. How am I supposed to work?"

Ivan chuckled. "Like people did for thousands of years before computers."

"There was no life before computers." She huffed and looked at Manny. "My system is running background on Jan Novotný, but I can help it along when I'm focused on it. Do you want me to do that or let my system run and see what dirt I can dig up on Antonin online?"

"Antonin." Manny looked at me. "Doc?"

I thought about this. “Both are important. Since we have basic background on Doctor Novotný and you’re already searching for more, I concur with Manny.”

“Well, it’s settled then.” Francine wrinkled her nose as she looked around the office space. “I’m going to sit in that comfy-looking sofa in the gallery and work on my tablet—on something that will give me results.”

“Good afternoon, everyone.” Phillip walked into the office. He was holding his dark blue wool coat over one arm, his bespoke suit fitting in well with the elegant surroundings. He glanced around the room, then stared at me for a second. “Are you well?”

“Hi and bye.” Francine smiled at him. “I’m outta here. If you need me, I’ll be in there.” She nodded at the gallery and left.

“I’m well. Did you learn anything of use?”

“Unfortunately not.” The frustration was not only in his body language, but also in his clipped words.

Manny briefed Phillip on everything that had taken place at the police station while I took a pair of latex gloves from their designated space in my handbag and put them on before opening a cupboard across from the desk. Even though this room was spacious, I was already feeling crowded.

I turned my back on the others and narrowed my focus on the contents of the cupboard. Just like the cupboard Daniel was going through, this one also was filled with ring binders. I took the first one on the top shelf and exhaled in relief. It was not covered in dust.

"What can you tell us about Antonin?" Daniel paused his search through the cupboard briefly as he looked at Phillip.

Phillip pulled at his cuffs. "I've known him professionally for… hmm… I would say eleven or so years. I can't remember the first time we met, but I remember the first time he pushed me for business. By that time I'd heard rumours that he was not always doing everything above board."

"Colin told us about some rumours." Manny closed one desk drawer and opened another one. "But what rumours are *you* talking about?"

"Well, it was whispered that Ant sometimes worked with art that didn't have clear provenance. Some of his clients also had reputations for white-collar crime, but few of them were ever charged, much less found guilty. There have always been rumours of illegal activities around him and some of his clients, but nothing that could be proven."

"That is why you always had the clients he referred to you so thoroughly vetted." It all made sense now.

Phillip nodded. "Not only the clients, but the art as well. I didn't want to be anywhere close to illegal art deals. But as you know, we never found anything."

Daniel straightened. "The sign of a good criminal. Hide in plain sight, continue doing transparent, legal business and be loud about it."

"Oh, he's loud." Phillip's smile was not kind. "He's arrogant and has no trouble telling anyone that he is the most successful art dealer in Europe."

"Is that true?" I never knew whether people were being truthful or merely boasting with hyperbole.

"Hmm… I wouldn't say he is the most successful." Phillip tilted his head as he took a moment before he nodded. "But I would say he is the most successful dealer in Near Eastern antiquities."

"Near Eastern antiquities?" Daniel put his hands on his hips. "Shahab dealt in that stuff. All looted artworks."

Manny swore and Phillip's lips thinned. He nodded. "Then Shahab might have known Antonin."

"I'm sure of it." Colin was leaning against the doorframe, not entering the room. He smiled at me. "Ant has a reputation for his expertise. That was how I first heard about him. I had"—he glanced at Manny, his smile widening into a smug grin—"a sculpture that needed to find its way back to its original owners. Ant met with me and I must admit, I was impressed by his exhaustive knowledge about the area, the artists, the eras as well as individual pieces. He was like an encyclopaedia."

"We have to keep in mind that Ant didn't only sell Near Eastern antiquities." Phillip looked at me. "How many of the pieces we insured are Near Eastern antiquities?"

"Two." I remembered the detail of each case I'd investigated. "The others are masterpieces from different eras, all of them European in origin though."

"So what are we thinking now?" Manny closed a desk drawer and leaned back in the chair. "That Antonin Korn deals in legit art from Europe, but is also the middleman for looted art from the Middle East?"

"Some of the Near Eastern pieces he sold were one hundred percent legal, but I wouldn't put it past him to deal in looted art. Not at all." Phillip shook his head. "I always had a bad feeling about him."

"Then why did you take on his clients?" Ivan asked.

I thought about this. "Those eleven clients had other works insured by you."

Phillip looked at me, his smile slight. "And they begged me to insure those pieces. It was only because I had done business with them before and I knew their integrity that I accepted them. Ant must have sent maybe fifty more clients my way, but I rejected them without any further consideration."

Colin and Phillip started talking about the many artefacts Ant had sold and ventured further off topic, discussing Near Eastern art. Ivan, Daniel and Manny returned to searching through the office. I turned my attention back to the binders in front of me.

An hour later, Phillip and Colin had left and I was looking through the last binder. I was doing a simple scan through each one, hoping to get an overall sense of Antonin Korn's filing system.

All the binders in this cupboard held paper copies of receipts for transactions dating back as far as 1995. But it was the binder I was currently paging through that held the most interesting information so far. I took another five minutes before I was satisfied that my conclusions were as near to accurate as possible. And that was when I saw something that sent a rush of adrenaline through my body.

I reached for Mozart's Symphony in F major, closed my eyes and focused on mentally writing the first three lines of the Allegro.

Only when I felt calmer did I look up. Ivan and Daniel were paging through what looked like an accounting ledger. Manny was sitting on the leather chair behind the desk looking through an open briefcase on his lap.

"I think I have a list of Antonin Korn's clients." I blinked when everyone's heads jerked towards me. I looked down to the binder in front of me. "I also think there's a list of his suppliers in here."

"Well, let's have a look at it." Manny put the briefcase on the desk and walked towards me.

I shrank back. A quick look around confirmed that the office had remained the same size as before. Yet it felt smaller. I swallowed and looked towards the door. "Can we meet with the others out there?"

"Oh, bloody hell, Doc." Manny sighed. "Of course. I could take a break from getting killed by papercut."

"It would have to become severely infected to kil…" I sighed and picked up the binder. Once again I'd taken someone's words literally.

Daniel and Ivan chuckled as they followed Manny out of the office. I held the binder away from my body in the likely case of it containing germs. The yellowed pages with the darker sections on the edges were proof of a lot of contact with hands that had not been gloved and very likely not been clean.

"What's cookin', good-lookin'?" Francine looked up

from her tablet and smiled at Manny as he sat down on the large leather sofa next to her. This was the living area, the first display when entering the gallery. Two uniformed officers were standing in front of the shop window, watching the street. Their postures appeared relaxed, but I saw the tightness in their shoulders as they took note of everyone passing them on both sides of the street.

"Doc found something." Manny lifted his chin towards me.

"Ooh!" Francine looked at the binder in my hands and frowned. "Paper? Really? Man, I hate this old-school system."

"What did you find, love?" Colin left the large landscape painting he'd been looking at and joined us. He pulled two beautifully carved wooden dining room chairs closer and put one down next to me. "Sit and tell us."

I inspected the tapestry-covered seat and decided it looked clean enough, so I sat down. "There seem to be two lists in this binder. One I assume is a list of clients. I came to that conclusion because I saw the names of the eleven clients Antonin had referred to Phillip. A lot of the names on the other list appear to be Arabic, which leads me to believe they might be his suppliers of Near Eastern antiquities."

"Give the lists to Francine." Manny ignored Francine's melodramatic mumbling about having to copy everything from paper. "She'll check them all out."

I pulled the binder a bit closer to my body, but still made sure it didn't touch me. "Shahab is on the second list."

"Motherfucker." Vinnie's nostrils flared as he crossed his arms over his chest.

"Bloody hellfire, Doc! Why didn't you say so earlier?"

Because it would've led to a shutdown. "I…"

I didn't know whether it was the movement on the street that caught my attention or the one officer's shoulders tensing even more. The shock of seeing Shahab's name and now this? I froze.

"Jenny?" Colin put his hand on my forearm. "Love?"

I focused on my breathing. Thirteen slow breaths later, I raised a shaking hand and point at the street. "Her."

"Who do you see, Jen-girl?" Vinnie walked to the shop window and looked up and down the street. His whole body jerked. "Fuck!"

"The hell?" Manny jumped up, but Vinnie was already out the door, running down the street. Manny swung around, stared at me, then looked at Colin. "Get her to talk."

"Millard." The reprimand was clear in Colin's tone.

I mentally wrote next two lines of the Symphony's Allegro. "I saw the woman from the police station."

"Bloody hellfire." Manny walked to the gallery door and looked out. He shook his head. "I don't think the big guy found her."

"How did she know to come here?" Colin took my hand between both his and rubbed it as if I was cold. "Tomas told us he'd revealed nothing to her when she'd questioned him."

"He's a bloody thief, Frey. He lied."

"He didn't." I was sure of it. "But I don't think he told us everything."

I thought about this some more. The woman from the police station had been leaning against the building across the street, eating a cupcake. She hadn't looked worried or expecting danger. "There are other possibilities. She could've followed us, she could've found out about Antonin Korn's reputation and decided to question him or..." I looked at Francine. "If she was the one who hacked the police system and deleted the footage of Tomas Broz's interviews and her presence, she could also have listened in on our interview with him."

"Holy mother of all the saints." Manny rubbed his hand hard over his face and stepped away from the door. I frowned. Manny looked pale.

Vinnie opened the door, the scar running down the left side of his face white. "She's gone."

"What do you mean she's gone?" Manny tried to push his hands in his trouser pockets, but missed. Then he swayed on his feet. His usual scowl changed to a confused frown. "I don't fee..."

His eyes rolled in his head and his legs crumpled under him.

Vinnie moved faster than I'd thought possible in time to catch Manny and gently lowered him to the ground. "Old man?"

"Manny!" Francine jumped up and ran to them.

Colin was already on his knees next to Vinnie, his fingers pressed against Manny's neck. "He has a pulse, but it feels very weak."

I couldn't move. It felt like my body had locked itself into this position. The only voluntary movement I could manage was blinking. And no amount of blinking forced Manny to stand up, scowl at me and demand illogical answers from me.

"We need to get him to a hospital." Daniel pushed Vinnie and Colin out the way.

"I'll drive. It will be faster than waiting for an ambulance." Ivan was already out the door, keys in his hand.

"I'll carry him." Vinnie elbowed Daniel out the way when the latter lifted Manny's arm. With the same tender care he showed towards Eric, Vinnie lifted Manny from the floor and rushed out the door. Francine ran behind him, swearing at Manny, using language I hadn't known she would utilise on a loved one.

I wanted to go with them. I wanted to shake Manny and demand he wake up. I wanted to make sure only the best doctors took care of him. I couldn't. My brain held my body hostage while it reeled from being overloaded with strong emotions.

My breathing was shallow and I had nothing grounding me. I blinked non-stop and looked around me. Everyone had left the gallery. Francine's laptop and tablet were abandoned on the sofa, Manny's coat carelessly thrown over the sofa's armrest. I was alone.

Everything went black.

Chapter SEVEN

"JENNY." COLIN RUBBED my hand between his. "Come on, love. Millard is going to be okay."

My eyelids refused to open. I had no idea how long I'd been shut down. I didn't even know where I was. Colin continued to talk to me as I forced Mozart's Symphony in F major into my mind.

I wrote the first three lines of the unusual second movement—the Menuetto—before my body obeyed the messages sent from my brain and I opened my eyes. I looked at Colin. "Manny."

"Hey there."

"Manny."

His smile was understanding. "He tested positive for an opioid overdose and the doctors gave him Naloxone to neutralise the overdose."

"Is he conscious?" One of the many articles I'd read about the opioid crisis was an in-depth look into what happened once Naloxone reversed the depression of the central nervous and respiratory systems caused by the use of opioids.

In limited cases the use of Naloxone caused nausea,

sweating, trembling and headaches. Those were the milder side effects. I was more concerned with the adverse cardiovascular effects it could have, including the very rare possibility of a coma.

"He was feeling a bit shaky and complained about a headache. Now he's sleeping." Colin narrowed his eyes. "How are you?"

"Well enough." I shifted in the chair and looked around me. "Where are we and how long have we been here?"

"In the hospital staff conference room. Daniel and Ivan should be on their way back from the police station. Francine went to the washroom and Vinnie went to get coffee. Phillip is taking a call outside."

"How long?"

Colin knew what I was asking. I hated shutdowns—losing the time, losing control over my body and environment, being vulnerable and exposed. He squeezed my hand. "I went back into the gallery as soon as Vin and the others left with Millard. You were… it was a rough one."

I swallowed. That meant I had been rocking and keening loudly. I nodded for him to continue.

"I decided it was best to stay put, but after about twenty minutes Vin phoned and told me to get out of there. Manny got exposed by touching something."

I crossed my arms. "That means it had to be very strong for Manny to react so quickly and badly by only touching it. But wait. He was wearing gloves."

"Yeah. We've been speculating about it a lot." He smiled

at my frown. "We're thinking that either he touched the powder when he took off his gloves or it might have transferred to his clothes and he touched his clothes with his bare hands."

"Do you…" I stopped when he kissed my knuckles.

"Let me finish telling the story. I'll be quick." He waited until I nodded. I wanted—no, *needed*—to know the details, yet was impatient and at risk of dismissing possible important information. "I brought you here and the decontamination team went through the gallery. They found concentrated levels of fentanyl on the briefcase Manny had been going through. Only on the briefcase though. Nowhere else."

I blinked a few times. "How long?"

"Altogether now, five and a half hours." He glanced at the door. "The others were worried."

"But you said Manny will be well."

He moved closer until our noses almost touched. "They're worried about you, love."

"She's with us?" Vinnie rushed over, placed a tray of steaming coffee mugs on the table and sat down on the chair on my other side. "I was so lonely without you, Jen-girl. There was no one here to debate the fourth dimension of the truth behind unicorns and energy fields causing lovesickness."

I frowned. "There is no…" My lips thinned. "Why didn't you just say you were worried?"

His smile was wide, genuine and relieved. "Because teasing you is a little bit of fun and also because it's your punishment for adding to my worries. It's bad enough the old man gave us such a scare."

I followed his glance towards the door and for the first time paid attention to my surroundings. The large room we were in was bright and airy, a landscape painting on one wall the only decoration. Eighteen chairs stood around the oval wooden table. The shiny surface was covered in takeaway boxes, empty water bottles and a few documents.

It was clear Francine had made herself at home across from where we were sitting. Her laptop was open, her tablet next to it and three phones on the other side of the laptop. Behind us were large windows overlooking a dimly lit courtyard. It was dark outside.

"My sugar bunny pumpkin love is coming home with us…" Francine stopped two strides into the room, her shoulders sagging in relief. Then she straightened and smiled at me. "Hey, you."

"Who or what is a sugar bunny pumpkin?"

Vinnie barked a laugh. "I'm totally using that on the old man."

"Ooh, don… no, please do!" Francine grabbed a cup of coffee and walked to her seat. "I'm using all kinds of ridiculous names on Manny to irritate him."

"Why would you do that?" Shouldn't she be loving and caring?

"Because the son of a bitch scared the living trees out of me."

I leaned away from her. "That doesn't make sense."

"None of this does."

I stared at her. Despite her immaculate make-up, she looked exhausted. This unusual and extremely stressful situation was likely the reason for her greater than usual melodrama. "What did the doctor say? Exactly."

"Exactly?" She leaned back in her chair and looked up and left. "Manny's headache should ease by tomorrow, but she doesn't know about his nausea. He doesn't want to take any medication for it, so we'll just have to keep an eye on him. She's happy with his ECG results, but also said we should keep an eye on his blood pressure and heart rate."

"I'll do that," Roxy said from the door.

"Rox!" Vinnie jumped up and walked to the door, his arms wide open.

Roxy's face relaxed into an affectionate smile as she walked into his arms and hugged him back. "Man, what an afternoon this was."

"Did you enjoy the ride?" Francine's smile disappeared the moment she noticed Roxy's shoes. "My God. You could at least have made the time to wear some shoes worthy of the occasion."

"What ride and what occasion?" This was another reason I hated shutdowns. It meant that I missed out on a lot of action and felt like I was in a constant state of catching up.

"Vin asked and Émile sent Rox over in his private plane." Francine sniffed. "An elegant private plane where one should wear elegant footwear. Not those horrid sneakers with all the beads and ribbons."

Émile Roche was a wealthy businessman we'd befriended after a case in which he'd been involved. At that time he'd had a reputation for questionable business deals, but had since worked hard to ensure that all his business was conducted in a legal and transparent manner.

"They're so comfy though." Roxy lifted her foot and twisted it from side to side. "I think they're pretty."

"Pretty horrid." Francine turned away from Roxy. "As I was saying—Manny is coming home with us tonight. The doctor wanted to keep him overnight for observation, but I convinced her that Rox and her bad shoes will look after him."

"I knew you loved me." Roxy walked to the table and sat down next to me. "How're you doing?"

"I'm well."

She leaned in and studied me. At first I had found it both interesting and disconcerting to have a medical professional try to be covert while checking my heart rate and breathing. After I'd confronted her about it, she'd stopped being subtle. She stared at my neck for twenty seconds, then sat back and smiled. "Your heart rate is normal and your breathing strong."

"So when will the old man be discharged?" Vinnie handed out the coffee and sat down next to Roxy.

"In about two hours. The doctor wants to take a last blood sample before we go, but wants to wait three hours after the last one. So we're stuck here for a while longer."

"And Manny could do with the extra sleep," Roxy said.

"That really is the best way for the body to recover from any boo-boo."

"Boo-boo." Vinnie laughed when Roxy punched his arm. "What? It's funny. And you're the one who said it."

"Well, I meant it lovingly." She tapped his nose with her fingertip. "Not in the evil way you took it."

I looked at Francine's devices. "Did you uncover any new and useful information?"

"A bit."

"We come bearing gifts." Ivan and Daniel walked into the conference room. Ivan was carrying a tray with two large serving dishes. He put it on the table. "My wife made a vegetarian quiche and one with chicken."

Daniel put a bag with paper plates and juice on the table, then looked at me. "Hi."

"Hi." I was grateful for the size of the room we were in. Usually panic would start scratching at my brain with this many people in one space. But this room could easily accommodate all eighteen chairs filled as well as another ten people standing without making it crowded. I stared at the white serving dish as Ivan took the covering off.

"I can vouch for Ivan's kitchen and for his wife's cooking." Daniel knew that I seldom ate food prepared in kitchens and by people I didn't know. "I would recommend it above any restaurant in the area."

"Me too." Ivan's sigh was happy. "It's my wife's fault I have to go to the gym so often and for such intense sessions. She loves cooking and I love eating. We're a terrible match."

"That's a perfect match in my mind." Roxy waved at Ivan. "I'm Roxy."

"Doctor Roxanne Ferreira." Ivan nodded. "Daniel told me you would be joining us."

Had it not been for Colin taking my hand and tolerating my increased grip, I would've expressed my annoyance at this neurotypical need for socialising. Clenching my teeth, I waited for everyone to fill their plates before I turned to Francine again. "What did you find?"

"Ooh, yes." She put a large portion of the vegetarian quiche in her mouth and hummed her approval. "This is really good."

"Told you so." Ivan's chest widened in pride.

"Okay." Francine tapped on her tablet screen. "First thing: I couldn't locate the exact address from which the email was sent to Phillip."

"Good evening, everyone." Phillip walked into the conference room, putting his phone in the inside pocket of his bespoke suit jacket. He looked at me and smiled. "Genevieve."

"Francine is telling us her findings." I wanted us to stay on track.

"Please continue." Phillip sat down and accepted a paper plate from Daniel with a smile and put a slice of the chicken quiche on his plate.

"I tracked the email to Düsseldorf, but wasn't able to get an exact IP address." Francine's lips thinned. "Annoying. But that gave me an idea. I looked for private investigators working in and round Düsseldorf, but didn't find anyone who fits the description of the woman you saw at the police station and the gallery."

"Tell her about Jan." Vinnie turned to Ivan as he put another helping of quiche on his plate. "Dude, seriously. Your wife can cook."

"I'll tell her." Ivan nodded at Francine. "Did you get much more on Jan Novotný?"

She looked at me. "Ivan sent me everything they had on ol' Jan. It didn't really give me anything I didn't find myself. I put everything in a file and sent it to you. In my ever-so-humble opinion, the only information that is really relevant and helpful at the moment is that Doctor Jan was very close to developing a cure for opioid addiction."

"That is very relevant." I thought about this some more. "We need to know if there is a connection between Doctor Novotný's research and the fentanyl found in the gallery that caused Manny's overdose."

"Fentanyl is a son of gun." The corners of Roxy's mouth turned down. "It is the most widely used synthetic opioid and does what it's supposed to in terms of pain relief, but man, it comes from the blackest heart of evil. It's fifty to a hundred times more potent than morphine and the fentanyl analogues can be much stronger than that."

"What's a fentanyl analogue?" Francine asked.

"Drug analogues are developed to imitate a specific drug, but are not exactly the same. In the case of fentanyl, the effects are usually a hundred times stronger. Or when we're talking about carfentanyl, it's ten thousand times more potent than morphine."

"Shit." Ivan shook his head. "I've done my fair share of courses on drugs and their effects, but it still shocks me. It… man, it's a weapon."

"It is." Roxy put her hands on her hips. "And far too many people are killed by it every single year. America is suffering an epidemic at the moment. An estimated seventy thousand people die as a result of opioid overdoses in a year. In the whole of Europe, we're talking about fewer than ten thousand people in the same period. Globally, just under two hundred thousand people.

"Reasons for addiction are diverse, but once that beast has a hold on you, it's a ghastly battle to get out. And we have to keep in mind that this addiction is not limited to a lower income class. It's across the board and the wider effect it has on families and communities is devastating."

Colin straightened in his chair. "At this point, I think we all agree that the fentanyl on that briefcase was meant to kill Ant. The million-dollar question now is what the odds are of Shahab's victim—Doctor Jan—working on a cure for something that was supposed to kill another man—Ant—who we suspect sells the Near Eastern antiquities Shahab supplies. And of course Ant's connection to Tomas Broz and the stolen Sirani."

Even though Colin's theory was viable, I wanted something more concrete than speculation. I looked at Francine. "Did you find anything else?"

"I've been going through Doctor Jan's emails. Wow, did he like to send chatty emails." She paused dramatically. "But here's a question for you. He was about to publish his work on the cure for opioid addiction with the focus on fentanyl. It is something that would render fentanyl harmless altogether and would make the person taking this drug immune to its effects. My question is this: Why would Doctor Jan—out of the blue—take a sabbatical?"

"Strange indeed." Daniel looked at me. "You're more familiar with academia. Does this make sense? Have you seen something like this?"

I shook my head. "Not that I recall. But there is incredible pressure on people to publish. Depending on personality traits, some people thrive under this pressure and others can't handle it. This causes irrational behaviour which could explain a seemingly senseless sabbatical."

"Has he taken sabbaticals before?" Daniel asked.

"No." Francine tapped her tablet screen. "There are quite a few testimonials from former students and colleagues in articles about Doctor Jan's work. It looks like everyone feels like he's making them look bad because he works so much and loves his work more than anyone they know. A few of them even said that he never takes breaks."

"Well, if this is out of character for him, it definitely becomes more suspicious." I needed to know more about Jan Novotný's personality. I took a moment to go through everything I'd learned. "Tell me more about the type of emails he sent."

"Like I said, he was quite the chatter. He was in constant contact with his team and even former students. He also emailed a lot with someone I think might be family—a nephew maybe."

Ivan leaned back in his chair, his hands fisted. "Patrik Bakala?"

"Who's that?" Colin's harsh tone made Ivan lean back even more.

"The first victim we found." Ivan raised both hands, palms out. "I'm sorry I didn't give you the full details earlier. There's a lot going on."

I stared at him. It was time to confront him. "What are you hiding?"

"Dude!" Vinnie threw his knife and fork on his plate, got up and glared down at Ivan. "Was the old man right to distrust you?"

"Vin." Daniel waited until Vinnie looked at him. "Let's talk, not threaten."

Vinnie crossed his arms, but didn't sit down or say anything else. Instead he returned his hostile gaze to Ivan.

"Tell us what you know." I watched his reaction to my request closely. I wanted to take note of every half-truth, omission or deception.

Ivan looked at me. "I can't tell you everything."

"Truth." Not only did I notice his regret, I also saw his frustration. "Tell us everything you can."

His smile held relief. "Then I'll tell you what I know about Patrik Bakala. We found him in Divoká Šárka three days ago—Divoká Šárka is a park about thirty minutes northwest of the city centre. He was left under a bush just like Novotný."

"And Shahab's other victims." I studied his expression. "You made the connection then."

His lips thinned. "I had a hunch, so I checked Interpol for similar crime scenes."

"Not this morning like you said earlier." Daniel looked disappointed.

"And you found our notes from last year." Francine tapped her lips. "Is that why you wanted us here? Not for the art theft?"

The expression on Ivan's face was my answer. He sighed. "I got lucky. I was looking for a way to convince my bosses to call you in, but I didn't have to. Tomas Broz got himself arrested and that was the way I could get you here."

"What?" Daniel thought for a moment, then nodded his head. "You were stonewalled when you pursued the Shahab connection."

"Yes. I still don't know why the brass insists that we stay away from that line of inquiry." He touched his neck in an unmistakable cue of deception. "The moment I told them I thought Shahab might've killed Patrik, they reacted strongly. Which only made me more convinced of my theory. The last twenty-four hours have proven that my gut was right." His lips thinned even more, then he looked at Daniel. "They've been pressing hard for me to steer you away from Shahab."

"Well, if that doesn't get my Spidey senses all a-tingling, then nothing will." Francine's fingers hovered above her laptop's keyboard. "Should I hack your police system and see what they're hiding?"

"Oh, God, no." Ivan waved his hands, then lowered his hands and pressed them hard against his thighs. "Let's rather talk about Patrik's crime scene."

"Yes, let's." Colin's nod at Francine was subtle, her responding smile just as fleeting. I sighed. These people had a fluid concept of abiding by the law.

Ivan narrowed his eyes at Francine as she typed on her laptop, then looked away. "I was not on call when they found Patrik. If it hadn't been for his severe injuries, I would not have been called to the scene. His fingers had been broken as well as all but two of his ribs. The autopsy revealed that his spleen and liver had ruptured. He had been brutally beaten."

"What do you know about his life?" I asked.

"Well, he was twenty-three when he died. He was doing a postgraduate course in micro-biology and lived a quiet life. He had a driving license and a small car, never got as much as a parking ticket."

"Did you know about his relationship with Doctor Novotný?" I asked.

"Not until Francine told us about the emails a few seconds ago." Again his *orbicularis oris* muscles contracted his lips into a thin line. "We were only able to ID him the evening before you came. The evening before his uncle's death. But we still don't have an address for him. Yesterday, I requested access to his social media and other online accounts, but was denied. I was told that it was not relevant to his murder."

"Okay, stop." Francine rolled her eyes. "Come on. Did your bosses really think that would make a good detective ignore evidence that is always relevant? Especially if we're talking about a young person. They live on the internet."

"Clearly they hoped it would."

"Then they're stupid. Pah. If you were chosen to run such an elite team, they should know you would pu… hey! Maybe they were hoping you would ignore them."

It was fast, but I'd noticed Ivan's reaction.

"I didn't ignore them. Not technically." He glanced at Daniel. "I grabbed the first opportunity I could to call in reinforcements."

"Tomas Broz and his painting." Vinnie sat down. "You're just lucky that they are connected."

"Yeah, I didn't see that one coming."

"Do you know why they don't want you to look deeper into Shahab as a suspect?" I asked.

He rubbed his hand over his mouth. Typical gesture when someone wanted to hide their words. Then he raised his head. "I have some idea, but please don't press me to go into that. I will share it the moment I know it will help us. For now… just please don't ask me about it."

"Good evening, everyone." A woman in her mid-fifties walked into the conference room. Her unbuttoned white coat was without stain or wrinkle, but her short hair looked like she'd pushed her hands through it countless times. Her pastel-green blouse was rumpled and only tucked in on one side. She looked tired. "I'm Doctor Filipová. Mister Millard asked me to update you."

"He's awake?" Francine jumped up and walked to the door.

The doctor put her hand out to stop Francine. "He's

awake and getting dressed. He's also very difficult and insisted that we leave him alone and update you so he wouldn't have to do it."

"Sounds like the old man is almost back to his old happy self." Vinnie smirked. "What's the prognosis, Doctor? Will he become a happy and laid-back man, filled with the joys of life?"

The doctor smiled. "I doubt that. But he will make a full recovery."

Roxy got up and walked to the older woman. "I'm Doctor Roxanne Ferreira. What did you find in his blood?"

"Enough fentanyl to have ended his life and another three people the size of him." She looked at Vinnie, then took in everyone sitting around the table. "If you hadn't acted as fast as you did and brought him here, he wouldn't be complaining about everything at the moment."

"Aftercare?" Roxy asked.

"Rest and monitor his heart, but I'm confident he won't feel any aftereffects within another day or two." The doctor pushed her hand through her hair. "If I leave now, I might make it in time for a late dinner with my husband. If you'll excuse me."

Francine pulled the doctor into a tight embrace, then stepped back and wiped her cheeks. "Thank you."

"You're welcome." She turned to the door. "Now pack yourselves up and save my poor nurses from that man."

"It's I who needs saving." Manny was standing in the door, his hands in his trouser pockets. His pallor was alarming, but his smile genuine when Francine squealed and threw her arms around him. "Stop the fussing, woman. I'm fine."

The doctor looked at Roxy. "You can deal with him now. He's not fine yet and needs to rest, but I'm going home."

She waited for Manny to enter the room before she left. Manny allowed Francine to drag him to the table. He looked at everyone and nodded in response to the greetings and teasing. His glance landed on me. "Doc?"

I swallowed. It felt like a large piece of bread was stuck in my throat. The last hour had been a great distraction from the reason I'd gone into a shutdown. But seeing Manny walking towards me, concern on his face, brought the panic back. I shook my head and held out one hand as if it would stop his progress.

He didn't stop. Instead he leaned over me, his face filling my vision. "Look at me. Do your Doctor Face-reader thing and look at me."

I did. A lone tear rolled down my left cheek. I pushed Mozart's Quintet in E flat major for Piano and Winds into my mind and continued studying every micro-expression on his face until I could speak again. My words came out as a whisper. "I was scared."

"So was I, Doc," he also whispered. "But you're okay now and I'm almost okay. You heard that horrid doctor. A bit of rest and a lot of tea will fix me right up."

"She didn't say anything about tea." I exhaled heavily when I saw the fleeting amusement in Manny's eyes. It was reassuring to once again be annoyed by Manny.

He straightened. "She did. You just didn't hear it."

"You know I can see when you're lying, right?"

"Well, I'm not lying when I'm saying that I want to have a cup of tea before I go to sleep on the wrong side of that overpriced hotel bed."

"You can have my side, sugar-bear." Francine laughed when Manny swore rudely. "But I agree on getting out of here."

"We can all do with a good night's rest after today." Ivan got up. "Daniel and I will join you for breakfast tomorrow morning. Hopefully, we'll have some results on Doctor Novotný's autopsy. And more data."

Chapter EIGHT

"DID YOU SLEEP AT ALL?" I put my coffee mug under the coffee machine spout and turned to where Francine was sitting at the kitchenette counter.

"Nope." She flipped her hair over one shoulder. "It was either lie in bed and stare at Manny the whole night, worrying about him, or get dressed, pretend I'm fabulous and get work done."

I studied her. She'd clearly spent more time than usual on her appearance. Her make-up was slightly heavier than I was used to. I wondered if it was to hide the dark circles she always had under her eyes when she was tired and stressed.

Behind the façade of determination and focus, I could clearly see her fear. And I found this most disconcerting. My breathing increased with my heart rate as panic started pushing at my brain.

I inhaled deeply, then placed both palms on the countertop, reaching towards her. "I don't know how to do this. I'm not equipped to be a friend. The books I've read talk about supporting friends when they exhibit fear like you do now. I don't know how to support you."

Francine tightened her jaw and looked at the coffee

machine dripping out my coffee. I waited for her to compose herself. When she looked back at me, her eyes were shiny with unshed tears. "You're the bestest best friend anyone can ask for. And you're doing exactly what I need you to do. You're not fussing. That would turn me into a puddle of goo and then we won't be able to focus on work."

"You can't turn into a puddle of goo." I thought about this. "Unless you are talking about the decomposition process after death."

"Oh, God, Genevieve." Francine burst out laughing. "No, I was not talking about that, but thank you. All gooey emotions are now properly gone."

"Oh." I turned to get my coffee. "Okay."

"So I found something interesting." She pointed at the chair next to her.

I took it and placed it across from her. When she didn't say anything else, I sighed. This time I would play along with her melodrama. I knew she employed this to help her cope. "What did you find?"

"Ooh, I thought you'd never ask." She winked at me. "I found this just after two this morning while you were all snoring."

"I don't snore." I had an app that recorded my sleeping patterns. Also to monitor if I had any breathing, snoring or sleep apnoea problems.

"Hmm." She glanced at her silver wrist watch that matched the eight silver bracelets jingling every time she moved her hands. Which was all the time. "They're most likely still snoring. Hey, what are you doing up and ready at half past five in the morning?"

"I was going to work." I sighed angrily. "Tell me what you found."

She leaned forward and whispered loudly, "Patrik Bakala was Jan Novotný's nephew."

"There's more." I'd known her for long enough to recognise the signs.

"Oh, there is more and then some." She rubbed her palms together. "I used my social media and Google-fu and found quite a few gems." She leaned back in her chair. "Don't ask me how I got all this info, but about eleven years ago, Doctor Jan and his brother had a huge—I mean epic—fallout. There were quite a few ugly emails flying back and forth between them. All about their late father's estate.

"Jan didn't care about the inheritance. Since he had no-one and nothing but his work, he said that he had enough money and didn't need their dead father's. He was going to put his full inheritance into a trust for his nephew Patrik, who was then twelve years old. He wanted his brother to do the same, even if it was only part of his inheritance. Brother didn't want to do that. He wanted to sell their father's small house in Berlin and use that money as well as the cash inheritance to invest in his cleaning company. He even wanted Doctor Jan's inheritance as well."

She threw her hands in the air and rolled her eyes. "Well, that just blew up all over the place. Jan refused and even went to court. It went on and on and on and on. Should I tell you?"

"Please don't."

"Thought so. Anyhoo, Jan signed legal documents giving his brother everything. He disavowed his brother completely and cut off all communication. The same day, he established a trust for his nephew. He waited a year before reaching out to his nephew. I found that email and was quite touched. His nephew seemed totally ready to connect with his uncle and get away from his dad. Do you know why?"

"Of course not." What an absurd question.

"I know you don't know. That's why I'm going to tell you." Again she paused dramatically. "His dad—Jan's not-so-loving brother—had used all the money for his cleaning business and lost it all. In less than a year. In the process he took to the bottle and was by now a proper drunk. Patrik stayed with his dad until he was sixteen, then went to live with his uncle."

"Didn't that cause legal problems?"

"No. You know why? I'll tell you why." She smiled when my lips tightened and I frowned. "Patrik changed his name and appearance. Before that he had long hair and was totally into heavy metal—the look, black clothes and all. When he moved to live with Jan, he cut his hair short and went all preppy. His social media photos for the last nine years are all slacks, shirts and vests like a proper nerd in the movies would wear."

"Did he legally change his name?"

"After a few years, yes. He took his mother's maiden name, which is Bakala. And it seems like he and Jan were very careful to keep their lives separate in public. Nothing connected them on social media or anywhere else."

"What about the police? Wasn't there an investigation when he left home at sixteen?"

"Nope. Brother dear never reported his own son missing." The corners of her mouth turned down. "Bastard."

"Apart from the emails, did you find anything else to connect them?"

"No." Francine waved her index finger at me. "Don't even think it. Patrik's father didn't do any of this or have any contact with Shahab. He's been dead for four years."

I thought about this information. "You didn't mention the mother."

"Because she died when Patrik was three. Breast cancer." Her expression softened. "He'd had a rough start, but it really seemed like he found a home and love with Doctor Jan. And now they're both dead."

"Who's dead?" Manny walked out of their room.

My eyes widened. "You look different."

"Hmph." He glared at Francine. "This is what happens when she packs and tells me to trust her."

"Doesn't he look snappy?" She jumped up and hugged Manny before taking his face between her hands and studying him. "How are you feeling?"

"Downright daft in this outfit." He grumbled when she kissed him, but pulled her closer and closed his eyes.

When she moved back, he grumbled again. "I'm fine. I told you that yesterday."

"Blah, blah." She stepped back, but didn't take her eyes off him. "Your colour looks better. But it could be because for once you're wearing decent clothes."

The tan trousers were perfectly ironed as well as the fitted black shirt. His black shoes were not the scuffed brown slip-ons he usually wore and his belt looked new. His stubbled jaw and the scowl on his face had not changed though.

"Oh, this is…" Colin laughed as he walked towards us. "Millard, you look respectable for maybe the first time since I had the pleasure of making your friendly acquaintance."

"Go back to your room, Frey. And stay there." He turned to Francine. "Now I have to put up with this the whole day."

"Back to your sunny normal self, I see." Colin kissed my cheek and walked to the coffee machine. "I heard Vinnie in his room, so he should be out here soon."

"An early morning for all of us." Manny sat on the chair on Francine's other side and pointed his chin at her laptop. "Did you find something useful?"

She had to start her update three times, twice more when Vinnie, then Phillip joined us. Vinnie went straight to the kitchenette and started breakfast.

"Ooh, you're all up." Roxy walked into the shared area, still in her pyjamas. Pink llamas were chasing clouds on her flannel trousers and shirt. Francine's lip curled when she noticed Roxy's bulky blue woollen slippers. Roxy lifted her arms and pretended to sleepwalk towards Vinnie as she'd done a few times before. "Coffee. I need coffee. Now."

Vinnie held out a mug without turning around to face her. She giggled, took the mug and hugged him from behind. "You are my hero."

"Bloody hell." Manny's eyes were wide as he observed them. He turned to me. "Do they do this often?"

"All the time."

"Well, kudos to you, Doc." Manny rubbed his chin, then looked at Roxy. "Doctor Ferreira, can you tell me more about this rubbish that nearly killed me?"

"Why yes, I can, Colonel Millard." Roxy's faux British accent caused Manny's scowl to deepen. Francine snickered and held out her fist to bump it against Roxy's. The latter dragged a chair to my other side, but thankfully didn't sit too close. She took a sip of her coffee and sighed happily before she focused on Manny. "What would you like to know?"

"Let's start with the basics of fentanyl. I haven't had the need to learn about this before now."

"The Americans know much more about opioids." All jesting left Roxy's expression. "They've been running education campaigns and have produced a lot of documentaries in an attempt to teach people about all types of opioids. The current estimate is that about ten percent of people who are prescribed opioids to deal with post-surgery and other pain become addicted. I think it might be more than that, since there is such a stigma attached to addiction that people will do anything and everything to hide it.

"Very few people actually start on fentanyl. It's only after their prescribed medication runs out that they start looking for illegal substitutes. Then there are those who are on heroin or other opioids for a long enough time that they no longer get the effect they want from small doses, so the idea of getting more bang for your buck with fentanyl makes it attractive. It's cheaper than heroin and cocaine, so if you think about it, it is more cost-effective."

"But a lot of addicts don't even know they're using fentanyl, right?" Francine asked. "I read this morning that fentanyl is a favourite to use as a cutting agent when the dealers are making up their cocaine or meth batches."

"True." Roxy took a moment to think. "No, I can't remember the statistics of that. But I know that fentanyl as a cutting agent will result in an intense physical addiction to opioids. Over a longer period, addicts' bodies develop a tolerance for it and they need to up their doses all the time." She looked at Francine. "I would have to read Doctor Novotný's research, but if he was on the road to develop a drug that could counter the effects and build a resistance to opioids, it would make recovery for addicts so much easier." She frowned. "But it would be problematic if they ever needed surgery. Usual anaesthetics wouldn't work on them. Hmm."

Roxy presented plenty of information to consider. There were many complex elements to keep in mind. One of those elements was the growing list of people involved in this case. I thought about it some more. "We are working on very strong circumstantial evidence that Shahab killed Patrik Bakala three days ago and Doctor Jan Novotný yesterday morning. I'm willing to accept that speculation. We've also found evidence in Antonin Korn's gallery that Shahab was supplying him with Near Eastern antiquities for his black-market sales. What we don't know is if there is any connection between Antonin Korn and Doctor Novotný and his nephew."

"I haven't found anything at all," Francine said. "And I've looked. There have been no emails from Doctor Jan to Ant. And Jan emailed everyone."

"The connection we have—albeit tenuous—is the fentanyl on Antonin's briefcase and the fact that Doctor Novotný was working on a cure for opioid addiction." Roxy sat back in her chair. "A cure like that would be life-changing for so many people. Far too many people are caught in its awful web. And it's too easy to overdose."

"Holy hell." Manny rubbed his hand over his face. "Close call."

Francine slapped his shoulder with the back of her hand. "One you are not going to ever repeat. You are going to live forever, you hear me?"

"No one can li…" I nodded. She was speaking in hyperbole as she did so often.

"What's this?" Manny stared at the mug in front of him, then glared at Vinnie.

"Coffee." Vinnie shrugged. "I thought it might tide you

over until I put the croissants in the oven and run downstairs to get milk for your tea."

"There's no milk?" Manny looked around the large shared room. "What kind of place is this?"

"You finished the milk last night with your four cups of tea." Francine tapped on her tablet. "I can order room service."

"Nah." Vinnie opened the oven door and put a tray inside. "I'll pop downstairs quickly." He looked at Manny. "I'll be back in a jiffy."

Manny grunted. "You should stick with your terrible Texan accent. Your British accent sounds like you are in pain."

"With you around I am." Vinnie slapped his thigh as he laughed. "That was funny."

"Bugger off, the lot of you."

And so it went on. Vinnie left, but Colin and Roxy teased Manny about his outfit while Phillip complimented him. Francine exaggerated every word she said, but her nonverbal cues communicated less distress the longer they went on and the more Manny groused about everyone's disrespect.

Phillip's phone rang in his bedroom and he left, a soft smile on his face. It was good for me to see him this relaxed. The last two days had brought immense tension to his muscles. Watching his disquietude had eliminated the usual protective layers I had built up to keep shutdowns at bay. As he closed his bedroom door behind him, I turned my attention back to the bickering around the table.

The hotel door slammed open, causing all of us to jerk. Manny and Colin jumped up, Manny reaching for the back of his trousers where his handgun was holstered.

"Look who I found loitering around the lobby." Vinnie entered the room, dragging a woman behind him.

I gasped, my hand flying to my chest. Walking reluctantly into the room was the woman I'd seen at the police station and the gallery. Today she was wearing an orange-brown knitted dress, black tights, the same brown double-buckled boots, another bulky scarf and a brown fedora. This close, I noticed for the first time the pink, blue and green neon highlights in her thick braid draped over her shoulder.

She glanced at everyone in the room and seemed to relax. Until she noticed the gun in Manny's hand. She took a step back. Vinnie didn't allow it. He jerked her closer. "You've been wanting to meet us. Well, here we are."

"You can let go of my wrist now." Her voice made me gasp again, her neutral English accent unmistakable.

I pointed at her, but couldn't speak. No one noticed me.

Vinnie was waiting for Colin to place himself by the door before letting go of the woman. Even though Manny was pointing the weapon at the floor, everything in his posture communicated readiness to act. To shoot.

Francine jumped up with her phone in her hand. She walked straight to the woman and took a photo of her face. "Nice outfit. Very hipster."

"Um. Thanks?" The woman watched as Francine rushed back to her laptop and uploaded the image.

I'd worked with Francine long enough to know that she was running a facial recognition search for this woman on all the databases we had access to.

"Who are you?" Manny's tone was frigid as he nodded at Vinnie, who stepped away from the woman. Vinnie placed himself between the woman and me, Francine and Roxy.

"Are you okay now?" The woman studied Manny's face, seemingly recovered from her initial shock. "I was worried when I doubled back and saw you being taken to the hospital."

"Who the holy bleeding hell are you?" Manny's *masseter* muscles tightened his jaw until it looked like he might break his teeth. Roxy got up, her hand reaching towards Manny.

Phillip's bedroom door opened, drawing the woman's attention. Her eyes widened, her lips parted and her face turned ashen.

But it was the shock on Phillip's face that brought blackness to my peripheral vision. A deep sadness pulled the corners of his mouth down. He walked towards the woman, his head tilted. He stopped next to Manny, his expression soft as he shook his head in disbelief. "You look just like your mother."

Chapter NINE

"WHAT THE BLOODY HELL is going on here?"

"Who are you?"

"Wait. What?"

Shouted questions continued to go unanswered, but I could barely focus on anything except controlling my non-neurotypical reaction to sensory overload. I turned my back on everyone and concentrated on my breathing and Mozart.

"Jenny, I'm here." Colin's hand was warm on my shoulder. I let the Larghetto of Mozart's Quintet flow through my mind as I focused on Colin's hand slowly sliding down my arm. I opened my fist and gripped his hand.

I turned around and looked at Colin while I took three slow breaths. His attention had not drifted anywhere else. He smiled at me. "There you are."

"I didn't leave."

"I know." He took my hands in his and squeezed lightly. "Okay?"

I nodded. I took another three breaths, but didn't feel ready to look at the others. I moved closer to Colin, my voice quiet. "Is Phillip well?"

Colin twisted around and I stared at his ear. If I saw any

form of distress on Phillip—a man who'd become like a father to me—it would completely overwhelm me. Colin turned back, his smile genuine. "He's fine. Millard looks ready to go to war though."

That relaxed me. An angry Manny was familiar ground to me. I blinked a few times and looked around Colin. Everyone but Manny and Vinnie was sitting on the sofas in the centre of the area. Francine was tapping on her tablet screen, Roxy holding Vinnie's hand resting on her shoulder as he stood behind her.

Phillip was staring at the woman, his expression gentle as if recalling a memory. The sadness I saw was slight. He was not distraught.

Manny swung around when the woman's gaze turned to me. He shook his index finger at me. "Come sit down here and do your job, missy."

"How dare you." The woman moved to the edge of the seat. "She doesn't deserve such treatment."

Confusion pulled at the stranger's face when her comment caused a few snorts and chuckles. Francine fluttered her eyelids, but didn't look up from her tablet. "For the record, I agree. But you're never going to turn a Komodo dragon into a unicorn."

"Doc." Manny shook his finger at the sofa again. Colin and I sat down. Manny turned back to the woman. "Name."

"Bree."

"Gabriella Reuben." Francine's smile was smug when she lifted her tablet. "Got you here, girlie."

"Urgh." Gabriella Reuben faked a large shudder. "Only my mother ever called me Gabriella. And that was when I had done something really, really naughty."

Phillip shook his head, his smile nostalgic. "How is your mother?"

"No." Manny sliced his hand through the air. "No sweet stories. Why have you been following us?"

Bree looked at Francine's tablet. "Feel free to tell them."

"She's a journalist." Francine scrolled on the tablet screen. "Quite a well-respected one."

"I'm doing research on a story." Bree frowned at Francine, then looked at Manny and shook her head. "Don't even ask what it's about. I never reveal anything until I publish."

Manny turned to me. "Doc?"

By no means did I have enough information to give an accurate assessment of this woman's truthfulness. Instead I addressed something that seemed to have slipped everyone else's notice. "You are here because of your interest in Tomas Broz and the Elisabetta Sirani discovered under his bed. Aha. You're shocked. Then it would shock you even more that we know you've been considering setting up a meeting with Phillip. Hmm. Like I thought. But why are you scared?"

"Why?" Bree's eyes were wide, her arms crossed tightly across her chest. "I have no idea how you would know any of this."

"You don't know? Oh, boy, oh, boy." Francine leaned towards Bree. "Your AI sent Phillip an email."

"My what? How?" She looked at Phillip, then at me. "I really don't know what's going on."

"Truth."

Her expression relaxed. "You must be Doctor Lenard. The body language expert."

"You found this information while researching me." Phillip's eyes narrowed in thought. It took mere seconds, then regret filled his face. "I'm not your father, Bree."

"Bloody hell!"

"Oh, my God!"

"Shit, dude."

Bree didn't react to the exclamations. Her gaze remained steady on Phillip. "How can you be so sure? Mom talked about you a lot. I know she loved you."

"And I loved her." Phillip sighed deeply, then looked at us. "I think it's best to give context."

"Ooh, yes, please." Francine's eyes were wide with excitement, her smile joyous. She loved personal gossip.

Phillip looked up and left, recalling a memory. "Decades ago. I was working at a boutique insurance company. I was the manager at that stage. Laura was the curator at the small contemporary art gallery in London. We met when the gallery wanted to change insurance companies and also heighten their security. It was just after the famous Degas exhibition heist."

"She still tells that story." Bree's smile was genuine and filled with affection. "All the time."

"It caused great consternation in the art world at that time." Phillip leaned back in the sofa. "Laura was determined that her gallery would never be on the list of such heists. We worked together on their insurance package and got to know each other."

"Quite well," Bree added. "Mom told me about the many nights the two of you would sit and talk until sunrise."

"We never had intercourse."

"Bloody hell, Phillip." Manny pressed his fists against his eyes for two seconds. "There are some things we don't need to know."

"Shush." Francine waved one hand at Manny. "All data is relevant."

I ignored her when she winked at me. I didn't want Phillip to share anything that would cause him discomfort.

Phillip smiled at Bree. "Your mom and I… I've never had a connection like that with anyone else. She understood what I said without me ever having to explain, justify or give context. It was like she could see every intention in what I said."

"She's still like that."

"But there was never romance." There was no regret on Phillip's face. "We would've damaged… no, we would've destroyed our friendship if we'd taken it any further."

"But you lost contact."

"We did. On purpose. Your mom deserved to find a man who could love her and be with her the way she needed. Being friends with me held her back." This time his smile was sad. "She sent me an invitation to her wedding, but I thought it best not to go."

"Tom." Bree nodded. "He's the bee's knees."

"But not your father." Phillip narrowed his eyes. "Why did you think I was your dad?"

"Tom came three years after I was born." She pointed at her face. "And he's as black as Mom. This light skin and my light blue eyes came from someone else. The black and curly hair? That's all Mom."

"So why don't you ask your mom who your biological father is?" Roxy asked.

"She doesn't want to tell me." Bree shrugged. "She says he was a one-night stand to be forgotten."

"Do you believe her?" Francine asked.

"Yes." Bree glanced at Francine's tablet. "But the journalist in me is relentless. My mom always jokes that I got in the right profession because I'm so nosy."

Francine continued to scroll her tablet screen, stopping every now and then to read something before she continued.

"If Laura is the way I remember her, she would tell you if you really wanted to know who your father is." Phillip tilted his head. "Do you really want to know?"

Bree inhaled deeply and held her breath before exhaling loudly. "Maybe. I don't know. I suppose I just wanted to learn more about myself."

"Huh." Francine's eyes were wide, her mouth slightly agape as she stared at her tablet screen. She slowly looked up at Bree. "You gonna tell them or should I?"

Bree's shoulders slumped and she dropped her head back against the sofa. Then she sat up and straightened the fedora on her head, her mouth twisted in a wry smile. "I thought you saw it before. Surprised it took so long for you to say something. No matter where I go, it always follows me. Or even waits for me."

"Speak!" Manny took a step towards Bree, but stopped when Francine shook her head. The sympathy and discomfort on Francine's face were curious.

"It's no longer the first result when you Google my name, but it will be at the bottom of the first page at the very least." Bree raised her hands as if creating an air banner. "'Gabriella Reuben, scandalous transgender reporter.'"

"You're a dude?" Vinnie jerked when Roxy slapped his hand hard. "Uh, sorry."

"I don't care what you are." Manny stared at Vinnie then at Bree. "You still have a lot of explaining to do."

"I won't reveal m—"

"I don't bloody care how you think you do your work!" This time Manny walked right up to where Bree was sitting and glared down at her. "We know you're investigating the theft of the Sirani. That means you're now a person of interest in our investigation."

Bree raised her hand to stop Manny. It was interesting to observe that she didn't react like most people to Manny's intimidation. Instead her tone was calm and respectful, her nonverbal cues cautious, but not fearful. "I really don't understand how you can know this."

"Let me tell her." Francine waited until Manny nodded once and stepped back, then told Bree how her AI had sent a recording of her conversation to Phillip.

Bree's eyes grew wider the more Francine revealed about the AI system. "Oh, Tobie is going to be gutted."

"Tobie?" Manny asked.

"My assistant. I was talking to him. He's in our hotel at the moment doing more research." She scratched her head, then righted her fedora. "Tobie was the one who insisted I get the AI. It would streamline everything, he said. It would order food before I even knew I was hungry, he said. It would keep me ahead of the pack, he said. Hah."

"Well, it can do all that, but you need to have tight control over your AI, the programming as well as the security, to make sure the thing doesn't turn into a science fiction horror flick." Francine shared a smile with Bree. "Serious horror flick."

"Oh, I get that now." She looked down at her hands. "I think I will take great pleasure in crushing that device as soon as I get home."

"What's your connection to Hatami?" Manny's abrupt question froze Bree for a second.

Then her eyes narrowed. "Who's Hatami?"

It was most intriguing to observe her nonverbal cues. I didn't comment, trusting Manny to correctly analyse her reaction.

He slumped. "You mean to tell me you don't know who he is?"

"No." She bit down on her lips to prevent from further comment.

"But you're now interested in him and are thinking about how to find that information." Manny rubbed one hand over his face before he stepped back and looked at me. "Get her to talk."

I didn't respond to his irrational request.

"Okay, here's the thing." Francine put her tablet on the sofa next to her and sat on the edge, closer to Bree. "In order for us to let you leave here and not phone Ivan, our friend in the Czech police, to arrest your tiny, sexy butt, you need to talk to us."

Bree shook her head.

"Girl, you don't want these people to gang up on you. You'll lose. Whatever it is you think you're investigating at the moment, it's much larger than that."

Bree pressed her lips together.

"What about a compromise?" Phillip pulled at the cuffs of his shirt. "Bree tells us everything she knows and we will give her material for her article to publish after the case is closed."

"No." Manny crossed his arms.

"That's not a bad idea, old man." Vinnie was staring at Bree. At her throat, her chest, her hips and back at her throat.

Bree rolled her eyes at Vinnie, then looked at Manny. "I could agree. But then I want exclusive rights to everything you know."

"Why would you agree so easily?" Colin asked.

Bree shrugged, but didn't answer.

After a few seconds of silence, Francine sighed dramatically.

"Seems like I'm the only smart one here today." She pointed at Bree. "That one is trying to look all innocent and pretty, but her investigative articles and the scandals that she's uncovered tell me that she knows about us."

I didn't even have to concentrate to see the truth in Bree's reaction. "She knows."

"Okay, fine!" Bree fell back in the sofa and narrowed her eyes at Francine. "We could've been friends, you know."

"Oh, we'll be best buds soon." Francine winked at her. "After you tell us all your deepest darkest secrets." She winced. "Not those ones. I'm talking about the article you're investigating at the moment."

"Anything that was deep, dark and secret was in that tell-all article about my gender. With a lot of added rubbish. I have nothing to hide about my life."

"Just your work," Francine said. "Well, spill."

Bree closed her eyes and shook her head. Working on what she'd revealed, this would be the first or maybe one of the few times she'd shared details about a story she was developing. I could appreciate doing something new that felt wrong and uncomfortable.

"Okay." Bree clapped her hands and sat up straight. "But before I tell you, I want some form of guarantee that I'll have my story."

"No." Manny held out his hand when Francine inhaled loudly. "Hold your horses for a sec." He looked at Bree. "First, I'm going to have you vetted. What we are working on at the moment deals with issues of national security."

"Which nation?"

Manny ignored her question. "If, and I reiterate, *if* you pass our vetting, we'll be able to share some intel with you. But you can't just go and publish what you want all willy-nilly."

"I know how this works, Colonel Millard." She nodded at Francine's tablet. "I've published articles about peacekeeping efforts in Sudan and war crimes in Bulgaria. I've worked with MI5 and MI6 as well as the International Criminal Court. I know how to maintain the trust of those who allow me to enter an area deeply confidential, fraught with possibilities of great destruction to lives and careers."

"We'll be the judge of that." Manny waited until Bree nodded. "Now talk."

"Okay. I'm working on an in-depth article into the use of art as currency for the black market. With black market, I'm talking about drugs, guns, political bribes and the like. But I find myself currently more focused on the drug trade. It seems like these guys really like their art. While looking into that, I came across Tomas Broz's name."

"You mean a drug dealer told you about him," Vinnie said.

"Anyway, that was a few weeks ago and Tomas Broz had become a legend. No one had heard from or seen him in three years. Not after the Sirani was stolen. And by the way, if he hadn't disappeared off the face of the earth at the same time as the Sirani, he wouldn't have been the main suspect."

"True." Colin nodded. "Not a smart move."

"Which made me wonder why such a successful thief would do something so stupid after years of evading authorities." She smiled. "Imagine my joy when he was arrested. I knew he would be a wealth of information and just had to speak to him."

"How did you get into the police station?" Manny's tone and posture was still hostile, but had relaxed marginally.

"I walked in with a group of officers. No one even looked at me funny." She raised one shoulder. "You just have to look like you belong. And being short always helps."

"What did Broz tell you?"

Her eyes narrowed. "You don't know?"

"Why would we?"

"Uh, I saw cameras everywhere."

The room fell silent. Bree looked from Manny to Phillip to me. Then she looked at Francine, confusion drawing her eyebrows together. I made sure to observe every micro-expression. I shook my head. "She doesn't know about the footage."

"What about what footage?" Her head swung from me to Manny and back. "Please tell me what's going on."

I had a deep appreciation for the need to know, but through experience knew to wait with my answer. It was difficult not to answer and tell the truth. I pressed my fist against my mouth and looked at Manny.

"Hellfire." He sat down next to Francine, still looking at Bree. "This doesn't mean I trust you."

"Okay."

"All footage of you in the police station is gone. Deleted the moment you left the station."

"What? Why?"

"Well, I was hoping you were going to tell us. But since you don't know this, you can now tell us everyone you've spoken to about your article."

Bree smiled, then twisted her mouth in an expression that was becoming familiar. "Only one person. My brother."

"He's a criminal?"

She laughed. "Oh, God, no. He's in Scotland Yard. And, well, I didn't really speak to him. I overheard him on the phone over Christmas when he was speaking to one of his colleagues. It sounded like they were talking about a stolen clock or something like that from a burglary a few days before.

"My brother was going on about a memo he'd read the beginning of last year about an increase in the use of art as currency in the crime world. I thought that would make a great article."

"So you know diddly-squat."

"I've done a ton of research on this, but my information at the moment is only academic. I've yet to find an art thief or fence willing to talk to me about this."

"If you find a thief willing to talk, he will not be someone with reliable information." Colin lifted one shoulder. "I wouldn't trust a thief if I were you."

Manny snorted.

"So, sadly, I don't have much to tell you."

I studied her. Then recalled every micro-expression I'd seen on her face since the first time I'd noticed her in the police station. She was embarrassed, but she was being truthful. But I had many questions, most of which I doubted she could answer. So I thought about ones she could. "How did you know to go to Antonin Korn's gallery?"

"Oh, that was one of two things Tomas told me." She raised her chin when Manny swore. "You've been shouting at me so much, you didn't give me time to tell you what Tomas said."

"Well, we're bloody waiting, your highness."

"Only in my dreams." She smiled when Francine laughed. "Seriously though, no matter what and how I asked Tomas, he only said that I should go to Korn's Art and that I should stay out of this altogether. Those were the two things he repeated a few times."

"What was your impression of him?" I wondered what her abilities were when it came to reading people.

She thought about this for a few seconds. "He's full of himself. But I got the impression that under all his bravado, he was scared. I don't know. There was something off in the way he treated me like a bimbo one moment, telling me I should back away and go find something else to write about. Then the next moment, he would glance at the door and tell me I should visit Korn's Art while I was visiting Prague."

"If you're so innocent, why did you run?" Vinnie asked.

"Gut feeling?" She shrugged. "Something is off here. And now that I know you guys are looking into this, I know my gut was right. This is going to be quite the story."

"That you will not tell until you have full permission." Manny stared at her until she nodded. "Not a word."

Bree rolled her eyes. "Yes, Master."

"Ooh, I like her." Francine laughed. "Can we keep her?"

"No, you can't." Bree got up. "I'm going to my hotel to freak Tobie out about the AI. And just to spare you the trouble, I'm staying at the Castle Hotel, room 416."

Her micro-expression gave me pause. I pointed at her face. "You plan something."

"Oh, for all the saints on this planet." Manny got up, both hands resting on his hips as he scowled at her. "Missy, I'm telling you this only once. If I find you doing something stupid, I will lock you up."

"Then I'd better make sure you don't catch me." She winked at Manny, smiled at Francine, then looked at me. "I plan to do as much research as I can without making anyone take notice." She turned to Manny. "I've built a career on the trust of people who don't always follow the rules. I will reach out to those contacts. Maybe I'll find something that could help you."

"Or maybe you'll do or say something that will jeopardise our investigation or get you killed," Vinnie said.

"Let her go." Manny's nonchalance was convincing, but not genuine. "We'll be in touch if we need her."

"Or maybe I'll contact you first." Bree smiled as Phillip

got up and walked to her. "I would love for us to have lunch."

"No!" Manny's and Vinnie's answers boomed through the room. Manny stepped between Phillip and Bree, glaring at her. "You're not speaking to one of us unless all of us are there."

"Scared of little ol' me?" She laughed, then walked to the door. "I have that effect on people."

The door barely closed behind her when Colin turned to Manny. "I know someone here in Prague."

"Do you trust them?"

"Yes."

"Do it."

"Um, what are we doing?" Roxy pulled her feet under her on the sofa.

"We're getting Bree protection." Vinnie nodded at Colin. "Ty is perfect for this. I swear the dude is invisible."

"Nothing criminal, Frey." Manny sat down heavily on the sofa. "My drugged brain can only handle so much stress before I lock every bloody one of you up."

"How're you feeling?" Roxy leaned a bit forward to look into Manny's eyes.

He recoiled and turned away from her. "Irritated."

"Back to normal, then." Roxy giggled and got up. "I feel a bit er… overdressed here. I'm going to get ready for the day."

"I don't suppose you got milk?" Manny looked at Vinnie.

"Of course I did." Vinnie turned to the kitchen. "But

breakfast is ruined."

"Or we could just have everything else you prepared," Francine said. "There's a lot of fruit, cereals and yogurt in the fridge as well. I'm sure we'll survive."

Vinnie scratched the back of his neck, then rolled his shoulders as if uncomfortable. "Look, if no one is going to say anything, I'll just come out and say it. She's a dude!"

"Vin!" Francine kicked out at him, but missed. "That's just ignorant."

"What? She's gorgeous." He glanced at the room he shared with Roxy. "Not as beautiful as my Rox, but I would never have pegged her as anything but a woman."

"That's because she *is* a woman." Francine shook her head. "You know my friend, Lucille?"

"The blonde hacker?"

"She's also transgender."

"No fucking way!"

"Oh, yes way." Francine went into a lengthy explanation of her friend's journey to make peace with who she was and live her life as normally as she could.

The transgender conversation would be interesting, but now I was more concerned about Phillip. I looked at him, still standing where he'd stopped before Bree had left. "Phillip?"

He looked down at me for a few seconds. He shook his head. "She looks so much like her mother. Lighter skin and those blue eyes, but her smile and gestures—one hundred percent Laura."

I wanted to say something supportive, but everything

I'd heard other people say sounded trite. I didn't know how to support my friends. Instead I just stared at Phillip.

His cheeks lifted in a smile. "I'm fine, Genevieve. Bree has brought back a lot of memories, mostly good. I didn't even get to ask her where Laura is now. Or how she's doing." He glanced at Vinnie and Manny arguing. "After this I'll make time to catch up with her."

I thought of what he'd said. And of my relationship with Colin. "It's good to have someone who understands you."

"It was. But I was honest when I said it would never have worked out between us if we'd become romantically involved." He watched the others bicker for a few seconds, then looked at me. "Everything turned out well for me. I'm now surrounded by people who understand me. My new family."

Chapter TEN

"AT BLOODY LAST." Manny took a sip of his milky tea and sighed deeply. "Thanks, big guy."

"No problem, old man." Vinnie smirked when Manny grumbled. "There's a lot more food if you want."

Vinnie had laid out a large breakfast on the kitchenette counter. I'd only had a bowl of fruit and yogurt, but Roxy and Francine were both on their third croissants with strawberry jam. Vinnie had reluctantly included his pastries, complaining that he'd wanted to serve them straight from the oven. They were all still warm.

Ivan and Daniel had joined us three minutes ago, both still standing at the counter, filling their plates.

"You outdid yourself, Vin." Colin rubbed his stomach. "Those little pastries with the bacon were really good."

"They are good." Daniel walked to where we were sitting on the sofas, taking another bite of the small pastry and nodding at Vinnie.

"Okay, so where were we?" Ivan sat down next to Daniel.

"Well, that's pretty much it." Francine smiled at Phillip, who'd been elected to brief Daniel and Ivan on our meeting with Bree. Manny had insisted that Phillip would be the one to least irritate him. I'd agreed.

"At least now we know who sent that email," Ivan said.

"Technically, it wasn't Bree who sent it. Her AI did." Francine's smile widened. "But I'm not going to split hairs. Not on this one. I actually like the woman."

"Only because you liked her clothes." Manny shook his head. "Why don't you be more useful and tell us what you found in your research."

She laughed. "Okey-dokey. Tell me who you would like me to start with."

"Jan Novotný," I said before Manny could answer. For once I hoped we could stay on track and even follow the evidence in chronological order, the way we discovered the information.

"Doctor Jan Novotný." Francine winked at me and looked at her tablet. "I looked far and wide, but didn't find anything significant to add to his social life. The man lived for his work and only his work, it seems. And boy, am I now excited about his work." She shifted on the sofa, her eyes wide. "He wasn't working on just a boring old cure for opioid addiction. He did his research and discoveries using AI and deep learning."

"Deep learning?" Ivan asked.

"You don't know what deep learning is? Ooh!" She clapped her hands. "I get to explain it. Okay, deep learning is when AI has networks that can extrapolate data that is unstructured or not labelled. This helps us then to train AI to predict an outcome or outputs when it is given inputs."

"Holy hell." Manny's top lip curled in disgust. "That doesn't mean anything to me."

"Maybe I can simplify it." Roxy said. "Deep learning is when computers learn by example. Facial recognition is a perfect illustration of deep learning. Once the computer correctly recognises a face, it goes a level deeper, taking the first lesson with it to build on top of that. Each success is stored and used as a reference."

Francine looked at me. "You should understand. It works like our brain. Deep learning even uses the term 'artificial neural networks'. It's essential to voice control in phones, tablets and even the AI that sent Bree's email to Phillip."

"It's an exciting development in the medical field," Roxy said. "Deep learning is being used to find cures for cancer. It can do the work of many scientists, doctors or experts in minimal time. And sometimes the accuracy exceeds that of human experts."

"Yet a scientist from a Houston university has recently warned peers about using this." I'd been alarmed when I'd read that article. "She found numerous instances where the results given from deep learning were misleading and often wrong. She called it a crisis in science."

Ivan blinked a few times. "Look, I consider myself quite smart, but this just flew right over my head."

"You and me both, dude." Vinnie scratched his head and the two men laughed.

"Hmm." Manny looked at me. "Doc? Is this useful? Do we need to understand this twaddle?"

"I don't know yet." We still had far too little data. My theory about how Jan Novotný's victimology could differ so much from the Strasbourg case was still fluid, without any evidence.

"I have more technical detail about Doctor Jan's work." Francine looked at Manny. "Should I continue or would you rather hear about Patrik?"

"Patrik."

"Doc." Manny's lips twitched. "I might get a complex if you keep answering for me."

"You won't."

Everyone laughed. Manny smiled.

"Okey-dokey." She looked at her tablet. "Patrik registered here in Prague as a resident under his new name, but the address turned out to be a home-sharing place."

"My team checked it out and found no trace of Patrik," Ivan said.

"He never revealed any location on his few social media posts." Francine's eyes stretched with disbelief. "What kind of student isn't active on social media? Mind you, he wasn't really posting that often before he ran away from his dad. Once here in Prague, he posted a few times on Instagram and Twitter, but nothing significant. The only friends he had were classmates. His posts were months apart, the longest period three months and a few days. But he hasn't posted in six months."

"Six months." Colin leaned back in the sofa and looked at the ceiling. "Jan Novotný went on a sabbatical six months ago. Coincidence?"

"Okay, so what do we think happened to him?" Ivan asked, looking at me.

Francine snapped her fingers to get his attention. "You are so asking the wrong person. Genevieve doesn't speculate. But I do. I really do. Want to hear my theory?"

"Oh, boy." Roxy smiled when Manny swore and Ivan nodded.

"So…" Francine wriggled in her seat. "Six months ago, Shahab wanted Doctor Jan to do something for him." She lifted her manicured index finger. "I don't know what yet, but I'm working on a theory for that too. Anyhoo. Doctor Jan gave Shahab a hard no. Shahab didn't like that and looked for leverage to convince Doctor Jan. He found Patrik."

"You think Shahab kidnapped Patrik to get Doctor Novotný to work for him?" Ivan rubbed the scar on his hand.

"But what would Shahab want from Doctor Novotný?" Daniel asked. "I mean, Shahab has been dealing in heroin for a decade and looting his own country's art for a few years. What would he want with someone who is working on a way to end an international epidemic? A way to nullify the effects of the drugs he was selling?"

No one answered Daniel. I assumed it was a rhetorical question since we had no means to find an answer. Not yet. It remained quiet in the large room for a few more seconds.

Manny turned to Francine. "What did you learn about the Korn Art fellow?"

"I learned that no one on this planet should work without any computer." She rolled her eyes. "Apart from that, I was looking through those lists Genevieve found." She looked at me. "You were right. The one list is the names of clients. I haven't done a deep-deep dive into these people, but my light-deep dive tells me all of the people on the list are on the up and up."

"Light-deep?" I knew my expression conveyed my dismay. "You're too intelligent to be using such a contradictory term."

"Pah. Everyone knows what I mean." She glanced at her tablet again. "But the second list is the interesting one. It definitely has some suspicious characters. I sent the list to Ivan."

"My people are checking through it. Already Antonin's correspondence has given us a lot of useable evidence against numerous individuals."

Francine looked at me. "These are the people on the list you thought could be Ant's suppliers."

"So far we think you were right about this as well." Ivan smiled at me. "There are seven names of people we've already suspected deal in black-market art. We are looking into the other names, but I'm confident we'll find enough to make my superiors very happy."

I took a moment to analyse his nonverbal cues. There was something connected to his superiors that made Ivan uncomfortable. I wondered if this was related to the issue he had asked us to refrain from pursuing for the time being.

Then I thought about something else. "Have you received information about Doctor Jan Novotný's autopsy?"

"I did." He took his smartphone from his trouser pocket and swiped the screen a few times. "Ah, here it is. He died from a fatal dose of opioids, but the ME said that if that hadn't killed him, his injuries would have. He had seven broken ribs and two of those ribs didn't just puncture his left lung, they tore through it. The damage was terrible. His spleen, liver and one kidney were so badly injured that he could've died from any of those internal traumas as well."

"There is something else," I said when he paused. His creased forehead and tilted head revealed his puzzlement.

"It will really take me a long time to get used to being so easily read." His smile was genuine. "You're right. Of course. The ME was a bit mystified by what he'd found. He took a good look at it and told me that he's convinced it was self-inflicted." He tapped on his phone and turned it towards me. "This is a photo of Doctor Novotný's left hip."

I leaned forward, but the screen was small and I couldn't see the detail. What I could see was letters and numbers on the skin—red and risen as if they were burn wounds. I shuddered and shifted as far back on the sofa as I could. "What am I looking at?"

He tapped the screen a few times. "I'm sending this to Francine and she can forward this to you for a better look." He looked at his phone again. "The ME thinks Doctor Novotný burned these letters and numbers onto his skin with acid."

"Bloody hell." Manny pushed back into the sofa. "That had to hurt."

"Oh, the ME assured me it did," Ivan said. "But this happened around the same time as the torture, so Doctor Novotný was already in great pain."

"Why didn't the dude just use a sharpie?" Vinnie grimaced as if he was feeling the acid burning on his skin.

"No idea." Ivan shrugged. "Maybe he was scared it would wash off? I really don't know. What I am sure of is that this had to be something very important for him to put this onto his body for us to see."

"How do we know he did it for us to see?" Manny asked.

"Good question. I'm working on the assumption that he knew he was going to die and he was hoping that the police would find his body and there would be an autopsy that would reveal this… key? Password?"

Francine finished tapping her phone's screen. "PY%7H-A07P. I'm thinking this is a password for something. If this is GPS coordinates or an IP address, we would need another key to decipher this. Which kind of makes it stupid. Yup, I'm thinking password."

"Do we have his devices?" Colin asked Ivan.

"The forensics team went through his house yesterday afternoon while we were at the hospital and didn't find any personal devices." The corners of Ivan's mouth turned down. "They did find Patrik's room. At least now we know where he lived. There were also no devices there. It is most unusual to not find a single computer, tablet or phone in someone's house. We know that Doctor Novotný sent a lot of emails, so we know that he used a computer."

"And Patrik had social media accounts." Francine shook her head. "Shahab must have taken all their devices. This will make things more difficult. I was hoping to have a look-see into Doctor Jan's personal emails. I only have his work emails and those were already personal. I was hoping to find some juicy things that could help us with the case."

"If Shahab took their devices, then that password could be for his phone or tablet or some encrypted data or files on his computer." Colin frowned. "Or it could be for an online account or a cloud account. Damn. It could really be for anything."

"Let's take one problem at a time," Ivan said. "We know that Doctor Novotný left us a clue. Now we can move onto the next… er… challenge."

"Please tell me you found a magical way to deal with all Antonin's papers?" Francine pressed her palms against the sides of her head. "There's no way I would ever be able to get data from all those destroyed trees."

Ivan chuckled. "I have young officers scanning all the documents. Last year we got very lucky. We were given two large scanners. My team is telling me that it's taking them about thirty minutes to scan all the pages in one of those ring binders we found in Antonin Korn's office."

"Have they scanned his correspondence yet?" Francine leaned forward. "If they did, please send it to me."

"Yes. My apologies. I should've mentioned it earlier. That's why we've found incriminating evidence already. Those letters are going to send a few people to prison."

Ivan blinked a few times. "You know what, I'll just tell my team to email you the contents of each binder as soon as it's scanned."

"Or even better." Francine tapped on her phone. "Let them upload it to a shared cloud folder. I'm sending you the link now. It's completely secure, so no worries about any data getting lost or into the wrong hands."

The more they talked, the tenser I became. It was extremely difficult for me to trust anyone with collecting data. How did I know they scanned every page and didn't miss a page by accident? That overlooked page could hold key information that would help us catch Shahab and stop whatever he was planning.

Yet I was realistic enough to know that we needed all the help we could get. If I wanted to scan those documents by myself, then analyse them, it would take weeks, if not months. So I forced my shoulders to relax and took three slow, deep breaths.

"I have some information on Antonin." Phillip put his empty tea cup on the coffee table next to the sofa. "I was on a call with Adam Lendl from the National Gallery Salm Palace when Vinnie brought Bree in. With all the excitement, I almost forgot about it. Adam is the curator at the National Gallery and an old friend of mine. He immediately recognised Antonin's name when I asked about him.

"Apparently, Antonin had become the go-to expert on Iranian art, especially Near Eastern antiquities. Adam said he had a feeling that Antonin had been in close contact with these artefacts. There was something in the way he talked about the works. Adam thought that Antonin had not only studied the era, but worked with and on some of these pieces."

"Does he have any idea where we can find Antonin?" Manny asked.

"No. I asked, but he said that his relationship with Antonin has been that of a professional acquaintance. Nothing more." Phillip's *depressor anguli oris* muscles turned the corners of his mouth down in disappointment. "I'm sorry that this is not of more help."

An unfamiliar electronic notification sounded and Ivan lifted his phone. "Oh, good." He tapped on the screen and looked at Francine. "Last night I asked for access to Antonin Korn's bank accounts. I just got it. We have three bank accounts that we can work through. Do you want to do this or should I ask my team?"

"I'll do it." I took a breath when I noticed the reaction to my abrupt response. "We'll do it. Your team is already busy with scanning and working through the paper documents."

"Yeah, Genevieve and I just love digging through other people's finances." Even though Francine was presenting this in jest, I knew she was being completely truthful. Whereas I thrived on facts, data and statistics, she took alarming pleasure in knowing about people's habits and more intimate activities.

"Done." Ivan got up. "Vinnie, thank you for this breakfast. I'm heading in to meet with my team and help them work through that mountain of paper."

"Rather you than me." Francine picked up her tablet. "I prefer a paperless office."

Vinnie and Roxy got busy cleaning up after breakfast and I went to my room to collect my laptop. I loved working through data. It was a safe place for me and I was looking forward to working through Antonin Korn's financial data. Hopefully Francine and I would find something that could take us a step closer to finding Shahab.

Four hours later, we had not found anything yet. It had been a bit easier to trace transactions since Ivan's team had sent us scans of his sales records. It had helped to connect each bank transfer or deposit to the sales he had meticulously recorded. Francine had eventually admitted that even though it was inconvenient, Antonin Korn's paper records were so well kept that it made the task a simple one.

Simple as it was, there had been no sign of any illegal activities. We'd looked at transactions of the last three years and I found it highly improbable that we had not come across any irregularities so far.

I wondered if Colin had found any useful information. He'd been on his phone for hours, using different accents and different levels of charm. At the moment he was in our bedroom, speaking as Sean with an Irish accent. Daniel was sitting next to Manny on the sofa across from me, both of them busy on their tablets.

I sat back on the sofa and closed my eyes. Mentally I

pulled up an empty music sheet and slowly drew the F, then the G clefs. With great care, I wrote the first line of Mozart's Piano Concerto No.5 in D Major. And smiled.

I opened my eyes and pulled my laptop closer.

"Have you got something, girlfriend?" Francine leaned closer to look at my laptop's screen. She'd insisted on sitting next to me on the sofa so we could work as 'bestest besties'.

I moved away and frowned when she giggled. It didn't take me long to highlight the transactions that had eluded our attention. "This is what I have."

"Share with us all, Doc." Manny looked up from his tablet.

"I don't know yet exactly what this is. Give me a moment." I went into our case files that we had been working on the last year. Researching every movement Shahab had made in the last nine years had been a lengthy process and there were numerous periods in this time that we couldn't account for, but my memory for dates was such that I was confident in what I was about to find. I opened the right file and sat back. "I was right."

"For the love of the saints, Doc." Manny got up and sat down on my other side, then grunted angrily when I cringed. He moved closer to the arm of the sofa. "See? Bloody fifty centimetres or even more. Now talk."

I moved my laptop to rest on my knees. That way both Francine and Manny could see the screen. "Look at these transactions. They all went to the same account. The expense in Antonin's record is listed as office equipment and the account name is for a company called Seppo-Tommi."

"I checked the company. It's in Finland. It's legit." Francine held up one finger. "But I didn't do a deep-deep check. I'll do that now."

I highlighted one specific transaction. "See the date of this transfer?" I changed windows and pointed at the timeline we had built for Shahab's movements. "He was in Finland at that time."

"Huh." Manny nodded at my computer. "Are all the other transfers to that company at the same time Shahab was in Finland?"

"No." A small smile lifted the corners of my mouth. "Not all. Some of those dates he was in Norway, Denmark, Estonia or Sweden."

"All a hop, skip and a jump away from Finland." Manny leaned forward to look at Francine. "What is that company?"

"Seppo-Tommi." Her fingers were flying over her laptop's keyboard. "What I have so far is that the owners of this company are a Seppo Vauramo and a Tommi Harlen. It seems like they are not the founders. Wait. Huh. I have to go back in the registration records to find out what's what."

"Do it." Manny lifted his smartphone and looked at me. "Do we want access to Sonny-Tammy bank accounts?"

I thought about this. "Yes. And it's Seppo-Tommi."

"I will need some time," Francine said. "If there's more to this company, it's well hidden. I'll have to dig more."

Manny got up and stiffened when there was a knock on the door. "Are we expecting anyone?"

"Not me." Francine didn't look up from her laptop.

"I'll check." Vinnie walked out of his room to the door, his weapon in his hand. Daniel also got up and joined Vinnie at the door.

Vinnie lifted the intercom phone and the camera engaged, but I couldn't see the small screen. I relaxed when Vinnie's posture lost its readiness to act. He put his handgun in the holster behind his back and opened the door.

"Hi! Did you miss me?" Bree walked into the room, her smile warm and genuine. "I missed you guys." She lifted a pink confectionary box. "I brought cupcakes."

Chapter ELEVEN

"OOH! CUPCAKES." Francine's smile widened when Bree opened the box and offered it to her. She took one with chocolate icing. "We are so going to be friends."

Bree's laughter was genuine and loud. She turned to me, but stopped when I shook my head. I didn't want a cupcake. She put the box on the low table in the centre of the sofas and sat down on the only empty sofa, glancing around.

"Phillip is in his room." Manny glowered at the box, then at her. "What are you doing here?"

"Your warm hospitality must be such a boon when you're building rapport with people." Her sardonic expression alerted me to her sarcasm. I made a note to reconsider all her statements before I took them literally. She seemed to be prone to overuse irony. "You'll be pleased to know that I come bearing tides of joy."

The door to Phillip's room opened and Bree's eyes immediately widened in recognition, her dilated pupils an indication of her pleasure to see Phillip again.

Phillip's reaction mirrored hers. His step faltered, then he walked towards her. "I'm glad to see you again, Bree."

She smiled and nodded at the box. "I brought cupcakes."

Phillip sat down next to her. "I heard you saying that you have good news for us."

"Indeed." She glanced at Vinnie and Daniel still standing by the door, their postures more relaxed. Her eyes rested on Daniel. "Hi! I'm Bree. Who are you?"

"Daniel Cassel." His smile was small, but genuine. "I'm Strasbourg police."

"Aha. Okay. Want a cupcake?" She pointed at the box, then shrugged when Daniel shook his head. She leaned forward, took a pink cupcake and looked at Manny. "I had a breakthrough with a source. Right now I'm waiting for a call from him to give me a time and place for a meeting. I thought you might like to join me." She took a large bite from the sweet cake.

"What meeting?" I hated it when people gave incomplete information, whether it was to be cryptic or merely negligent. "With whom? About what?"

Bree smiled at me, not offended at my inpatient tone. She inhaled to speak, but waited when Colin came in from our bedroom.

Colin blinked when he saw her. "Bree. How are you?"

She looked at Vinnie, then at the kitchenette, then back at Colin. "Parched. Dying of thirst. Desert-dry."

"Bloody hell." Manny pointed his finger at Vinnie when the latter turned to the kitchenette. "Don't you dare. She needs to speak."

Bree put her cupcake down, grabbed her throat and uttered a dramatic and fake cough. "Water. Water."

Vinnie tried unsuccessfully to hide his smile as he walked

to the kitchenette. "Why don't I make us all some coffee?"

Bree smiled warmly at Vinnie, picked up her cupcake and turned to look at me, glancing at Colin sitting down next to her. Her expression sobered. "I arranged a meeting with Karel Maslák."

Colin froze for a second, then frowned. "Karel retired more than seven years ago."

"Yes, but the relationships he'd built over the last five and a half decades have not disappeared." She shifted on the sofa to fully look at Colin as she took another bite. After a few seconds of evaluation while she chewed, she nodded as if to herself. "You might know that he keeps in touch with his most trusted business acquaintances."

"Who the bloody hell is this Carl?" Manny demanded. "And how do you know anything about him?"

Bree turned back in her seat to look at Manny. "Part of my job as an investigative journalist has always been to do in-depth research. If I want to write an article about art being used as currency in the crime, especially the drug-world, I need to know all the players. That includes people who are working in the light."

Colin nodded. "Karel is a legend in the art industry. You might not get art thieves or fences to talk to you, but he loves to share his amazing stories."

Her fleeting pout caught my attention. "He didn't want to share with you?"

"Apparently, he doesn't like being interviewed for articles. He told my assistant he was misquoted in an article in 1976 and since then he refused to speak to journalists."

She made a sound of derision. "Talk about throwing the baby out with the bathwater." She pushed the last of the cupcake in her mouth.

I ignored her last statement. "If he refuses to speak to journalists, how did you get him to agree to meet with you?"

"Oh, bloody hell." Manny slumped deeper into the sofa. "What have you done?"

"What any respectable journalist would do." She raised one shoulder and put the empty cupcake paper on the coffee table. "I told him I was doing research for my master's thesis about the art industry and wanted to interview a legend."

"How did you know it would work?" Vinnie put a tray of coffee mugs on the coffee table.

"Research." She thanked Vinnie for saving her from dying of thirst and took a mug. "One of the art gallery owners talked about what an amazing fountain of information Karel would be and that he loved talking about the historic deals he'd been part of. I got the impression he has quite an ego."

Colin nodded. "Oh, he definitely loves telling stories. I've only met him three times and each time he thrived on people listening to his anecdotes. I must add though that in all three of those occasions he blew me away with his incredible insight. Someone told me that Karel is considered an encyclopaedia for art deals in Western Europe. Those three meetings made me agree."

"Then you should go with Gabriella." Manny's lips

twitched when Bree groaned. "It is your name, right?"

"Only when I've done something bad." She laughed when Manny just stared at her. "I was hoping I could take your art expert."

"You were hoping to take Phillip." It had been clear in her quick glance towards Phillip and regret when she looked at Colin.

She turned to me. "Can I ever lie to you?"

"Yes, you can."

She laughed. "Okay, but can I do this and you won't see it?"

"It's possible, but not probable."

"Well then." She looked at Phillip. "Would you consider coming?"

Phillip shook his head. "This is not my expertise. Colin is far more qualified than me to go to that meeting."

"And he already has a previous relationship with Karel." I thought about what she'd told us. "But Karel is expecting a student to interview him."

"Yeah, I was kind of planning an ambush." She didn't look contrite, even though her tone implied it. "I've done a few of those in the past and the honest reactions might have been hostile, but it always got me what I needed and often more."

I didn't like this confrontational approach to glean information from someone. I knew it was a style that worked, but I preferred something more professional.

"Would you mind horribly if I take the lead on this?" Colin's question was phrased in a way different to his usual manner of speech. "I might have an idea that would make Karel more amenable to sharing with us."

"Sure." Her answer was immediate. "I'm not one of those who always need to take the lead. I need to get the job done—which means getting as much information as quickly as possible."

"Then it's done." Manny looked at me. "You're also going, Doc."

"Colin is more than competent." I stopped when he raised his palm to stop me.

"I know, Doc. But I want you to see the things us mere mortals can't. And don't even think about arguing with me right now. I still have a headache from yesterday's débacle."

Bree's phone rang and I swallowed my response to Manny's statements. She swiped her phone's screen. "Hello? Yes, sir… That would be my pleasure… In half an hour?" She looked at us and Colin nodded. "Not a problem at all. Sir, I wonder if it would be okay if I can bring my professor and her husband to meet you as well. They were curious when I told them I would meet you… No? Fantastic. We'll see you soon."

"I'm not your professor." Horror filled me. "I cannot pretend to be someone I'm not."

"Oh." Her eyes widened, then she tilted her head. "You are a doctor, right?"

"Yes. Not a professor."

"Then I'll say I consider *you* my mentor." She leaned towards me, her face open for me to read. "Which, in all honesty, I would be so honoured. But we can say that I mentioned to you that I was going to speak to Karel and your husband overheard. He's the one insisting on coming with, because he'd met Karel before." She looked at Colin. "I have a feeling you will be okay with that deception?"

Colin took my hand. "Want to be married for a few hours?"

"No." My immediate reaction elicited snorts of laughter and shock on Bree's face. She took another cupcake. A white one.

I didn't like any of this. I had not mastered the diplomatic deceptions, exaggerations and politenesses neurotypicals employed in everyday communication. The few times I'd had to engage in such activities had been most trying.

Colin kissed the back of my hand. "Do you want us to stay? Bree can reschedule or we can find a different way."

I considered this. Finding Antonin as soon as possible would greatly aid us in having a better understanding of Shahab's art trade here in Prague. He might even give us insight into Shahab's motivation or his end goal. Or why Shahab had tried to kill him. I sighed deeply. "No. I'll do this."

"Then we'd better get going." Bree got up. "It's a good twenty minutes to drive to his house."

"Vin?" Colin also got up. "Dan?"

Daniel was still standing at the door. "I'll pick Ivan up and meet you there."

"I'll take the old man with me." Vinnie looked at me.

"We've got your back, Jen-girl."

"I know." And I understood the meaning of his words in all its nuances. I truly trusted Vinnie to protect me, not just physically, but in all ways. He was a good friend.

It took us eighteen minutes to reach Karel Maslák's house. Colin parked his SUV in a clearly affluent street. The only other vehicles here were in a price class not within reach for the average wage earner. Not even the above-average wage earner.

We were parked across from a house with large tinted windows. A small balcony led from the top floor to overlook the greenery on our side of the street. It was quiet and peaceful here.

"Give me a minute." Colin opened the back of the SUV and took out a small case he always kept there. Four minutes later, a thin moustache rested on his upper lip, his dark hair now had blond streaks in it and was combed tightly against his skull to the side. The hazel contact lenses and wire-frame glasses completed the transformation. He looked the same, yet very different. He took out a wooden walking stick and leaned heavily on it. "Let's go."

"Colour me impressed." Bree nodded in admiration. "Maybe I should make you my mentor."

"If you hadn't used a feminine pronoun, it would've been much better. Karel met me as Professor John Sandford, a scholar of Roman antiquities from Oxford University." He looked at me. "We'll make this work, love."

I had used the drive here to mentally prepare myself for

the deception that was about to ensue. I didn't feel ready for it, but knowing all the micro-expressions and nonverbal cues that revealed untruthfulness was a tool I could use to deceive.

Colin's gait looked painful as he followed Bree to the front door two houses down from where we'd parked. He looked down at the pavement. "Don't look, but Daniel and Ivan just parked up ahead. Millard and Vinnie parked two cars behind us and I think they're already somewhere close. We're safe."

"I'm not concerned about my physical safety." Maybe I should've been, but it was the least of my concerns. "I need to know that you'll do most of the communication."

"Absolutely." Colin's smile was genuine. "It won't be hard to get Karel to chat about his exploits in the sixties, seventies and eighties. I'll make sure to lead the conversation." He looked over at Bree. "You're still good with that?"

"Completely, Professor Sandford." She knocked on the front door, then rang the doorbell. "I'm here to listen and learn."

The door opened before either of us could reply. An elegantly dressed older man swung the door wider and smiled. "Bree?"

"Mister Maslák, it is an incredible honour to meet you." She stepped to the side. "This is my mentor, Doctor Genevieve Lenard."

"And I am her husband Professor John Sandford." Colin's Received Pronunciation was often referred to as posh, heard from those in the higher echelons of British society. It grated on my mind.

"I know you." Karel Maslák stared at Colin. "We met in 2001 at the Ancient Rome exhibition."

"In London. I remember." Colin shifted to lean more on his walking stick. "I was impressed by your memory then and even more so now. It's an honour, sir."

"Well, come in, come in." He stepped away from the door and waved us inside.

I was tempted to look back into the street to reassure myself of Vinnie, Manny, Daniel and Ivan's presence, but managed to simply nod and follow Colin into the foyer of the house. Colin's eyes widened and his smile was genuine as he walked to the antique wall unit facing the front door. His attention was wholly on a bronze sculpture of a walking man. "Not my field of expertise, but I'd recognise an Alberto Giacometti sculpture anywhere. It's breathtaking."

"One of the few pieces I've collected over the years." Karel closed the front door and walked to join Colin. "Oh, I'm lying. I've lived a life of indulging myself by collecting many pieces. Let's go into the salon. My most valued artworks are there."

Karel Maslák's English was heavily accented, but spoken with ease. He walked into a large room to the left of the foyer and immediately started pointing out different artworks to Colin. Bree turned to me and rolled her eyes before she followed them into the room.

It was interesting to watch this older man strive to

impress Colin. Or rather the alias Colin used—Professor John Sandford, who had been a seventeenth-century English clergyman and academic as well as a neo-Latin poet.

For a man who had a well-known reputation, one could easily assume Karel Maslák would be completely confident in his achievements. Yet he was regaling us with stories of how each piece was obtained, pausing frequently and only continuing once Colin exclaimed wonder and awe.

"And this Matisse I got from a countess in Poland. Mind you, her title was defunct, but she still referred to herself as a countess." He pulled at the lapels of his tailored blazer. "I spent a Christmas Eve in her house. The décor was horrid. It looked like a cream monster had vomited all over the place. Puffy cream curtains, cream and gold wallpaper, so many embroidered cream cushions there was hardly space to sit." He pointed at the leather wingback chairs placed to face the stone fireplace and waited for us to sit. "Dinner was a hoody-doo affair. The Italian ambassador was there as well as some famous film director and some other people. She spent the whole evening talking about herself, telling us about her four marriages. The last one was to a world-famous opera singer who had left her a fortune and a scandal."

He leaned forward. "Three children born out of wedlock, while he was married to the countess." He straightened and looked back at the colourful painting. "I was just going through my own divorce at the time and could really empathise with her. I think that is why she sold me this Matisse for such a good price. Or maybe it was because her husband had bought this for her after she found him kissing a mezzo-soprano in their kitchen."

Now I understood his reputation. The animation with which he talked and his ability to engage with us made him a great storyteller. But if all his stories were like the one he'd just told, I could not bear to spend unnecessary time with him. Francine would love hearing such gossip. Bree did. Her inability to sit still and the quick swipe of her tongue over her lips was a clear giveaway of her anticipation for the next anecdote.

Colin also enjoyed it. The pleasure on his face was sincere and plain to see. He asked Karel about the Degas painting hanging above the fireplace and sat back to enjoy the story. I didn't enjoy it. It did, however, give me more than sufficient time to create a baseline for Karel's non-verbal communication and better understand the nuances of his discourse.

"I'm talking too much again." Karel chuckled, then looked at Bree. "You said you wanted to ask me questions."

"I did, but I think I'll leave it to Professor Sandford."

Karel shifted slightly back and put one arm across his body. He was closing up. "What is this really about?"

"You are indeed as observant as your reputation tells us." Colin fiddled with the copper handle of his walking stick. "I had ulterior motives coming here. After the amazing life you've lived in the art world, I know that you have contacts everywhere. I also think I am right to assume that you keep tabs on everything and everyone noteworthy."

"Go on." Karel rested both elbows on the arms of his chair, displaying his growing confidence.

"I need to find Antonin Korn."

"Go to his gallery."

"He's not there." Colin leaned forward and lowered his head as if to impart a secret. "This is a matter of utmost importance, one I wish I could tell you about, but the confidentiality agreement with the other party and my lawyer's advice prevents me from sharing. For now."

Karel's eyes widened slightly, then he nodded once in understand of Colin's unspoken message. It was now clear to me that this man lived for information few others had. "Antonin is very much like the countess' baritone husband."

"He's with a lover?"

Karel's shrug was unsuccessfully nonchalant. "I know that opera singers like visiting historic villages around Prague when they're here. There is one such village. Its history of wealth and what is now perceived as horror draws hundreds of thousands of tourists every year. People love the morbid chandeliers and Halloween-type abbey. You might want to visit it yourself. It's beautiful in spring."

"That's very kind of you, Karel." Colin rested his hand on his chest. "It would be a privilege to visit you in the future to hear more of your amazing adventures. And to tell you how we enjoyed our visit to the villages surrounding Prague."

Karel studied Colin for a few seconds, then got up. "I

would like that. Very much."

It took us eleven minutes to leave Karel Maslák's house. He told Colin three more stories and warmed up to Bree when she laughed at his humour. He looked at me only twice. Neither time was with cordiality. I didn't care.

As soon as we left the house, Colin shook his head. "Wait until we're in the car."

It was hard. I had many questions. Colin walked with difficulty to the SUV and got in after he put his walking stick in the back. As soon as he closed his door, he turned to me, but frowned when I leaned away from him.

I pointed at his face. "Take off the moustache."

He laughed and carefully removed this part of his disguise. He took off the glasses, removed the contact lenses and pushed his fingers through his hair a few times. The colour was still not right, but it looked more like his usual style. I nodded. "Do you know to which village he was referring?"

"Kutná Hora." Colin took out his phone. "Let's get a quick open line with everyone." He phoned Francine and within a minute she'd put all of us on a conference call. "Okay everyone, I'll give a detailed account of our meeting with Karel later, but for now I need Francine and Ivan to find out who Antonin's lover is and where she lives in Kutná Hora."

"Is Korn there?" Manny asked.

"Karel thinks so," Colin said. "He didn't come out and say it in so many words, but his hints were quite clear."

"Doc?"

I considered my answer for a moment. "Karel was being cryptic. His nonverbal communication was truthful, but his words unclear."

"What the hell does that mean?"

"May I?" Colin waited until I nodded. "I think Karel doesn't like Antonin. That is my gut feeling without any real evidence. But what I'm one hundred percent sure of is that Karel wants more gossip stories to tell. And it would be even better for him if he could be the star of that story. He quickly gave me hints as to Antonin's whereabouts when I said I would be back to tell him about it. I swear he got stars in his eyes the moment I said that."

"Francine?" I preferred to hear from Francine rather than pontificate about the silly star expression. "Do you have anything yet?"

"One… mo… yes!" Her bracelets jingled through the speakers. She must've thrown her hands up in victory. "Antonin's company records show that he paid a salary to a Hana Zonová for three years as a gallery assistant. She resigned last year and moved to Kutná Hora. Since then her bank records show monthly payments from Antonin's private bank account. And she also owns a house in the village. That also magically appeared in her name last year."

"Okay, I'll get the right legal paperwork for us to go there." Ivan paused. "Francine, how did you get access to Hana Zonová's bank records?"

"Hello? Hello? Oh, darn it! We have a bad connection. I have to go." A click sounded.

Vinnie's chuckle was accompanied by Manny's swearing. "Bloody hell. Ivan, I apologise. We'll make this right."

"Please don't." Ivan's tone confused me. I wished I could see his face to determine whether he was annoyed or amused. "I'll make sure everything is done legally."

"What now, oh fearless leader?" Colin asked.

"Bugger off, Frey." Manny was silent for a moment. "Ivan, how soon can you get your paperwork done?"

"My team will do it. It should be ready by the time we reach Kutná Hora."

"Then this is what we are doing, Frey." Manny mumbled an insult which had Vinnie chuckling again.

"Love you too, Millard." Colin ended the call and started his SUV.

Chapter TWELVE

"UM, YOU KNOW I'm still here, right?"

I turned around to look at Bree sitting cross-legged on the back seat. "Of course we know you're still here." Where else would she be?

We'd left Karel Maslák's house and had been driving towards Kutná Hora for the last seventeen minutes. We'd just left the outskirts of Prague and were travelling east on a highway. This seemed to be mostly flat farmland interrupted by small villages.

Colin was following Ivan's SUV, driving at a speed that was at the limit of my comfort zone. The few vehicles that were travelling in the same direction as us quickly made way when they noticed the flashing police light on the roof of Ivan's SUV. Vinnie and Manny were behind us in the silver rental sedan.

"I think it might've slipped Millard's mind." Colin's smile deepened when he glanced at Bree in the rear-view mirror. "He's going to be pissed."

"He really is a huggable, sweet porcupine, isn't he?" Bree's expression held the same glee as Colin's. I didn't understand.

"That's Millard in a nutshell for you." He glanced again

in the rear-view mirror. "Why did you choose Düsseldorf?"

"Honest answer? My brother hates Düsseldorf."

"That doesn't make sense." I thought about this. "Unless you have a bad relationship with your brother and don't want him to visit you."

"Nah." She lifted her braid and twirled it around her finger in what seemed a habit. Her posture and this unconscious action while she thought were interesting indicators of a feeling of safety and comfort. "I get on very well with my brother. Even though he is a huge pain in my butt."

"Why's that?" Colin asked.

"The little shit is five years younger than me. Gareth is Tom's son, so that makes him my half-brother. My much younger brother. When he turned thirteen, he was taller than me. Not that it's very hard to be taller than me. When he turned fifteen, he started treating me like his baby sister. Being all protective and uggha-uggha."

"What's uggha-uggha?" I was not familiar with this vocabulary.

Bree laughed. "Like he's the big man protecting me, the little girl."

"Were you already living as a female?" I asked.

Her eyes stretched wide, then narrowed until she studied me through slits. "When I did my research on Phillip and I learned about you, I had to read up on autism. You're very frank, right?"

I nodded.

"And there's no malice," Colin said. "Genevieve's questions

and comments are without judgement."

"Why would I judge?" I didn't understand why Colin thought this important to point out. Yet the relief on Bree's face showed it had been her concern. I turned even more in my seat to fully observe her. "Being transgender is only judged by people who don't understand, appreciate and fully embrace the complexity and difference within the human species."

She stared at me, eyes wide. "Wow. That's… I think I love you."

I jerked back, then relaxed when I registered her expression. "You're jesting."

"Only a little. There are very few people with such an open mind." She glanced at Colin. "My brother has an open mind, but he tells me that his job in Scotland Yard has shown him how horrid people can be."

"And that's why he's taken on the role of your protector."

"Much to my dismay." She rolled her eyes. "I'm a big girl and can take care of myself." She snorted. "Okay, maybe not physically big. But I *can* look after myself."

I thought of the people who had become my family. "It's important in a relationship to trust other parties to look out for you."

She was quiet for a minute. "Is it easy for you?"

"No." Not even after six and half years with them. "But I'm determined to learn."

"Gareth is a little bit right about people being awful to me. He saw how I was treated in school while I was finding myself." She sighed. "It was difficult for him as well. We moved a lot and in every new school, he was the freak's little brother."

There was so much I needed to say that I didn't know where to begin. "There is no such thing as a little bit right. It's either right or wrong."

"That's what you're going with?" She laughed. "Not telling me I'm not a freak?"

"You're not and you know you're not."

She slapped both hands on her thighs. "That's it. I love you. Completely. Fully."

Colin smiled. "How long have you been in Düsseldorf?"

The levity in her expression disappeared. "I moved there after the article was written about my gender. The trolling became intolerable and Gareth became overbearing. He was in my flat every day, insisting that I move in with him, his wife and three children. God help me. I mean, I love the brats, but no. Just no."

I turned back to face the front, lowered the visor and tilted it to be able to see Bree's face. After a few minutes of comfortable silence, Colin glanced again in the rear-view mirror. "Do you still publish under the name you used before?"

"Most definitely, yes. Those bastards might've dented me a bit, but I'm not going to give up my name or the pride I take in the quality of my work."

Colin and Bree talked about the articles she'd written and her investigative processes. It was fascinating. She was fascinating. I listened quietly while looking at the tilled fields flanking the highway, small villages as far as the eye could see. We approached a forested area and I felt my muscles relax. Driving through such greenery was good for my mind.

The road curved to the left and a small village lay ahead of us.

"Ooh, that's fairy-tale pretty." Bree leaned forward until she was between the two front seats. I pushed myself against the passenger door and looked at the awe on her face. "Man, I so have to come back here to write something about this little place. I wonder what the history is."

"It's called the city of silver," Colin said. "It was established in the twelfth century with the settlement of the Sedlec Abbey. In the thirteenth century Germans started mining the area for silver. It is believed that this wealth helped the Czech Kingdom boom."

"Why does the Sedlec Abbey sound familiar?" Bree tapped her index finger on her lips. "Hmm."

"Think harder." Colin waited, a smile lifting the corners of his mouth. He enjoyed Bree's company.

"Blimey! It's the skeleton skull place."

"Well, I wouldn't exactly phrase it like that." His smile widened. "The small Roman Catholic chapel has incredible artistic as well as historic value. It's the art that first drew me here. Underneath the chapel is the Ossuary, which they estimate contains the skeletons of between forty and seventy thousand people. The bones of these people have been used artistically to decorate and furnish the chapel. The enormous chandelier of bones alone is worth seeing.

This chandelier has at least one of all two hundred and six bones in the human body. Then there are the garlands of skulls draping the vault. No, really. It's an amazing place to visit."

"Have you been there?" Bree asked me.

"No." But after Colin's enthusiastic description I might consider visiting something that was now thought to be morbid, but had once been considered artistic and beautiful. Karel Maslák's cryptic descriptions now made sense. I wondered though why he hadn't just given us the village's name. It seemed he was a man who greatly enjoyed playing games.

We entered the village and Colin slowed down to follow Ivan's SUV, turning right into a narrow street. The little I had seen so far of Kutná Hora reminded me of our visit to the historic artists' village of Szentendre in Hungary. Our holiday there had been interrupted by a case that had been both interesting and horrifying.

Colin's phone rang and he pressed the answer button on the steering wheel. "You're on speaker, Millard."

"Can that bloody paparazzo be trusted?"

Bree burst out laughing. "Huggable porcupine."

"Doctor Face-reader?" His demand boomed through the interior.

"Paparazzo is male. Bree would be a paparazza, but she isn't. She's an investigative journalist." I sighed when Bree snickered and Manny swore. "She has proven herself to be trustworthy, but within limits. I don't know to what kind of trust you are referring."

"Details of this case, missy." It sounded like he was clenching his teeth.

I looked at Bree in the visor's mirror. She stared back at me, her expression open to read, her smile genuine. "We can trust her."

"Are you listening, Ms Reuben?"

"Sir, yes, sir!"

"Oh, hell. Another comedian." Manny swore again. "Well, let me tell you this. If you even think about interfering in our investigation, doing or saying anything stupid, I'll throw your arse in jail faster than you can say 'porcupine'."

Bree's smile brightened for a second, then her expression sobered. She leaned forward to speak closer to the car's mic. "I value the trust anyone puts in me. Whether it is my brother to babysit his children or a whistle-blower hoping I will keep his name out of my article so he can stay safe—hell, so he can stay alive—I will honour that trust. And something tells me that this case you guys are busy with might be up there with the most sensitive information I've ever worked with." She paused. "I won't betray your trust in me."

"Hmm." Manny cleared his throat. "Well, then. You stay put with Frey and Doc. Ivan, Daniel, myself and the big guy are going to the address we have for Hana Zonová. We'll let you know as soon as we've cleared the property."

"And hopefully have Ant squashed under our boots." Vinnie's chuckle came over the speakers. "See what I did there?"

"Put a sock in it and drive." Manny said something else, but it was too muffled to hear. "Frey, find a place here to park and wait for my call."

"Done." Colin slowed down even more and parked in front of a sadly neglected building. Large chunks of plaster had fallen off its façade, revealing the raw brick underneath. On the top right corner of a building, a groove had been cut into the wall to accommodate a nest of cables running to the roof. I doubted this building had seen any maintenance in the last five decades.

"You guys seem really close." Bree looked at my reflection in the visor mirror. "Closer than other teams I've seen."

"We're family," Colin said. "Not the blood-related kind."

"Yeah, I understand that kind of family. I'm lucky that I'm close to my mom, Tom and my brother. When that story broke, their support carried me through." She smiled. "That and hugs from my brother's three monsters."

"Monsters?" I asked.

"Kids." She frowned. "You take everything literally, don't you?"

"Words have meaning. I interpret that meaning." Trying to comprehend the legion of nuances possible in one sentence was exhausting and I'd been wrong on too many occasions.

"Do you feel different to normal people?"

"'Normal' is a word too broad and generally subjective to use. If I understand your question correctly, I don't feel different than neurotypical people. I am different. This is my normal."

"Yeah, I understand about having one's own normal. My normal has not been easy to explain to people."

"Why do you need to explain it?"

"Why indeed." She paused when Colin's phone rang.

He pressed the answer button. "On speaker, Vin."

"It's clear, dude. The old man wants you guys here in a jiffy." He laughed when Manny said something in the background. "That overdose really gave him a hangover from hell. I didn't think it was possible for him to be grumpier than he usually is. But… here we are."

Colin started the SUV engine. Fifteen metres ahead of us was a park. We turned right into a narrow, cobblestone street. On our left, the park was green and appeared minimally maintained. It was nothing like the manicured parks close to our flat in Strasbourg. On our right were two-story houses, some as dilapidated as the one where we'd parked earlier.

A few houses were beautifully restored, cream- and peach-coloured paints making them look new. One house had flowerboxes in the windows—a bit early in the season, but I imagined it looked charming in summer with flowers flowing down to the pavement.

Colin drove towards the peach-coloured house at the end of the street. He tilted his head up to speak towards the SUV's mic. "I see your car, Vin. Tell Millard we'll be there in a minute."

Ivan's SUV and the rental car Vinnie and Manny used

were in front of the park, three parking spaces next to them still open. Colin stopped next to the silver rental car.

"As much as I would love to go in with you, I will stay here." Bree crossed her legs, settling deeper into the back seat. She looked at Colin. "But I really want to know all the details."

"As much as we can tell you, as soon as we can."

"Thanks." She sighed heavily, her shoulders dropping. "Man, I'm starving. I should've brought that box of cupcakes. Hey, do you think they sell cupcakes here?"

Colin laughed as he shook his head and opened his door. We got out and joined Vinnie by the wooden front door. This was the only house on the street with wooden window frames. The ground-floor windows had burglar-proofing—something I had not noticed in the other houses.

Vinnie was leaning against the doorframe and lifted his chin towards Colin's SUV. "She's staying put?"

"Yeah." Colin glanced at the vehicle. "I think she's hoping to build more trust, to prove to us that we can allow her into this case."

"Not going to bloody happen." Manny stood in the hallway and waved us in. "We can worry about sharing information with a journalist later. Right now I need you, Doc."

I nodded and walked with everyone to the back of the house. Even though the outside façade and wooden door and window frames blended well with the historical ambience of the village, the inside of this house could be any modern home in any city.

Rugs with abstract patterns were scattered on white glossy tiled floors. Recessed lighting, mirrors and modern art were well matched to the battleship-gray walls. We passed a room that had a large flat screen television against a wall. The room at the end of the hallway was the kitchen. The black and white floor tiles were matt, but the modern white kitchen units were as glossy as the tiles in the other rooms. All the appliances were top of the range.

A small round table stood in the centre of the room. Only when I saw a man sitting at the table did I realise that I had not yet seen a photo of Antonin Korn. He was shorter than average with a petite build. Francine would insist on describing his features as 'not an oil painting'. His eyes were close-set, his nose wide and his cheeks ruddy. But his short, styled hair and designer clothes made him appear like a wealthy, well-groomed man.

The kitchen was crowded and I walked to stand next to the back door. An overfull travel bag rested on three large suitcases by the door. I leaned back against the kitchen counter and further studied the man who had a reputation of great self-confidence. There was no evidence of that right now. Only fear. Immense fear.

He clenched his trembling hands into fists, his breathing was shallow and I could see his racing pulse beating in his neck. He was pushing himself against the back of the chair and it appeared like he was trying to make himself look smaller by hunching over.

Manny sat down at the table with Antonin and Ivan joined Vinnie in the hallway, leaning against the opposite wall and looking into the kitchen.

"Is Hana okay? What did you do with her?" Antonin's English was without accent, his voice high from stress. "I want to speak to her."

"Hana is in her bedroom." Manny slumped in the chair. "Why do you want to speak to her?"

"I want to make sure she understands how serious this is. She needs to go somewhere safe." He glanced at the suitcases and his expression turned pleading. "You have to keep her safe. Her and my wife and children. I was going to take them away, but you can keep them safer. You have to."

"That's a lot to demand when you're a criminal."

"I'm not a criminal." His slammed his fist on the table.

"No? Then explain why you have a business relationship with Vittorio Sordi, Mirek Havel and Jeroen Verhoeven."

Antonin crossed his arms. "You've been in my office, my records."

"Yes." Manny didn't say anything else. He waited quietly, one eyebrow raised.

It was easy to see Antonin adding the information to form a conclusion. A conclusion that caused him a series of emotions—fear, hope, relief, anger, regret. He swallowed, his shoulders sagging. "Shahab Hatami."

"Yes?"

"That's why you're here." The fear on his face intensified. "You know what he's done, don't you? You're here to stop him. Please tell me you're here to stop him spreading the poison. He's got everything ready, you know. The way he was talking, this is going to be worse than Moscow. I tried to convince him not to kill innocent people. He completely lost it. He told me that he would do whatever he wanted and if I wanted to stay alive, I should stay out of his way. But I had a feeling he was going to come back for me. The moment I heard that Doctor Novotný had been found dead, I knew I was next. Shahab has never been one to leave loose ends lying around. No, sir."

His eyes grew wide, his gaze frantic. "If you found me, that means that he will find me too. Oh, God. You have to keep me safe. Me and my family. And Hana. He's going to kill us. He's a psychopath. A madman. First he's going to kill me, then he's going to do whatever it is he's planning with all the stuff he created. Oh, man. We're all going to die."

I was the only one who didn't outwardly react to his rambling. Manny swore, Vinnie and Colin gasped and Ivan ran outside, his phone in his hand.

Manny turned to me. He inhaled, then frowned and looked at Ivan, who rushed back in. His eyes were stretched wide, his eyebrows high on his forehead, his jaw slack. Shock. I took a step back. Away from Ivan and whatever bad news he had.

"We have a problem." Ivan glanced at Antonin. "Three hours ago, a man died in one of the five-star hotels on the riverbank. Preliminary tests are coming back as an opioid overdose, but the ME is worried. There's something about this opioid."

"It's started. It's Shahab's poison. Oh, God. You have to keep me safe." Antonin got up. "Hana! Oh, God, Shahab is going to kill us."

Chapter THIRTEEN

"WE'VE TOLD GUESTS it's a gas leak." Ivan looked towards the wide staircase in the centre of the hotel's foyer. Dozens of people were coming down, some with their suitcases. I detected no panic, just looks of annoyance, confusion and curiosity.

"That is always the simplest and fastest way to get a large group of people to evacuate an area." Daniel was standing with us next to the beautiful mahogany reception desk. Even though he was wearing jeans and a thick jacket, his posture was exactly the same as the specialised police officers calmly leading the guests outside.

"Have you heard from the hospital?" Colin asked Ivan.

"Yes." Ivan had tried to calm Antonin down in gently spoken Czech, but Antonin had been hysterical. I'd recognised that level of debilitating panic. The state he'd been in had reminded me of my meltdowns. When Antonin had started crying and rocking in his chair, Manny had told Ivan to order an ambulance. "They've sedated Antonin and he's sleeping."

"If they've sedated him, he'll most likely sleep until tomorrow morning." Daniel shook his head. "I usually see such breakdowns only in traumatised children."

"His fear was real." It had affected me greatly. Even now, I was mentally listening to Mozart's String Quartet No. 1 in G major to slow my breathing and heart rate.

"We're here! We're here!" Roxy rushed over from the front entrance and went on her toes to kiss Vinnie. "How can I help?"

Francine stopped next to Roxy and looked at me. "Are you okay?"

"I'm well." Anxious and trying to process all the new information, but I was managing. For now.

Roxy took a step closer to me and stared at me, then nodded. "You're good to go."

I leaned away from her. "I'm not going anywhere."

She smiled and moved back to Vinnie's side. "Where's Bree?"

"Her hotel is three blocks away." Colin nodded with his chin towards the street. "She said she was going to walk there and do some more research. And eat. She was hungry."

"Good riddance." Manny jerked when Francine slapped his shoulder. "I don't trust that journalist."

"Not yet, but you'll come around." Francine turned to Ivan. "What do we know about this death?"

"He wasn't tortured like Shahab's other victims." That had been the first question Ivan had asked the first responders. "He had been exposed to some form of opioid, collapsed in his room and died there."

"Is this the poison Antonin was talking about?" Vinnie asked.

Ivan raised both shoulders. "We need autopsy results to know that."

"Who found him?" Francine asked.

"The hotel received a call from the victim's business partner. The victim was supposed to be at a meeting, but didn't show and wasn't answering his phone. The partner managed to convince the hotel to check his room."

Francine lifted her tablet. "What's the victim's name?"

"Jarda Zonyga." Ivan looked at Francine tapping on her tablet, closed his eyes for a second and sighed. "I don't know what you're doing now, but I hope you'll find more than we've done so far."

"What do you know?" Manny asked.

"Zonyga was a partner in a toy company. My team is looking into him, but so far they tell me they can't find a connection to Shahab." He swiped his smartphone screen and held it out for us to see. A handsome man in his late thirties was smiling at the camera. "This is Zonyga. Too young to be dead."

I studied Ivan's expression. "You're frustrated about something."

"I am." He looked at the last of the guests leaving the hotel. "It's hard to do my job when my bosses are trying to prevent me from doing it."

"The thing you don't want to talk about." Vinnie crossed his arms. "Dude, you might want to tell us soon."

The regret on Ivan's face was real. "If I do…" He shook his head. "I can't."

"Bloody hell." Manny turned to Roxy. "Maybe you can

be more useful, Roxanne."

"I hope so, Manfred." Her smile lifted her cheeks and crinkled the corners of her eyes when she used his full name.

"Oh, bugger off." Manny pushed his hands in his trouser pockets. "Tell me what kind of weapon was used in Moscow that is also related to our case."

"You know this." My frown was deep and my tone impatient. "The moment Antonin referred to Moscow, I saw the recognition on your face. You know he was talking about Kolo…" My frown disappeared when I registered his expression. "You wanted Roxy to confirm your theory."

"Well, you just did, missy."

"Wait. What?" Roxy's eyes were wide as she looked from me to Manny and back. "Are you talking about Kolokol-1?"

"Um, I don't know what you guys are talking about." Ivan looked at Roxy.

"In 2002, Kolokol-1 was speculated to be the agent used in the Russian theatre hostage crisis." Roxy's lips thinned. "Eight hundred and fifty people attending a performance were taken hostage by around fifty armed men. On day four, the Russian government pumped some chemical into the complex. Official numbers put the death toll at a hundred and seventy people, but it's highly disputed." Her curly hair bounced as she shook her head. "Not relevant, I know. What's relevant is that the Russian media reported the drug used to be Kolokol-1. It's deadly."

"Doctor Ferreira." Ivan studied Roxy for a few seconds. "If you take into account Shahab, Doctor Jan Novotný, his research and everything else you know about him, what conclusions do you reach about a poison Shahab is said to have created?"

"Firstly, call me Roxy." She paused and pulled at one of her wayward curls. "Secondly, hmm. If I take everything you just mentioned and I add your talk about Kolokol-1 and your visit with Antonin, it's easy to jump to conclusions about a chemical weapon that could wipe out as few or as many people as Shahab wants."

"Do you think Novotný could've developed this weapon for Shahab while held hostage?" Manny asked.

"Without a doubt." Roxy looked at me. "What do you think?"

"And don't say you're not going to speculate, Doc." Manny lowered his chin to stare at me. "We need something to work on, so share whatever theory you have."

"It's not difficult to come to a theory similar to Roxy's." It might not be based on irrefutable evidence and facts, but there was far too much circumstantial evidence not to reach these conclusions. "In order for Doctor Novotný to develop a cure for opioid addiction, he would've needed exhaustive knowledge of all forms of opioids, their effects on the human body and much more we're not even thinking of at the moment. All of this can be used in reverse as well. Not as a cure, but as a weapon."

"Bloody hellfire." Manny looked around the empty foyer. "What numbers are we looking at?"

"Numbers?" I wished people would be more specific in their questions.

"What kind of casualties?" Roxy inhaled deeply. "It could be catastrophic, depending on what kind of agent or narcotic Shahab has weaponised."

"This is too much speculation." I didn't feel comfortable talking about theory as if it were fact. I inhaled to continue, but paused when a man still dressed in his hazmat suit walked towards us.

"Ivan." The man continued talking in Czech, his non-verbal cues clearly communicating his respect for Ivan. I also detected puzzlement and concern.

Ivan held up his hand to stop the man and turned to us. "My apologies. Václav doesn't speak English. As soon as he's debriefed me, I'll share."

Immediately, Václav continued talking, his eyes frequently going towards the elevators.

"While they're talking, I have a question." Roxy waited until we looked at her. "Where is Shahab getting money to do all of this? Scientific research and development is awfully pricey. Since he's not paying Doctor Novotný, I'm not talking about labour, but rather the outrageous cost for the equipment Doctor Novotný would need to do this kind of work. We're not talking about things the price of a computer or smartphone. This equipment can easily reach half a million euros each."

"Seppo-Tommi." Francine smiled when we looked at her. "What? You think I was sitting in the hotel painting my toenails while you were speaking to Antonin?"

Manny swore under his breath. "Speak."

"So, I found out that Seppo-Tommi is a small, but ridiculously successful company. It was established in Finland three and a half years ago and registered to trade in the fields of research and development and human resources."

"That's vague," Daniel said.

"Absolutely." Francine nodded. "And of course I think it was done on purpose."

"Do you have any useful information?" I wanted her to get to the point.

"I do, my bestest bestie." She winked at me. "The real owners of the company are Anna Elg and Sven Laakso. The Seppo and Tommi who are listed as owners are false identities. Those people don't exist. I looked Anna and Sven up and they are as good as married. They have been a couple for fifty-three years."

"Huh? How old are they?" Vinnie asked.

"Anna is eighty-one and Sven is seventy-nine."

"There's more." I recognised the look on her face. She enjoyed building up the anticipation.

She rubbed her hands. "Anna and Sven are both in a care home in Vaasa, a small city on the west coast of Finland. This care home is an exclusive place where the richest of the rich put their parents."

"So who are their children?" Manny glanced at the hazmat official leaving and Ivan turning back to us.

"They don't have any." Francine's eyes were wide with enjoyment. "Anna and Sven met at university when they both studied optometry. They opened consulting rooms and worked together until their retirement. They did a lot of charity work, gave a lot of free eye-care and donated a lot of glasses to refugees. I didn't find one negative thing about them."

"Are they paying for their care?" I asked.

"Nope." Francine leaned forward. "They were put in the care home, guess when?"

"Three and a half years ago," Daniel said.

"Ding-ding! You win the prize." Francine spread her hands as if to emphasise the obvious. "Someone used their identities to register a company and as payment put them in the best possible care home."

"Can we interview them?" I asked.

"I suppose we could, but it wouldn't help much. Sven has advanced Alzheimer's and Anna suffers from dementia." Her pause and micro-expressions warned me. "I phoned the home and asked a few questions. They said both Anna and Sven were in a very bad state when they arrived. It took four months just to deal with their malnutrition."

"You didn't phone." Why would she lie? "Did you hack the home's system?"

"Never!" Her eyes shot to Ivan before she looked at me, her eyes widened in an expression I was familiar with.

I pointed at her face. "You're a terrible liar. And your threats don't work on me."

"You're the worst bestest bestie."

Manny glared at her, then looked at Ivan. "See what I have to deal with all the time?"

"I don't agree with this illegal action, but we got answers." Ivan cleared his throat. "What else did you learn?"

Francine smiled. "Not much more on the care home's system. There are loads of internet search results about them—lots of newspaper articles. I'll go through those later. But once I learned all of this, I looked a bit deeper." She glanced at Manny. "And you can shout all you want, but I got us great intel."

Manny sighed. "What did you do now?"

"I might've peeked into the care home's bank records."

"Dammit, Francine." He rubbed his hands over his face. "What did you find?"

"Anna and Sven's bill is being paid by a company that is registered in Cyprus. That company is owned by a company that is registered in Turkey. And that company is owned by a company registered in guess where?"

"Iran," Colin said quietly.

"Yuppers. And what's even more exciting is when I took a quick peek at Seppo-Tommi's finances. Guess who their main client is?" She didn't wait for an answer. "Yes, you are right. This Iranian company. Almost eighty percent of their financial transactions is with them."

"Do you think Shahab has a relationship with Anna and Sven?" Daniel scratched his chin. "No, I can't see it."

Neither could I. "Nothing in our research about Shahab revealed any such connection." I looked at Francine. "Did you check the timelines we built about his whereabouts when he was in Finland?"

"I did. And no, Shahab was never close to the care home. He didn't buy any old-people stuff, didn't mail anything, didn't hire a car to go there. Nothing."

"Then what is this connection?" Ivan rubbed the scar on his hand. "Do you know who owns or is connected to the company in Iran?"

"Uhm. Yeah. About that." Francine raised both shoulders. "I tried to get into the registration records, but this is Iran. I need to finesse my way around their system a bit more and you guys phoned about this." She waved her hand towards the hotel foyer. "I'll get into that later."

"Let me see if I can look into it through legal channels." Ivan waited for her to nod, then looked at Roxy. "We need to know much more about the research Doctor Novotný developed."

"Oh, I agree." Roxy's curly hair bobbed as she nodded. "It would be ideal if we could go to his workplace and speak to his boss, look at his lab and nose around. We will learn a lot more than just reading their website."

"I thought you would say that." Ivan glanced at his watch. "It's almost five, so we won't make it to the company before they close. But I phoned them earlier and asked if they would stay until we got there. Everyone agreed. It seems like Doctor Novotný was very popular with his colleagues. They want to do everything they can to help us find out what happened to him and why."

"We're not going anywhere until we've eaten." Vinnie looked at me. "You haven't eaten since breakfast and that was just a puny bit of fruit."

Had this been seven years ago, this case would've sent me into a state of hyperfocus and I wouldn't eat, sleep or shower for days on end. Being in a team with neuro-typicals had taught me the importance of breaks, meals and taking a step back to regain perspective.

"We're not bloody going anywhere until I know what happened here." Manny looked at the staircase, then at Ivan. "What did your pal have to say?"

"They've cleared the building. The only place they found the opioid that killed Jarda Zonyga was in his hotel room." His lips thinned. "It was aerosolised. They took samples and are going to test it find out exactly what it is." He looked at Roxy. "And whether it is an opioid analogue."

"Why did your colleague look perplexed?" I became concerned when experts looked confused.

"He told me he's never seen anything like this before. I've asked the ME to rush this autopsy. We need to know as much as possible about this." Ivan took out his smartphone. "I think I'll just phone them again."

"Do we still need to be here?" Colin turned to me. "Do you want to see something? Ask anything?"

I considered my answer, then shook my head. "I would rather go to Doctor Novotný's laboratory in Prokop Industries."

"First food." Vinnie put his hands on his hips. "No arguments from anyone. The only choice you get is to choose restaurant food or my cooking."

I had enough occupying my brain space without having

to obsess over the cleanliness of an unknown restaurant. "Your cooking."

His pleased smile brought a soft feeling to my chest.

Chapter FOURTEEN

"SHE DOESN'T SPEAK English." Petra Sudova pointed at the shortest woman in the laboratory, who was looking at us with tears in her eyes. "Nikola worked with Doctor Jan on a daily basis. She's heartbroken."

"We all are." Dominik fiddled with a ballpoint pen that was adding to the stains on his fingers. He'd introduced himself as Doctor Novotný's work neighbour. Their offices were next to each other. Of all Doctor Novotný's colleagues, only Petra had introduced herself giving her surname. The others had said foreigners found their surnames too hard to pronounce. Dominik had said his was the hardest. "The rest of us speak English and will translate for Nikola."

"Doctor Jan loved English." Tears formed in Petra's eyes. "He said it was a noble language. International. He insisted we use it as much as possible. He did all his work, all his writing, everything in English."

We were in a large open workspace. Long work tables ran along the walls as well as across the room. The florescent lighting made it easy to forget that it was dark outside. After one of Vinnie's quick pasta dinners, we'd arrived here no more than an hour and a half after we'd left the hotel crime scene.

Francine, Vinnie and Daniel had stayed behind. Ivan had made a valid argument that we should not arrive in a large group to interview the scientists. Manny had insisted I join him and Ivan, and had agreed when Colin had stated he would travel with us, but wait in the car. But Manny had argued with Vinnie when Roxy had agreed to join us. It had taken a threat from Roxy before Vinnie had relented in his insistence on accompanying us as protection.

Roxy and I were standing behind Ivan and Manny as the two men spoke to Doctor Jan's colleagues. This allowed me to observe their nonverbal cues.

I witnessed a lot of deep sadness.

"How can we help?" Emil Nedvěd had met us at the entrance of the four-story building and had introduced himself as the director of Prokop Industries and Doctor Novotný's friend.

"What can you tell us about Patrik?" Ivan asked.

"Who's Patrik?" Emil—the man who'd told us no more than seven minutes ago he knew everything about Doctor Novotný—frowned.

"A person of interest." Manny took his time looking at all eight individuals in the room. "Any of you know about Patrik?"

They silently shook their heads. I observed no deception cues.

"Hmm." Manny leaned against one of the long tables. "Can you tell us exactly what Doctor Jan was working on?"

"I'll do it." Petra took one step forward. "I had to give a presentation to our investors and had to change the scientific language to something non-scientists would understand."

"That will be greatly appreciated." Ivan heaved an exaggerated sigh of relief that made the scientists laugh.

"Okay, so Doctor Jan started this research four years ago, but it was only the year before his sabbatical that he started making significant breakthroughs." Petra paused and shook her head. "We never understood why he took a sabbatical. He just disappeared."

"Now we know." Dominik, standing next to Nikola, paused in his translation, his fist on his hip. "He was being used by a madman and then killed."

"What do you mean used by a madman?" Manny's question came out slow and soft. Angry.

"It's on the news." Dominik took out his smartphone. "It was breaking news early this evening."

Manny jerked and turned to me, his lips in a thin line. "Did she do this?"

"I don't know." I wouldn't have expected this from Bree. I'd only witnessed sincerity when she'd given her word not to betray our trust in her.

Manny turned back to the group, his body tense, but his expression open when he looked at Petra. "You were telling us about Doctor Jan's work."

"Yes. Well. Um. Where was I?" She snapped her fingers. "Yes, he started out using machine learning, but then chose deep learning to search for links between genomes and the proclivity to addiction. He was part of the study that showed some people's genomes carried a type of ancient retrovirus called HERV-K HML-2 which made them more likely to become drug addicts because this virus affected the production of dopamine."

Manny just stared at Petra. Then he turned to Roxy. "I think it's best if Doctor Ferreira translates what you just said into a language I understand."

Roxy smiled at him, then at Petra. "Can you explain artificial intelligence, machine learning and deep learning in one sentence?"

"No."

"Exactly. These are extremely complex fields to define." Roxy put her hand on her chest and looked at the scientists. "Please forgive me for how much I'm about to simplify this."

Petra smiled. "Oh, please go ahead. It's too hard for me to skip all the defining detail."

Roxy turned to Manny. "Okay. Hmm. Artificial intelligence is like an umbrella term. If we had a diagram, AI would be the encapsulating circle that contains machine learning and deep learning. The basics of AI is a machine that shows a form of intelligence by solving a problem. Are we good so far?"

Manny nodded once and pushed his hands in his trouser pockets.

"Great." She smiled. "Now, at its very most basic, machine learning uses algorithms to analyse data, learn from it and then make a prediction or determination based on the results. This is when machines are learning by experience and acquiring skills without human involvement."

"This sounds like a horror sci-fi movie." Ivan's arms were crossed, his brow furrowed.

"Ooh, then you're really going to like deep learning." Roxy giggled when Ivan shook his head. "Deep learning was inspired by the human brain and all the inter-connected neural paths. In deep learning we have neural networks that are algorithms that look very much like the biological structure of the brain.

"A deep learning algorithm learns from large amounts of data. I'm talking ridiculously large. The same as we as humans learn from experience, a deep learning algorithm repeats a task, but each time, it tweaks it a little bit to improve the outcome.

"Deep learning is actually machine learning on steroids. Deep learning has many more layers than machine learning to process data. Basically each layer extracts different pieces of important information. A good example here would be a self-driving car. One layer would detect the edges of the road, another layer the lane lines, another the distance between cars ahead, another the distance between cars behind and so on and so forth. Still with me?"

"Hmm." Manny nodded.

"Deep learning is used in many, many things we use today. Virtual assistants like Alexa or Siri, computer translations—"

"They're sometimes really bad," Dominik said. "We tried once to use it for an email in English. It was terrible."

"True. But if you were to correct those mistakes, the machine would learn and the next translation would be better. Another example relevant to this moment is how great deep learning is in medicine and pharmaceuticals. It does all kinds of diagnoses for diseases and tumours and is also able to create personalised medicine for an individual genome."

"That's what Doctor Jan was doing." Petra's mouth was slightly agape. "That was the best short description of AI, ML and DL I've ever heard. Can I please steal it?"

Roxy giggled. "Oh, please do. I did a lot of reading and learning about this when I realised how much it could help in my field."

"Doc?" Manny turned his back on the scientists and stepped into my personal space. I leaned back, but he moved even closer. "Can we trust these people?"

"I need context." I didn't know what kind of information Manny wanted to share with them.

"You can trust us," Emil said. "We work with projects that have the potential to earn millions of euros. The non-disclosure agreements we sign threaten us with our livelyhoods if we so much as breathe a word of the projects we are working on."

"Which brings me to a question." Roxy tilted her head. "Why are you so readily answering all our questions about Doctor Novotný's work? Isn't his cure also protected?"

"Not any more." Emil crossed one arm in half a body

hug. "The whole project rested on his shoulders. He was the only one capable of making this work. The investors knew the potential this had and gave him everything he needed and more. And he never demanded anything he didn't need. Just the best equipment and people."

"And pay," Petra said softly. "He fought for us to be paid far above the average salary for scientists here. He believed that people should be paid their worth. He valued each one of us."

"Not one of us would betray him, his work." The director looked at his scientists as they all nodded enthusiastically. "And now we won't betray the trust of whatever it is you need to ask or share."

Manny turned to look at me.

"I don't see any signs of deception." Or inappropriate eagerness to gain information.

He turned back to the scientists. "How loyal was Doctor Jan?"

"Very." Emil's answer was immediate and confident. "He'd adopted us as his tribe and treated us as such. If one of us published in a journal, he would go to great lengths to defend us and our article to any critics. That was one of the reasons we loved him. He made us feel important to him."

"Just how great would those lengths be?"

Emil, Petra and Nikola were shaking their heads. The others looked disgusted.

"He would never do anything illegal, never something that could harm others. Never." Petra's voice got firmer and louder as she spoke. "If anyone says that he did something bad, and that after his death, we will not stand for that."

Emil put his hand on Petra's shoulder. "Petra's right. We won't stand for it. The man we knew and loved was working on a cure for opioid addiction because he wanted to help people."

Manny glanced at me and I nodded. I only saw truth in their nonverbal cues.

"Did Doctor Jan leave any of his personal effects here when he went on sabbatical?" Ivan asked.

"His tablet." Dominik turned towards the door. "He left it in my office. When I phoned him the next day to ask if I could bring it to him, he told me to keep it until he returned."

"Can we have it?" Ivan looked at Emil. "We can go through legal channels if it will help protect you."

"That won't be necessary." Emil shook his head. "I'll deal with any investor or anyone who has anything to say about us co-operating with the police. I pride myself in running a company that is completely transparent in our ethics and goals. It's only in the development phases that we have to keep things very confidential in case of intellectual property theft. No. You can have his tablet."

"I'll go get it." Dominik left the room.

Roxy looked at Emil. "We'll treat any information we find in there with the utmost sensitivity and confidentiality."

"I know." He paused when Dominik came rushing back

into the room. He took the tablet from Dominik and handed it to Ivan. "The news said Doctor Jan was working for a psychopath, creating a drug that the psychopath believed would cure fanaticism."

"What?" The corners of Roxy's mouth turned down. "Being fanatical about something cannot be found in a virus, genomes or genetics. That doesn't make sense at all."

"That's why we don't believe it." It wasn't Emil's tone as much as his micro-expressions that caught my attention.

"Who believes this?"

"Conspiracy theorists are already jumping on this. They are saying this is a sign they were right all along—being a liberal, a fascist or an extremist of any kind is genetic."

"Bloody hell." Manny turned to the director. "Emil, am I right to think that we can call at any time if we have more questions?"

"Absolutely."

"Doc? Roxanne? Any more questions?"

"No." I looked at Roxy who was shaking her head.

We left the building five minutes later. Colin was standing outside his SUV waiting for us. He straightened when he saw us. "How did it go?"

"We have a gift for Francine." Roxy pointed at Ivan. "We have Doctor Jan's tablet."

"Frey." Manny stopped in front of Colin. "Do you know where that paparazza is staying?"

"Yes. Why?"

"Take me there. Now."

"Okay." Colin drew out the last syllable as he opened the passenger door for me. "You can tell me about it on the way there."

Chapter FIFTEEN

"ANYTHING?" MANNY STORMED into our hotel rooms, going straight to where Francine was sitting on one of the sofas. "Do you know where that bloody woman is?"

Roxy shook her head with a smile and walked to Vinnie in the kitchenette. Colin closed the door behind us and took my hand with a reassuring squeeze. We settled on the sofa across from Francine. Ivan sat down next to Daniel on the other sofa, Phillip reading a newspaper on the third sofa.

"She's turned off her phone, so the virus I put on her phone is useless. And before you ask, I tried to power it up, but I think she's removed the battery." The admiration was clear on Francine's face. "She knows how to disappear."

"Not what I want to hear." Manny rubbed both hands over his head.

Ivan frowned. "Wait. You put a virus on her phone?"

"Just a little one." She winked and looked at Colin. "Ty lost Bree? How's that possible?"

"Clearly he's an incompetent criminal." Manny sat down next to Francine.

"He's not a convicted criminal, Millard." Colin's tone was terse, his facial muscles tense. "But he's one of the best if you want someone followed."

"And she gave him the slip." Francine smiled. "That's my kinda girl."

"Do you have anything on his assistant?" Daniel asked.

"Let me ask." Ivan got up and swiped his smartphone screen. He walked to the large windows overlooking the park behind the hotel and spoke quietly in Czech.

Manny continued his grumbling about wasting time going to Bree's hotel only to find that she'd gone in shortly after we'd stopped at Jarda Zonyga's hotel. But she'd left again twenty minutes later. I thought about her sitting alone in Colin's SUV while we interviewed Antonin Korn.

"Have you looked at Bree's incoming and outgoing calls?" I wasn't surprised when Francine nodded. "Anything interesting?"

"In my opinion, yes." She glanced at Ivan when he asked a loud question into his phone, his posture tense. "For an investigative journalist who is here to investigate a story, she made very, very, very few calls. And received even fewer. I counted seven outgoing calls in the last twenty-four hours and nine incoming. I checked the numbers and they're nothing to pay attention to."

"Are you sure?" I needed to know that she had done her due diligence.

"Oh, I made very sure of that. I have a bad feeling about this and don't want anything to happen to Bree."

She rolled her eyes when Manny swore. "I like her."

Ivan walked back from the window, putting his smartphone in his trouser pocket. "My team found Bree's assistant, Tobie, in an Italian restaurant having dinner. He was expecting Bree to join him, but he said that he's used to her not showing up. Usually, that means she's following a lead."

I uncrossed my arms when I realised I had folded them tightly across my chest to protect myself from the angry expression on Ivan's face. "What else did you find out?"

"Our IT guys traced the hack." He sat down, but didn't relax into the sofa. "The person who hacked our police station and deleted all the footage of Tomas Broz and of Bree coming in and leaving… that person was in Bree's hotel."

"Holy hell."

"My team did some more checking and found that a call had been made from that hotel to the news station that first reported about Doctor Novotný's death and that he'd been working under duress for a madman." His lips tightened. "We can't say for sure it was Bree, because the call originated from the hotel's phone system, not a mobile phone. And the hotel's system is old—too old to pinpoint from which room a specific call was made. All local calls are free and unregistered. Only international calls are registered on the system."

"I want that paparazza arrested." Manny pushed his fists on his thighs. "Tonight."

"I don't know about this." Francine looked at me. "What

do you think, girlfriend? Did Bree hack the police station? Did she leak the story about Doctor Jan's death?"

I took my time to consider everything I'd learned about Gabriella Reuben. And everything I'd observed in the time we'd spent together. "There are no absolutes in human behaviour analysis, but in my experience and opinion, Bree showed no indication of deceit or that she was conspiring against us."

"You think she's being set up, Doc? By whom?" Manny's frown deepened, then he looked at Francine. "Do you think Shahab has the computer and technical skills to do this?"

"We know that he worked in Iran's cybercrimes division for a few years when he just started out." Francine shrugged. "It's not that hard to hack a police station, or to reroute a phone call so it looks like it came from a different country."

"Not hard for you maybe," Daniel said. "I'm pretty decent with computers, but I can't do that."

"I can sho—"

"Please don't continue." Ivan pretended to shudder. "I don't want to have to arrest you."

"Ooh, that would be fun." Francine winked at him. "But Daniel is right. Maybe this is too far above Shahab's skillset."

"He could've hidden his skills. I know some extremely smart people who play dumb all the time." Roxy's attempt not to look at Vinnie was so obvious, my eyes immediately went to him as she tilted her head away from him.

Daniel and Ivan chuckled when Vinnie shook a spoon at Roxy.

"Do we need to worry about Bree?" Phillip had been quiet this whole time. "Is her life in danger?"

"I would say yes," Daniel said. "But I have a feeling she can look out for herself."

"I did more digging into Bree." Francine's voice was just above a whisper. "She was terribly bullied and attacked when she was a child. When she was seventeen, she started taking self-defence lessons."

"What kind of self-defence?" Vinnie asked.

"Krav Maga." Francine winced. "She only took a few lessons. Said she wasn't made for violence."

"Huh." Vinnie was disappointed. "Krav Maga would've been perfect for such a pint-sized woman. Man-woman. Shit. For Bree."

"She's a woman, honey." Roxy put her hand on Vinnie's chest and looked into his eyes. "A woman."

"Yeah, I'm still trying to wrap my head around all of that." He looked over her head at us. "So what do we do? Should we look for her?"

For a few seconds no one spoke.

"If that paparazza is everything you're telling me, then we should maybe give her some rope." Manny grunted and looked at me. "Some space to do whatever the blazes she's doing." He looked at Francine. "Are you going to just sit there and look pretty or are you going to tell us what is on Novotný's tablet?"

Francine fluttered her eyelids and pressed her palm

against her chest. "You think I'm pretty."

When Manny swore, she smiled and held out her hand towards Ivan, wriggling her fingers. "Gimme."

Ivan got up and handed Francine Doctor Jan Novotný's tablet. "Don't upload anything to that cloud folder you created. I would like to keep a very tight lid on whatever we find and I'm not as confident in your cloud as you are."

"Non-believer." Francine's revulsion was exaggerated and so fake, it made Ivan smile. She took the tablet and tapped the screen. "Don't worry. I'll keep all the secrets I find here safe."

"Why don't I find that reassuring?" Ivan's relaxed expression belied his words. A small frown formed when his phone pinged. He swiped the screen, his frown deepening. "I have to go." He looked at Daniel, then at Manny. "My boss said the bigger bosses want to see me."

"Do you need me to intervene?" Manny moved to the edge of the sofa.

Ivan's eyes narrowed for a moment in thought, then he shook his head. "Let me first see what this is about. I'll let you know if I need reinforcements."

"Hmm." Francine tapped the screen of Doctor Novotný's tablet, her mouth twisting. "It's password-protected."

"That's my cue." Ivan nodded at us and walked to the door. "I'll let you know what the bosses say."

There were a few murmured greetings, but our attention was mostly on Francine. She continued tapping. "I tried that crazy code Doctor Jan burned on his skin, but it's not working. I need time."

"And here you thought it was going to be easy." Roxy giggled when Francine threw a cushion towards the kitchenette. She pulled at Vinnie's arm. "I'm hungry. Cook for me. Now. Feed me."

"You ate dinner."

"That was three days ago!" She put her fists on her hips. "I'm going to wither and die if I don't have… pumpkin chip cream pie! Yes, that's what I need to keep me alive."

Vinnie laughed. "I don't have the ingredients for that, Rox."

"They're working." She nodded towards us. "We can go shopping."

"Don't go too far." Francine glanced up. "I plan to crack this baby quickly and we might need you and your terrible shoes to make sense of any science stuff."

"Ten minutes?" Roxy looked at Vinnie. "There's that twenty-four-hour shop two blocks away."

They continued talking, but I lost interest. I sat back in the sofa and let Mozart's Symphony No.14 in A major flow through my mind. I went through everything I'd learned so far. Doctor Novotný's work that involved the worrisome ability to create a chemical weapon that could kill one or thousands depending on the targeting and the delivery method. Antonin's unadulterated fear of Shahab. The role Antonin as well as the thief Tomas Broz had played in Shahab's plan.

But this was where I stalled. We didn't know what

Shahab's end plan was. Of equal importance, we didn't know what motivated him. My assessment of Shahab was that he wouldn't execute a terrible act just because he could. He was driven by a strong motivation and in the year we'd investigated and searched for him, we'd not once come across something that could explain his plans for a chemical weapon.

We'd been able to create an acceptable profile of Shahab's professional life, but his personal life had proven problematic. The Iranian authorities had given us his date of birth and parents' information, nothing else. They'd said that after carefully going through everything they had on his personal life, they'd come to the conclusion that none of that would assist us in finding him. Not even President Godard had been able to get us information about his life outside of work. And Francine's efforts had been fruitless—there was nothing about Shahab's private life stored in any of the places she'd hacked.

I moved on to go through all the data we'd gleaned from Antonin's operation. I'd just started contemplating the probability of Shahab working with a partner when Roxy and Vinnie returned, laughing and carrying three large shopping bags.

They went to the kitchenette and Phillip joined them, smiling when Vinnie forced Roxy into a chair by the kitchenette counter and made her promise not to help him. Colin and Daniel started talking about ingress and egress methods when stealth was required in an operation.

I went back to Mozart.

An hour and twenty minutes later, we'd all had a slice of Roxy's pie and the others were in their bedrooms. Colin had convinced everyone that it would be to our benefit to rest while we could. At least until Francine had gained access to Doctor Novotný's tablet. No one had seemed enthused about leaving all the work to Francine, but had reluctantly agreed to rest.

I hadn't.

My mind would not allow me to sleep, so I had a relaxing bath and returned to the living area to Francine punching the air and hopping in her seat. "I knew I would get you, you Evel Knievel."

"What's an Evel Knievel?"

"Ooh!" She started, then smiled at me. "Didn't see you sneaking up on me there, girl. Don't worry about Evel. I got into Doctor Novotný's system."

I sat down on the sofa next to her. "Have you had time to look around?"

"Nope. Just got in this very second." She grabbed an unfamiliar tablet and held it out to me. When I leaned away from it, she snorted. "It's not going to bite you. It's brand new and I'm the only one who's touched it. If you put your grubby hands on it now and take it, I'll quickly clone Doctor Novotný's tablet onto that one and you'll have what I have."

"I don't have grubby hands." I took the tablet. "I just bathed."

She stopped and looked at me. "Right now, I'm a little

jealous. The ugly kind. A soak would be heavenly right now."

"You can indulge in spa treatment later." I knew she wouldn't consider taking a break to rest. Not at this moment. The information we could get from this tablet was too important. "I will give you another voucher for that spa you like so much."

"And this"—she shook her index finger at me—"is why you are my bestest bestie in the whole wide world."

"Have you cloned the tablet yet?"

She laughed at my irritated tone and shook her head at me. Then she started tapping on Doctor Novotný's tablet. "You know I love you, right?"

"Yes."

She laughed again. "Glad we're clear on that." She raised her hand and dramatically tapped the tablet screen. "There. You now have everything I have on this tablet."

I swiped the screen and started looking through the files stored on the tablet. I exhaled in relief. Doctor Jan Novotný had been organised. He had a few apps that organised his folders under different headings. Within a folder, the files were clearly named and when I opened the files, their names correctly indicated the content.

Five and a half hours later, Francine was in the kitchenette making another cup of coffee and I was staring at the tablet screen. We'd divided the content and I'd finished working through my folders. And had found nothing of significance. Everything I'd looked at was related to his work in Prokop Industries and his work on the cure for opioid addiction. There were also a lot of his personal thoughts on deep learning, machine learning and artificial intelligence.

"Here you go." Francine handed me a mug. "Maybe this coffee round will give us something."

"Not in any of the folders I've been through."

"Nothing?" She winced. "Damn."

"How far are you with yours?"

"I have another"—she looked at the tablet screen—"three to go."

"Which ones?"

She gave me the names and I took the largest folder. She worked through the first one and again found nothing. I was two-thirds through my folder when Francine jerked. I looked up. She was staring wide-eyed at the tablet screen. "That wily old scientist."

"What did you find?"

"He named the folder ThisIs and the file TheKey. Open that document."

I found the file and opened it. It was a word document with only one line written on it. "What does this mean?"

"It's the address to a cloud folder." Francine's fingers flew over her laptop keys. "It's an extremely secure cloud storage in the internet—one of the best. I know quite a few hackers who use it because they've not been able to hack it."

"You've hacked it." I'd seen it on her face.

"Of course." She winked at me and returned her focus on her laptop. "Aha, here it is. Okay, now we have his account name. We need a password."

"His hip," we both said at the same time. Her smile was wide when she entered the code into the allocated place and pressed enter. She shifted so it was easier for me to see her screen.

It took two seconds before a new window opened on her laptop screen, listing seventeen documents. She frowned. "This is not a lot. This cloud has room for much, much more than this."

She clicked on one document. It opened to a spreadsheet with a lot of technical data, a lot of medical terminology and scientific terms I'd not come across before. "We need Roxy."

"In a mo." Francine opened another document, but returned to the listing. "Wait. Look at the date stamps on these documents."

My eyes widened. "These were uploaded in the last two weeks."

"Updated. Not uploaded." She turned to me. "You know what this means, right?"

"I have a theory."

"Oh, let me just come out and say it. Doctor Jan found a way to link Shahab's computers to this cloud network. All Shahab's stuff is here. All the work Doctor Jan did for him."

"We don't know this."

She pressed her index finger against her chest. "I know this. Give me ten minutes and I'll prove to you this came from Shahab's system."

"Before you do, send those documents to this tablet so I can go through them."

She did that and I opened the most recent document. One glance at it told me it was a journal. Each section started with a date and a time, followed by paragraphs of writing. It would appear that even in captivity Doctor Novotný continued his wordiness. I started reading.

"Jenny?" Colin's hand on my forearm jerked me out of the focused space I'd been in. I looked up and saw everyone dressed and seated on the sofas, including Daniel. Vinnie was in the kitchenette making coffee.

"Where's Ivan?" I asked.

"Checking in with his team," Daniel said before Colin could answer.

"Francine updated us." Roxy had a tablet on her lap. "I'm going through the medical data now. There's a lot here."

"It's not good." It was clear on her face.

"No." She pushed the tablet to rest on her knees, away from her. "I would have to confirm my findings, but I'm quite confident that Doctor Novotný successfully developed a drug similar to Kolokol-1. It's an opioid analogue and seems even stronger than carfentanyl. He finalised the delivery system and it seems ready to be used."

"What delivery system?" Manny asked.

"Aerosol. It can be sprayed from a normal spray bottle that you use to spray house plants or it can be placed in a pressurised can to release on a timer."

"Oh, hell."

"Hmm-mm." None of Roxy's usual good humour was evident. "This is lethal. Kolokol-1 was developed by the Russians as an aerosolisable incapacitating agent—a sleeping gas. This one has no such benevolent uses. Looking at the chemical structure Doctor Novotný uploaded here, this is deadly. Completely deadly."

"He tested it." The words came out hoarse and I cleared my throat. "I've been reading Doctor Novotný's journal. He's been extremely thorough in detailing everything Shahab made him do." I swallowed. "And everything Shahab did to him."

"Oh, hon." Roxy's expression conveyed her sympathy. "That had to be hard to read."

It had been. "I only have three more pages to read. Doctor Novotný started journaling a week after he started working for Shahab."

"That's peculiar wording." Daniel was sitting next to Phillip. Not only had I not heard anyone move around, I also hadn't heard Daniel join us. "He wasn't kidnapped like we thought?"

"No." I remembered the distressing phrases Doctor Novotný had used. "Shahab contacted him and blackmailed him into taking a sabbatical and starting the work on this weapon."

"Blackmail?" Roxy asked. "How?"

"No, wait." Francine held up her hand. "First finish telling us about the testing."

"Shahab started testing Doctor Novotný's weapon a month ago. The first time didn't work as fast as Shahab wanted and the doctor had to change the formula. Then it worked fine."

"Bloody hell." Manny closed his eyes for a moment. "How many people?"

"Doctor Novotný wasn't sure, but he wrote that Shahab had told him he'd killed one person at a time for the five tests they'd run. Shahab didn't want to attract attention by killing more than one person. One overdose victim found by the police didn't raise much suspicion."

"He's right," Roxy said. "I contacted my colleagues here in Prague and they told me that there were fewer than fifty opioid overdose cases last year. One more wouldn't raise any eyebrows, but a cluster at the same time would." She rubbed her upper arms as if she was cold. "How did Shahab blackmail Doctor Novotný?"

I'd read this on the first pages of the journal. "He had a long list of threats. Shahab laid out to Doctor Novotný how he had set up fake accounts in Doctor Novotný's name. Bank accounts that received a lot of bribe money, social media accounts with a lot of racist, homophobic and politically radical and very divisive rants. This went back years and Shahab had assured Doctor Novotný he would change the social media accounts' settings to public so everyone could see it. That would destroy him and his life's work.

"Shahab had done the same with Patrik—fake accounts, rants and bribes. He knew Doctor Novotný's colleagues didn't know about Patrik. He was going to use that to make his colleagues doubt everything else Doctor Novotný had told them. He threatened to use the social media manipulation against Doctor Novotný's nephew if he did not have full cooperation. He kidnapped Patrik and held him hostage, but wanted Doctor Novotný to voluntarily take the sabbatical and go to Shahab's laboratory." I shuddered at the memory of that page. "Doctor Novotný seemed to have suffered greatly from guilt for doing this and not going to the police."

"Why didn't he?" Colin looked at the tablet on my lap. "Did he say?"

I nodded. "Arrogance. He admitted as such. He thought he could outsmart Shahab. Doctor Novotný was highly intelligent and often these individuals put themselves above everyone else. Two months ago, he admitted Shahab was much more intelligent than he'd had originally thought. The doctor tried to work in a code that would diminish the effectiveness of the chemical weapon he'd created. Shahab found out and showed Doctor Novotný a video where he broke all Patrik's toes and the small bones in his feet. Shahab promised to do worse if Doctor Novotný didn't produce his absolute best work."

"Bloody hell."

"To answer Colin's question, at first Doctor Novotný was worried about his reputation and thought he could stop Shahab by quickly creating something that wouldn't work, but that Shahab wouldn't know. Two months in, he realised that wasn't going to happen, but it was too late to contact the police. Shahab was controlling Doctor Novotný's day completely. He had no access to a phone or anything that wouldn't alert Shahab."

"But he managed to have access to the cloud." Phillip looked at Francine. "How did he do this without notice?"

Francine looked at me. "Did he say?"

"Yes. In the last month Shahab disappeared sometimes for a few hours. It was one of those times that Doctor Novotný used his knowledge of artificial intelligence and computer technology to set this up."

"But why not contact the police then?" Daniel asked.

"I would also like to know that," Manny said.

"He didn't explain his reasoning for connecting these few folders to this cloud storage." I had wondered about this as well. "He also didn't explain why he didn't connect Shahab's entire computer network, why he didn't alert the authorities about Patrik's abduction or the many other questions I have. Some of his actions appear clearly thought out and logical and others don't make sense to me at all."

"Did he write any details about his work?" Roxy glanced at Francine's laptop. "It would be helpful to compare the data I have here with his thought process."

"He was quite detailed about his work." I didn't understand all the science, but had determined that he'd been successful in creating exactly what Shahab had asked of him.

"Is there any actionable intel, Doc?"

"Doctor Novotný didn't know what day and time Shahab would execute his plan. He also didn't know what the plan was exactly. He did know that Shahab is planning to kill as many people as possible." I thought back to everything I'd read. "Eight times Doctor Novotný wrote that Shahab said this was for Chabar."

"Chabar?" Roxy's frown pulled her brows down low over her eyes. "Who or what is that?"

Francine's fingers were flying over her laptop's keyboard. "I've got nothing here." She spelled it. "Like this?"

"Yes."

"Hmm."

"Hold on." Daniel leaned back and scratched his shaved head. "This might be Chabahar. It's Iran's most southern city and the port is a free trade zone."

"Ooh, let me check." Francine typed a few commands, then leaned closer to her screen. "Daniel is right. This is not a large place at all. Only around a hundred thousand residents. Ooh, there's a mangrove forest nearby and a lot of beautiful beaches."

"Now how the holy, bleeding hell does this fit in with everything else?" Manny rubbed both his hands over his face. "This is the first time we've heard about this city, right?"

"Yes." I had not come across it in any of our intelligence-gathering about Shahab.

"As far as we know, Shahab has no connection to this place," Francine said.

"We now know different." I pointed at the tablet on my lap. "Doctor Novotný connected Shahab to Chabahar. If indeed this is the correct interpretation of the word or name Doctor Novotný heard Shahab say."

"Okay, let's put that aside for only a sec." Again Roxy's lips pulled into a thin line. "We know the kind of weapon Shahab has created. But we don't know when or where it will be used."

And we didn't know the why.

No one answered her for a few seconds, everyone lost in their own thoughts.

I jerked when Daniel's phone rang. He lifted it and swiped the screen. "Ivan, I'm putting you on speaker."

"Oh, okay." He paused for two seconds. "Can I speak?"

Daniel chuckled. "Yes, we are all here."

"Well, good morning, everyone. Did you learn anything from Doctor Novotný's tablet?"

Daniel gave Ivan a summary of what I'd shared.

"Hmm." Ivan cleared his throat after a pause that had Daniel and Colin exchanging wary looks. "Well, I would like for you, Daniel, to bring Genevieve, Colin and Manny to the police station. Tomas Broz has been asking for John Dryden since four o'clock this morning."

"So early?" Daniel asked.

"Yes. And that made the officers suspicious, so they checked his cell and found a smartphone. The only calls were to and from his lawyer, which means the bosses are not firing anyone. Not yet anyway." He paused. "But I need you to come as soon as you can."

"We'll be on our way within five minutes." Daniel looked at me for confirmation and I nodded. "Five minutes."

"Okay. See you soon."

The call ended and Roxy leaned forward. "Am I the only one or did that sound very… secret-ey?"

"Secretive is the correct word." But I hadn't heard that in Ivan's tone. I would've needed to see his face to ascertain that.

"Yeah, I heard it too." Francine pushed her fingers through her long hair. "While you guys go and find out what secrets Ivan has, I'm going to jump in the shower."

"I need three minutes to finish reading Doctor Novotný's journal."

"You can do that in the car, Doc." Manny got up and waved his hand impatiently. "Come on. Let's go."

Chapter SIXTEEN

"MISTER DRYDEN!" TOMAS Broz's pupils dilated in pleasure and his shoulders relaxed. "Thank you for coming."

Colin stepped into the interview room and waited for me to be seated before he sat down. He groaned as he lowered himself with effort onto the steel chair.

This time Colin's deception didn't distract me as much. I was more interested in the severe change in Tomas' appearance. His shirt was rumpled, his hair appeared unwashed and uncombed, his nails bitten to the quick. Gone was his nonchalance as well as his easy confidence bordering on arrogance.

The fear he had managed to hide previously—albeit not always with great success—was now on full display. His hands were trembling, his shoulders hunched and his blinking increased. "Will you help me? I need you to help me."

"What kind of help?" Colin asked quietly, studying Tomas until he shifted in his seat and bit on his thumbnail.

He realised what he was doing and hid both hands under the table. "I want protection. I want to make a deal."

Colin leaned back in the chair and stared at Tomas for

several seconds. "Tell m-me about the phone you had."

"My lawyer gave it to me. I needed it." Words tumbled from his mouth. "When I was first arrested, I asked my lawyer to contact my… uh, my friend. This man is able to get all kinds of information."

"What kind of information?"

Tomas put his elbows on the table and leaned towards Colin. "I needed to know what was happening in my case. When we spoke three days ago, I told you everything I knew. I needed to know more."

"You're lying." I had no trouble discerning those markers, not with his fear hindering his ability to mask his deception.

"Huh?" He blinked a few times, then closed his eyes and slowly shook his head twice. When he looked up, he appeared completely defeated. "I told you *almost* everything I knew. Since then I learned a few more important things."

"Why d-don't you start with what you d-didn't tell us before?" Colin said.

He opened his mouth, then slammed it shut and shook his head. "No, I want a deal first." He pointed at his torso. "Look at me. I'm not made for a place like this. I won't survive in a prison. I don't know why, but they are still keeping me locked up in a private cell on this floor. It's not too bad, but I've heard talk that they want to transfer me. I won't make it. I can't do that." His fear was genuine as he leaned even closer to Colin. "You have to help me."

"I d-don't have the authority to m-make a d-deal with you. Not even the power to negotiate for you."

"She does." Tomas looked at me. "I asked my… friend to look into you. He told me that you work for the president of France. That means you have power. You can make a deal for me."

I didn't know how to answer. Our work for President Godard was not a secret, but it was not a well-known fact. I didn't want to confirm what he'd learned. And I definitely couldn't promise help.

"Why should we help you?" Colin put his hand on my knee, but was looking at Tomas. I exhaled heavily and realised I had been holding my breath. Colin squeezed my knee.

"I know things. Antonin liked to talk. He talked a lot. We've been working together for many years. In the last year or two, he's been telling me a lot about the people he did deals with. I can tell you everything he told me. It will help get a lot of people arrested. The police should love that. Just please get me out of here."

"Why such a great need to leave?" Colin's question was quiet and kind.

"He's going to get to me. I know it." Tomas nibbled on his thumbnail, then pushed the heels of his hands against his eyes for a moment. "My friend told my lawyer about Doctor Jan Novotný. They don't know this, but I know Shahab killed him. I know it. And then Shahab made Antonin crazy. My friend says Antonin is in a catatonic state in the hospital. I'm going to be next."

"How d-do you know Shahab killed D-doctor Novotný?" Colin asked.

"Who else? I've heard many stories about Shahab Hatami." He looked at me again. "Please say you'll help me. Get me out of here. I'll disappear. No one will find me."

"I believe you m-made it easy for the police to catch you with the Sirani," Colin said. "You evaded capture for years. Why let them catch you and now change your m-mind?"

"I made a mistake." He shook his head. "I thought the police might catch Shahab quickly and I would be safe in prison."

"Why did you want Shahab caught?"

"Ant knew." Tomas swallowed as if his throat was dry. "He knew Shahab was losing his frigging mind. Ant called me last week and said Shahab had been to his gallery and threw stuff around. Ant had been doing business with Shahab for years, but had never seen this crazy side of him. Ant was beyond rattled. He was freaking out and told me I had to make a plan to stay so far below the radar that Shahab could never find me." He took a deep, shaky breath. "That's when I decided to phone the police with an anonymous tip about the Sirani."

Colin lowered his head, his gaze conveying his disbelief. "That's far too naïve for someone of your intelligence."

"It was an irrational decision in a moment of great fear," I said. My theory was immediately confirmed when Tomas jerked and nodded once.

"In all the years I'd known Ant with all the jobs, he'd

never, ever been anything but cool and calm. When he phoned me that day, freaking out? It scared me. Really scared me. And now that Doctor Novotný's dead?" He shuddered. "I have never been so scared in my life. Never."

Colin narrowed his eyes. "How d-do I know we can trust you?"

"A show of good faith." Tomas' expression brightened. "I will tell you everything I know about Shahab—what I knew before and what I've learned since. You can follow up on it and if it proves helpful"—he looked at me—"you can negotiate a deal for me. Freedom for a lot of arrests."

"We can't promise anything," Colin said. "Tell m-me you understand that."

"I understand." Tomas looked at Colin, some of his confidence returning. "I've built my reputation over years of success because I've always followed my instincts. I'm extremely good at reading people. And I know that she will do everything she can to help me."

"Not m-me?" Colin's lips twitched with a smile.

"No." He swallowed. "I don't want to lose the rapport we've built, but to be honest, I see something of myself in you. Something I don't trust."

Colin's neutral expression didn't deny or confirm Tomas' astute observation. "Tell us what you know about Shahab."

"Thank you." Tomas collapsed against the back of his chair in relief. "Okay, you know that I stole Sirani's *Venus and Cupid* from the Zeman family house, right?"

"Yes."

"Do you know if they have it back yet?"

"I d-don't know. I can ask."

"Don't bother. Ant talked to me. When he gave me the job to steal the Sirani, he said that this was for one of his most important suppliers. But something was off with Ant that day. So I asked him what the problem was with that job." Again he bit his thumbnail. "I should've backed out right then. But Ant begged me to get the painting. He said Shahab had been supplying him with art for years. Valuable pieces. And Shahab gave Ant more than double the usual commission.

"Ant didn't want to work with Shahab and accept the double commission at first, but he's always been weak when it came to money. He loves it. So he accepted it even though he knew he would have to pay the price for it one day. That day came when Shahab demanded Ant find someone to steal the Sirani."

"Why that specific painting?"

"Because of who owns it."

Colin's eyebrows rose. "The Zemans? Shahab was after them? Whatever for?"

"Ant told me that he sold the Sirani to the Zemans ten years ago. They wanted the painting because Sirani painted it the year before she died. It shows her fine-tuned style, her accomplished technique."

"The way she used a simple palette of white, red and golds to effectively m-make the scene come to life." Colin's pleasure as he talked about this work of art was genuine. "It's no surprise that in her short life, she stood out in the Bolognese art world, not with her amazing talent and her fresh interpretations of old themes."

"Exactly. It wasn't just about owning the *Venus and Cupid* for the Zemans. It was about the value of the artist, who she was and what she accomplished."

"Then why d-did Shahab want to take it away from them?" Colin tilted his head. "You had it all these years. Why d-didn't you give it to Shahab?"

"He was using it to blackmail the Zemans. I don't know what he wanted from them, but I wasn't going to let Shahab use this masterpiece as a pawn." He rubbed the heel of his hand against his chest. "I had a feeling that it would be nothing for Shahab to damage or even destroy the painting just to get what he wanted."

"And you couldn't let such an amazing piece of art and piece of history get lost."

"Or get used in some sick person's game."

"Why d-disappear?"

Tomas swallowed. "He told Ant he'd take the painting the week after I'd stolen it. That was when Ant told me what he suspected would happen to the painting. I told Ant I would not stand for it and wouldn't hand over the art. Ant was horrified. He told me Shahab would kill him.

"So I told him that he could tell Shahab I had absconded with the painting and that once Ant had realised I was gone, he made some enquiries and found out that it was not the first time I did something like that."

"Is that true?" Colin asked.

"Of course not." Tomas looked offended. "A man is only as good as his word."

"I assume Shahab believed Antonin's story?"

"I contacted Ant two months after the theft. He told me that Shahab was at first angry, but then he thought it was funny. As long as the painting was nowhere near the Zemans, he was happy. But he did tell Ant I was a dead man if he ever found me."

Colin studied Tomas for a few seconds. "D-did you d-do any more jobs after that?"

"Three." Tomas blinked. "But I think I shouldn't say anything else now. Not until you organise a deal for me. And I should maybe phone my lawyer."

Colin lowered his chin, his expression stern. "If we find out that there is even the smallest d-detail you d-didn't share about Shahab, I will personally make sure you get no deal."

"I told you everything." He looked up and to the left, recalling information. "Yes, I can't remember anything else to do with Shahab." His expression turned pleading. "Please help me."

"Let's first see what your information gives us." Colin got up with a groan. "Until then, you m-might want to consult with your lawyer."

Tomas swallowed and nodded.

I followed Colin out of the interview room. He'd just closed the door when the door of the technical room opened and Manny rushed out.

Colin immediately raised one hand, palm out. "Before

you huff and puff, I didn't make any promises."

"Bugger off, Frey. I wasn't going to huff and puff." He turned to me. "I was going to ask Doctor Face-reader what she thought of all the blarney."

"If by blarney you mean dishonesty, you are wrong." I waited until Ivan and Daniel joined us in the hallway. "Tomas Broz's fear is real and I detected no deception when he spoke to us."

"Hmm."

Colin looked at Ivan. "Would you be able to work out a deal with him and his lawyer?"

"The bosses already approved it." Ivan nodded. "They're very pleased with the good PR it will give the department if there are such high-profile arrests."

I pointed at his face. "There is something about your bosses that is causing you great concern."

"Not here." Ivan nodded upwards, his eyes not making contact with the security cameras.

Manny was staring at Ivan. Usually, he would have a caustic remark, but now I observed empathy. He understood the intricacies of interdepartmental politics within law enforcement agencies. He'd even once admitted that the backstabbing and pettiness was the reason he would never go back to that line of work. And why he preferred working with a group of pseudo-criminals. That had elicited a loud and prolonged response.

Manny gave a curt nod. "Let's visit the Zeman couple and find out why Shahab targeted them specifically."

"They're not answering their phones." Ivan lifted the

smartphone in his hand. "But I got a patrol car to drive past their house. They saw the security shutters open, so the Zemans are at home."

Ivan's concern about his superiors and the information that he'd been withholding from us was becoming of greater interest to me. And concern. As soon as we finished speaking to the Zeman couple, I was going to confront him. We needed to know what he knew.

The drive to the exclusive area just west of the Old Town took us twenty-three minutes due to heavy traffic this time of the morning. The street we were in was unlike the affluent area where Karel Maslák lived. These properties had higher walls, larger areas with sprawling lawns surrounding houses that could easily be defined as mansions.

We slowed down and followed Ivan into the driveway of a house that looked like a grand country manor. From the street most of its glory was hidden, but as we followed the driveway around the side of the house, my appreciation grew. The mature garden at the back of the house flowed into a public park, separated by a palisade fence. All the ground-floor windows were large, looking out over the garden and the old Brevnov Quarter in the distance. The mansion had two long wings to the sides and a round central section with glass doors leading to a beautiful patio.

We parked in the circular driveway. Daniel, Ivan and Manny got out, both Manny and Daniel holding up their hands towards us. Colin opened his window when Manny stepped closer to our vehicle.

"Something is off here." Manny was looking at the patio door. "The gate is open and one patio door is ajar. We're going to clear the house first, then you can come in."

"Should I phone Vin?" Colin reached for his smartphone.

"Not yet." Manny slapped lightly on the SUV's roof. "Sit tight."

Manny walked away, taking his handgun from its holster. Ivan and Daniel were flanking the patio door, weapons in their hands. Manny stopped behind Daniel and tapped his shoulder. Ivan pushed the door wider and they disappeared into the house.

I crossed my arms. "Phone Vinnie."

"Yeah, I think so too. Millard can shout at me later." Colin made a quick call while I stared at the front door until my eyes felt dry from not blinking.

I looked away for a second to regain control over the panic building in my mind. Colin ended the call and nodded at me. "Vin's on his way."

Just then Daniel appeared on the patio and waved us over. We walked up the wide wooden pathway leading to the patio and the elegant furniture carefully arranged to make most of the view. If all the French doors to the patio were to be open, it would create a feeling that the garden flowed into the house.

Daniel stepped away from the door and walked towards the impressive staircase by the front door. "Manny wants you upstairs."

Cold dread entered my mind when I registered his expression. "They're dead."

Daniel nodded. "But it's not Shahab's usual MO. There's no torture or blood."

Colin and I walked past the dining room with a table that could easily seat twelve guests. To our right was the living area with large paintings on the walls, Persian rugs on the floor and exclusive furniture creating an entertainment area both warm and luxurious.

The stairs were on our right, sweeping to the top in a half-circle. The wall forming the right-hand side of the staircase was covered in art. Colin uttered a sound of surprise and stopped in front of a colourful portrait of an easily identifiable woman. "This is a Kahlo." He looked at the painting next to it. "Huh. This is a Cassatt. And the next one is a Fontana."

"What does that mean?" Manny asked from the top of the stairs.

Colin took a moment to look at all the paintings on the wall. "Wow. These are all masterpieces by female artists." One by one he pointed them out. "Frida Kahlo was known for self-portraits. Mary Cassatt was an American who moved to France in her adulthood and became close friends with Edgar Degas. She was known for her works depicting the social and private lives of women and had exhibitions among the masters of impressionism.

"Lavinia Fontana was an Italian artist who died twenty-four years before Elisabetta Sirani was born. But they lived and painted in the same era and Fontana is said to be the first female artist to have painted female nudes and possibly used live nude female models. She had quite a lot in common with Sirani. Or Sirani with her, depending on how you look at it."

"Hmph." Manny shook his head. "You two better come and look at this."

I didn't want to. But my desire to stop Shahab killing more people was stronger than my revulsion at seeing more dead bodies. I followed the men up the stairs and down a wide hallway. The décor was elegant and no effort had been made to disguise the wealth displayed on every wall, in the furniture and ornaments. Colin's eyebrows kept shooting up as he passed more artworks and sculptures.

"They're in here." Manny walked into the room at the end of the hallway. The open double doors revealed a king-size bed, antique nightstands, a Victorian-era chaise longue and paintings that made the walls look like a gallery exhibition. There was only one painting above the bed.

It was easy to identify Elisabetta Sirani's *Venus and Cupid*.

A lavish and sophisticated Venus was looking into the room, her right hand pointing towards a cupid whose micro-expressions were hard for me to reconcile. They vacillated between playful mischief and deep concern. In the background two arrows were lodged in a tree, a quiver with more arrows resting on Cupid's hip. The bright, warm colours brought the scene to life.

It was beautiful.

I kept staring at Cupid's face, trying to understand which emotion Elisabetta Sirani had tried to convey. Looking anywhere else was going to draw my eyes to where Ivan, Daniel and Manny were looking at the floor. Colin took my hand, interlaced our fingers and tightened his grip. "Want to leave?"

"No." I inhaled deeply and started mentally playing Mozart's Violin Sonata No. 18 in G Major. After the first two lines of the Allegro con Spirito, I looked away from the painting and stepped deeper into the room.

On each side of the bedside tables were large windows with views of the landscaped garden. The window on the right looked badly damaged, cracks marring it and the wooden frame broken in places. Under the window were two bodies.

"This is Marta Zemanová and Radek Zeman." Ivan was on his haunches, taking care not to touch anything, but trying to see as much as possible. "I'm no expert, but I've seen enough overdose victims to think that is not what killed them."

The woman was a bit overweight, her features softened by the extra few kilograms. A scattering of freckles on her rounded cheeks provided evidence of time in the sun, wrinkles around her eyes evidence of laughter. But in death her eyes were stretched wide open, her gaze empty. The man had the same expression on his handsome face.

But what distressed me most was their position. Marta was lying in Radek's arms, her head resting on his chest, her hand fallen to the side of his face as if she'd been touching his cheek. Radek's left arm had fallen to his side, but his right arm was still around Marta, his eyes staring unseeing to the ceiling, tracks of tears dried on their faces.

Daniel walked around to Marta, leaned over and studied her face. "I don't see any of that foamy stuff around their mouths. That is what is usual with opioid deaths. The petechiae around their eyes and their blue fingernails show a lack of oxygen, but that can also be due to opioids."

"That's what I'm thinking too, but we will have to wait for the ME to give us a real cause of death." Ivan got up and looked around. "How did they suffocate to death?"

"And why does it look like they tried to break out?" Colin pointed at the damaged window.

"What the bleeding hell happened here?" Manny stepped away from the bodies and looked around the room. He took his smartphone from his trouser pocket and swiped the screen. Ringing sounded through the phone.

"Hey, sexy." Francine sounded distracted.

"You're on speaker, woman." Manny stared hard at his phone. "We found the Zemans." His tone softened. "They're dead. What did you find out about them?"

"Oh, no. That's so sad. I researched them as soon as you told me, but I've only had twenty-five minutes." It sounded like she was typing on her laptop. "Okay, what I have so far: The Zemans are the ninth richest couple in Czech. An interesting Czech language titbit is that Marta's surname changed to Zemanová, the female version of Zeman. Anyhoo, their wealth comes from construction. It seems like Marta got lucky when she invested in a project through her first job. They had been married for six years by then and had just a small bit of savings, but she put everything in it.

"Eight years later, they got their first payout of hundreds of thousands. Radek used half of that to start his construction company and within fifteen years they were number fifty on the rich list. He sold his construction company ten years ago and invested heavily in a tech start-up. In a recent article, they boasted that their home was almost completely a smart home. They have AI for all their appliances and… the list is long, so I'm just going to say you are standing in one of the most technologically advanced homes in Prague.

"A few interesting titbits I found: They don't have separate finances, even though Marta said in an interview they had both been advised to change this many times by their lawyers and financial advisers. They liked being connected in all ways.

"They have one daughter who took after her mother. Ooh, I forgot to be more chronological. Sorry, Genevieve. To backtrack, once they made their fifth million, Marta stopped working altogether and devoted herself completely to charities that focused on women's causes. It's estimated that the Zemans have donated around twenty million euros over the years to these foundations.

"Their daughter Natálie did her degree in some kind of women's studies and immediately got a job with an NGO, her work connected with CEDAW—that's the UN's Committee on the Elimination of Discrimination against

Women. She's now thirty-one and is still working for them. And here's where it gets really, really interesting. Natálie has done a lot of work with Iranian women. She's part of a team that hel—"

"Francine?" Manny shook his phone after a second of silence. "What the hell? Hello?"

The call had been terminated. No sooner had I realised this than the security shutters closed with an alarming speed. All the windows in the bedroom were secured within four seconds, dumping the room in dark shadows.

"What's happening?" Ivan took his weapon from its holster and looked at Daniel.

"I locked all the doors before we came upstairs." He also unholstered his weapon.

"We cleared the house." Manny walked to the bedroom door and pressed the light switch. Nothing happened.

A hissing sound had all of us turning to the air vents. Colin took a step back. He looked at the vents, then walked closer and held his hand in front of one. "That's not good."

"Frey?"

"I've only seen this in art preservation rooms in museums and galleries." Colin walked back and took my hand. "If this is what I think it is, the shutters have made the house airtight and these vents are sucking out the oxygen. In museums and galleries, this is used in case of fire. These systems are extremely sophisticated and will never be triggered if they register human presence."

Daniel walked towards the door. "We need to split up

and find a way to stop this."

"I don't know if that's the best use of time." Colin looked at the air vents. "We might need Francine when we find the panel to the system. It might be better to find a weak window and break it open to allow air in."

"That's most likely what they were doing." Ivan pointed at the Zeman couple, then at the air vents. "And this is most likely what killed them."

"Bloody hell." Manny also took his gun out of its holster. "Frey, you and Doc come with me since you don't have weapons. Dan, you take this floor. Ivan and I will do the ground floor."

Daniel nodded and left the room. Ivan followed us out the bedroom and down the stairs. The whole house was in dark shadows as if it were dusk and not seventeen minutes to nine in the morning. There was still enough light to find our way around, but I didn't feel comfortable not being able to see clearly.

On the ground floor, Ivan went to the rooms on the left and we went right. Manny went into each room first, his posture alert and ready to act, his weapon held out in front of him. The first room we entered was an office. There was nobody and the two windows were locked and impossible to open.

Instead of spending more energy here, we went into the next room and then the next. By the time we'd circled back to the front door, I was feeling weak. My breathing was becoming shallow and it felt like I had been on an exceptionally long morning run.

"I found nothing upstairs." Daniel slipped on the last step, but steadied himself. "And I'm feeling the lack of oxygen."

"Me too." Ivan joined us.

Daniel and Ivan tried, but they couldn't unlock the front door and decided not to waste any more time on it. Ivan shook his head. "Everything is tightly locked."

"Not this window." Colin pointed at a long, narrow window to the left of the front door. The shutter appeared to have stopped five centimetres above the ground, light from the lower part reflecting on the tiled floor.

"Stand back." Ivan aimed his weapon at the window. He glanced at us and frowned. "No, even further back. Get behind the wall."

He waited until we were out of sight. The loud report of a gunshot rang through the house. Darkness entered my peripheral vision and I didn't know whether it was from a looming shutdown or the lack of breathable air. Or both.

"Fuck!" The anger was easy to hear in Ivan's voice. We stepped back into the entrance to see Ivan pressing his hand against his left upper arm.

"Bloody hell, man." Manny rushed forward and took Ivan by the shoulders. "Did you shoot yourself?"

Ivan burst out laughing. "Seems so." He lifted his hand to reveal a tear in his jacket and blood seeping through.

Manny leaned in closer. "Looks superficial."

"Yeah, it wasn't the bullet that got me. It was the ricochet off the wood it hit." He pointed at the damaged, but unbroken window. "These windows are bulletproof."

"Oh, man." Daniel sat down on the floor. "I'm not feeling so good."

"Makes two of us." The light coming from the narrow window highlighted Ivan's pallor. He was looking even paler than a minute ago.

Slight tremors started shaking my body and light-headedness overwhelmed me. I looked down at the ground, trying to slow my breathing. It didn't help. My lungs were gasping for more air.

Colin's grip on my hand loosened and he joined Daniel and Ivan on the ground. He looked up at me. "I can't any more, love."

"Holy hell." The desperate look on Manny's face as he took us in sent even more darkness into my peripheral vision. "We're not going to bloody, fucking die here."

I blinked and found myself sitting on the floor next to Colin. He was cradling me against his side. "We're still here, love. Millard is going to swear us out of this bloody place."

"Bugger off, Frey." Manny was swiping on his smart-phone screen.

I blinked again and found Colin lying on the floor next to me. His eyes were still open, but he was gasping. Manny was sitting on the floor, still swiping his phone screen, his actions no longer coordinated. Daniel and Ivan were both unconscious. Tears formed in my eyes as I fought against the blackness trying to take me away. I didn't want to die. And definitely not like this.

Manny jerked when there was loud banging on the door.

I concentrated to hear what was happening, but everything was fading. The banging stopped, but someone was shouting a lot of obscenities and something about moving away from the front door.

"Doc." Manny sounded completely out of breath. "We've got to move."

He crawled on the floor and pushed Ivan towards the stairs. His arm slipped out from under him and he fell flat on the floor. He pushed himself up and pushed Ivan even further away. "Doc! Get your lazy arse moving and get Frey away from the front door."

Colin's eyes were closed, but he was still breathing. Barely. Manny was now pushing Daniel's legs with weak movements. I forced myself to my knees and pulled Colin's legs towards the room on our left. It felt like I was trying to move a building.

I heaved again and his legs slid on the tiled floors. It took all my strength and felt like hours, but I managed to move him two metres. Sweating profusely and gasping for air, I collapsed on top of Colin just as I heard a loud crash at the front door.

I gave myself over to the darkness.

Chapter SEVENTEEN

I DIDN'T KNOW whether it was Manny's irritated tone, the sound of a lot of people moving around or Colin softly talking to me that pulled me out of my shutdown. The moment I became aware of my surroundings, I also became aware of the numbness in my legs.

I opened my eyes and winced as I lowered my legs to the ground. Then I frowned. How had I got to the sofa in the living area of the Zemans' house?

"I carried you here," Colin said and I realised I had asked the question out loud. He took my hand.

"How long?"

"It's now"—he glanced at his watch—"five past twelve." He squeezed my hand when my eyes widened. I had been in a shutdown for three hours. "No worries. We just needed to make space for the first responders and then the hazmat team, so I brought you here. You wouldn't let the paramedics touch you."

I looked beyond him towards the front door. People in hazmat suits were moving around. More tension left my body when I noticed they weren't wearing helmets and their nonverbal cues revealed no alarm. I looked back to where we were sitting and my frown deepened. Francine was sitting on the other sofa, her laptop on her lap. "Why are you here?"

"Hi to you too, girlfriend. It's good to see you." She raised one eyebrow and waited.

I sighed. "Hi, Francine. What are you doing here?"

Her smile was wide. "I came with Vin when you guys phoned. I didn't think we were going to walk into this."

"What is this?" I turned to Colin.

"A fucking house tried to kill you!" Vinnie stalked towards me from where he'd been pacing next to the patio doors and stopped next to Colin. "Do you have any idea how fucked up that is?"

"Easy, Vin." Colin's tone was gentle. "We're okay."

"Only by the skin of your teeth." He swung around and walked back to the doors leading to the patio and paced from one side to the next, his posture stiff.

"Teeth have no skin." I knew the expression, but like so many others it was ridiculous and almost impossible not to refute each time I heard it used.

Vinnie snorted and some of the tension left his body.

"Vinster is pissed that he wasn't the one to save you guys." Francine winked at Vinnie when he swore at her.

"Is she with us yet?" Manny didn't give me the same courtesy as Vinnie. He walked right into my personal space and leaned over to stare into my face. "You okay, Doc?"

I pushed myself deeper against the back of the sofa. "I'll be much better if you respect my space."

A small smile tugged at the corners of Manny's mouth.

He straightened. "She's back."

He stepped away and sat down next to Francine. Only now did I take note of the deep stress lines etched next to his mouth and the dark rings under his eyes. "Manny, are you well?"

"Peachy, Doc." He waved his hand at me. "I'm alive. We're all alive and that's all that counts."

"I'm fine!" Bree's husky voice travelled to us from deeper in the house. I turned in the sofa as she came out of a room and shook off a paramedic's hand on her arm. She turned around. "Touch me again and you're the one who's going to need pain medication."

He stepped back, both hands in the air. "Only trying to help, miss."

"Oh, dammit." Bree's shoulders dropped and she took a deep breath. "I'm sorry. I know you're doing your job, but that… that wasn't fun."

"Because you refused pain medication."

"What the hell is going on?" Manny stood up and glared at them.

Bree turned to us and I gasped. Her left eye was swollen so much, she was looking at us through a slit. Almost parallel to her eyebrow was a long cut that had been stitched. The blood from this injury stained her beige blouse, making it look as if her injuries were of such severity she needed to be in a hospital.

"This… patient refused any painkillers when I stitched that cut." The paramedic's expression vacillated between admiration and exasperation.

"Yeah. Maybe next time I should. That hurt like a son of a bitch." She leaned a bit towards him. "Thank you for doing it so quickly."

"You're welcome." He turned and walked back into the room, shaking his head.

Bree looked at Manny, then at the rest of us. She put a chocolate-brown fedora on her head, pulled her shoulders back and walked towards us. "Hello, beautiful people. Miss me? Anyone have a cupcake by any chance?"

"Shouldn't you be in the hospital?" Francine asked.

"Me? No. This is just a little scratch. I'm fine."

"You don't look fine." I pointed at her face. "Your frontal bone could be fractured."

"My what now?" Bree sat down on a wingback chair.

Manny stared at her for a few more seconds, then sat down next to Francine again.

"Your eye socket bone." I tilted my head. "How did you get that injury? Did someone attack you?"

"Hah!" She laughed, then winced and pressed gingerly against her temple. "Hmm. I shouldn't laugh. But yeah, I was attacked by an airbag."

"Bree crashed her rental car through the front door like a boss." The pride in Francine's expression was unmistakable. "That's when her airbag deployed and punched her in the face."

I leaned back against the sofa, exhausted. "There's so much wrong with what you just said."

Francine's smile was wide and relieved. "Everything I said is fabulous. Because Bree is a hero. She saved your lives." She pressed her elbow into Manny's side. "Yours too."

"You can be glad you still have your teeth." Vinnie stood next to Francine, his arms crossed in an uncommon display of discomfort. It appeared like he was trying to reach out to Bree, but was unsure how to relate to her. "And your nose isn't broken. Those airbags are bastards—they can really pack a punch."

Vinnie was right. I'd read an article about the dangers of airbags. They were triggered and deployed in an average of fifty milliseconds—less than the blink of an eye. It then immediately started deflating in order to absorb the shock and not act as a solid barrier to the passenger. Research had shown that people who were shorter or taller than average were at grave risk of injury when an airbag deployed. Vinnie and Colin were both above average height. It worried me. Yet the dangers were still outweighed by the safety provided by having something to cushion an impact.

I looked at Bree. "You purposely crashed your vehicle into the front door?"

"Yup." Her lips twisted. "I just hope the insurance will cover this."

"Don't worry about it." Colin looked at Francine and she nodded. He looked at Bree until she inclined her head. "We'll take care of your car. You saved our lives. Thank you."

"Any time." Her micro-expressions revealed slight embarrassment at the attention, but also pride and relief.

I frowned. "How did you know we needed oxygen?"

She looked at Manny. "That one was shouting at me when I knocked on the front door."

I hadn't heard any of that.

"Hazmat has cleared the whole house." Ivan walked in from the kitchen area and noticed me. "Are you okay?"

"I'm well."

"Thanks." Colin smiled at Ivan. "How's your arm?"

Ivan glanced at the white bandage peeking from under his torn sleeve. "Didn't need stitches, but that disinfectant stuff burned a swearword out of me."

Colin chuckled, then sobered. "Did they find any evidence of the opioid weapon used in the hotel?"

"None." Ivan sat down on the second wingback chair and glanced at Bree. "The ME looked at the Zemans and thinks they died from a lack of oxygen, but will confirm once he's done a full autopsy."

"Bloody house."

"Yeah." Vinnie was standing by the patio doors, but looked more relaxed. "Who would've thought we'd ever say that a house tried to kill you?"

"It wasn't the house." Francine's expression and tone indicated that this was not the first time she'd said this. "How many times do I have to repeat myself? Technology is only as useful, effective or dangerous as the user and his or her skills." She glanced at a panel against the wall next to one of the patio doors. "Shahab hacked the house and tried to kill you. The house didn't do it by itself."

Manny stared at Bree. "This doesn't mean I trust you."

"Hah!" Her smile was wide, pulling at her swollen eye. "You do. You trust me. And you like me." She looked at Francine. "He likes me."

"Bugger off, paparazza."

Their bantering didn't distract me from what Francine had said. I looked at her. "Do you have evidence that Shahab hacked the house?"

"Uh, not the kind you want." She pointed at her laptop. "But the signs are all here. This is circumstantial, but seriously? At this point in the game, it's really hard to not lay all this on Shahab."

"My team agrees with Francine." Ivan held out a hand towards Francine. "You tell them."

"So, Ivan's IT people are not too bad." She smiled when Ivan loudly cleared his throat. "Maybe a little better than not too bad. They managed to get a lot done and only needed my help at the very end. But we did trace the computer that hacked the police station and deleted the footage of Tomas Broz and Bree. That computer was dumped in a public bathroom in a shopping mall in the northern parts of the city. And before you ask, Ivan's team recovered it, but it's completely destroyed. We won't be able to get any data from it or any prints."

"If it's completely destroyed, how did you trace it?" This didn't make sense to me.

Ivan smiled when Francine pointed at him. "My team traced it to its last location, didn't find it there, looked at the CCTV footage and followed a teenager who was carrying a laptop to the shopping mall. He works for a delivery service and said a man paid him three hundred euros to dump it in the mall."

"Shahab was one of the best the police had," Daniel said from behind me. I twisted around. This was only the third time I'd seen him angry. "He would know how to take forensic countermeasures."

"Bastard." Manny turned to Ivan. "Did your team find the five people Shahab used as guinea pigs for his poison?"

Ivan nodded. "The ME had no problem pointing out the strange opioid deaths. These people had clearly died from an overdose, but they didn't have any signs of prior use. And the ME noticed something peculiar in the toxicology report. He didn't follow up on it, because then it just looked like a usual overdose. But now he's running full tests on all of the victims."

"I like Ivan's team," Francine said. "They're good. They immediately ran with the names and found that three of those victims had worked at or donated to women's shelters. The other two were rather loud activists for women's rights."

"He's killing people helping women?" Bree's *levator labii superioris* muscle raised her top lip in disgust. Vinnie swore and Bree nodded at him. "Sick, sick, sick."

"I also got an initial report back from the ME." Ivan glanced up. "He's still busy with the Zemans, but will rush their toxicology tests as soon as he gets them to his office. The report he gave me is for the hotel victim. He was definitely killed by an opioid analogue, but they haven't seen this specific analogue yet. They're trying to identify it, but the ME says it's more powerful and deadly than carfentanyl."

"And carfentanyl is ten thousand times stronger than morphine. This is the drug Roxy said Doctor Jan wrote about in his journal." Francine shook her head. "This has to stop."

Daniel walked around the sofa and placed a photo frame on the coffee table in the centre of the area. "I found this when I walked through the house."

Manny leaned forward and took it. A second later his eyes widened. "Holy Mother Mary and all the saints."

"What's that?" Francine leaned in and gasped. "I knew it!"

Manny turned the frame around for us to see. It was an enlargement of a Christmas photo. Radek and Marta were sitting at their dining room table laughing with two young people. It was easy to recognise Natálie as their daughter. She had all her mother's features, but her father's smile. Next to her with his arm around her was Jarda Zonyga, the man who'd died in the five-star hotel from the opioid weapon Doctor Novotný had created for Shahab.

"Well, I'll be." Colin rested his elbows on his knees and looked at Francine. "What do you know?"

"My Spidey sense was shouting at me, so I ran a check on everyone we've so far come across in the case. I wanted to see if anyone's paths have intersected." She turned her laptop for us to see the screen. "That's when I came across this photo on Jarda's social media. There's only this one photo and she's not clear in it, but I'm quite sure that the woman there is Natálie."

The photo had been taken at a house party. Everyone was standing around a living room with a glass of alcohol in their hands. This didn't look like a house party for friends. Most people were too formally dressed and their body language was too controlled and even withdrawn to display the kind of comfort people showed when with friends.

At the very left of the photo was a couple, the man smiling at the camera Jarda Zonyga. The woman was turned away and her long hair partially covered the side of her face. She was standing in Jarda's arms, his one hand resting low on her back, the other on her waist. Her arms were around his neck. After seeing her in the Christmas photo, it was easy to identify her features. This was Natálie.

"I got curious and started digging." Francine turned her laptop back. "Natálie and Jarda were a couple for almost six years, but ended it on very good terms last year. I spoke to his partner, who said that Jarda and Natálie were best friends. When they realised that the romance in their relationship was completely gone and they only loved each other as friends, they were determined to keep their friendship and not ruin it. They used to speak to each other at least once a week."

"Hmm." Manny scratched his cheek. "If Shahab is targeting people who help women, why target Jarda?" He looked at Francine. "Did he donate to some women's something?"

"Nope. Nothing I found. And his partner said he didn't know anything about Jarda's personal finances. But it could be his connection to Natálie that painted a target on his back." Francine's laptop pinged. She looked at the screen and her eyes narrowed. "Slap a rainbow horn on my forehead and call me a unicorn."

Manny sighed. "What now?"

"I've told you guys before that hackers often see themselves as artists. They like to sign their stuff. But not everyone does. Smart hackers won't leave any trace that it was them, but that's not always possible."

"Get to the point." Manny tapped his index finger on the sofa between them. "Now."

"My point"—she rolled her eyes at Manny—"is that as humans we don't realise when we form a habit. We don't realise when our work becomes our signature. There is something very specific about certain hackers' methods that makes it quite easy for me to tell whose work it is. I ran a program on the hacks of the police station and the house to compare the code. The person who hacked the police station is the same person who hacked this house. Shahab."

I still wasn't completely comfortable with the supposition without concrete evidence, but I agreed about the improbability of this being someone else. "That means he also killed the Zemans."

"And so his list of victims grows." Francine's lips thinned.

"If you are now able to identify his method of hacking—" I stopped when she gasped.

"Oh, my God! Of course." She bounced on the sofa. "I'm totally going to run a search for any other hacks he might be responsible for."

This day had started with a visit to Tomas Broz and had continued with numerous revelations. Bits of information we'd gathered that had seemed disconnected were becoming clearer in their connection to the case. Yet I felt as if there was an as of yet undiscovered element that linked all these loose pieces.

One of those loose pieces was Bree. I studied her. She was quietly listening to us in a manner that I was becoming familiar with. "How did you know to find us here?"

"Huh?" She looked at me and blinked, then swallowed when everyone turned to look at her.

"Well?" Manny shifted to the edge of the sofa, scowling at Bree. "Answer her."

"And while you're at it, tell us about your burner phone." Francine's innocent expression was blatantly false.

"Research. That's how I came here." Bree looked at Francine then back at me. "And I use an untraceable phone because I've been an investigative journalist for many years and have learned not to trust anyone or anything. When it comes to technology, the police have shown themselves to be horribly disrespectful of my privacy. I have one phone that I use to make calls to respectable members of society. A phone that won't be problematic if the police break into it."

"And you have another phone for your less kosher contacts." Francine nodded. "That way you can protect your sources and also stay out of trouble."

"Not always successfully, I might add."

"How did you get here?" I wasn't interested in her investigative methods. Not at the moment.

"I heard you guys talking about a Shahab guy. You also mentioned Hatami the first time we met. So I did some digging." She ignored Manny's swearing. "It wasn't hard to find out that he was part of the team that worked with you on a case last year. I have a friend at Interpol who told me that he's been on the most wanted list for a year now.

"So I got in touch with a colleague in Iran. And no, I'm not going to tell you anything about him. He's Iranian and works for a state media outlet. He does everything the government demands of him. But in his private time, he sends to a select few internationally renowned journalists the information he gets from the many people who want the unofficial tyranny to stop."

"He uses the dark web?" Francine asked.

Bree nodded. "That's one of the great things about the dark web. It's enabled him to shine light on a few terrible issues that the Iranian government doesn't want the world to know about. Well, I asked him if he knew about a Shahab Hatami, who is now on the most wanted list. He came back to me almost immediately, but gave me very little. He said he would find out more and send it to me.

"What he did tell me was that Shahab Hatami got extremely angry when he was overlooked for a promotion a bunch of years ago. The next week he started his drug-smuggling business. He stayed in law enforcement because that helped him to become very successful with his drug trade. But something happened seven years ago that broke him.

"My contact said that rumours are that he lost someone close to him. It's suggested that this event was the trigger that turned him into a psychopath. He carried on for a while, but some years after that he changed once again. He and his teammates were watching a travel documentary when he lost his mind. It took four of them to hold him down until he calmed enough to be sent home."

"What travel documentary?" Colin asked.

"It was about Prague and the surrounding areas. The scene that made him lose his marbles was one with a lot of people on Charles Bridge. No one knew what he saw and he refused to say anything."

"You're lying."

She huffed a laugh. "Man, I was about to correct myself. He didn't say anything more about the documentary, but when his bosses pushed him about his behaviour, he just said it was about Chabahar."

"Stop!" Ivan jumped up and looked towards the front door where the hazmat team were packing up. He sat down again and lowered his voice. "Not here."

Manny stared at him. "Are you finally going to tell us what the hell you've been hiding?"

Ivan nodded, concern pulling at his features. "But not here."

"Well, she said she's hungry." Vinnie pointed at Bree and took a step towards the patio doors. "And my Roxy is all alone in our hotel room still reading through Jan Novotný's journal."

"Good idea." Daniel got up. "We'll meet you guys at the hotel."

I took my time studying Bree, Daniel, Manny and Ivan. Daniel didn't appear to know what Ivan was about to share with us. And Manny's superior rank in an international agency apparently hadn't assisted him in gaining the needed information from Ivan's bosses either. Bree only exhibited curiosity. She didn't know.

I got up. I needed to know what this information was. I needed to find out if this was the missing piece tying it all together.

Chapter EIGHTEEN

"SPEAK." MANNY STORMED into the living area of our hotel accommodation and spun around. He looked at Ivan and pointed at a sofa. "Sit down and speak."

"Why don't I make coffee first?" Vinnie walked to the kitchenette area and opened his arms when Roxy walked to him. "And kiss my Rox."

"Good idea." Colin walked to a sofa. "Maybe we should all settle in first."

Manny grumbled, but also walked to the sofas. He didn't wait until Vinnie finished making coffee. As soon as we were all seated he looked at Ivan. "So?"

Ivan looked at Phillip, who had quietly placed a financial magazine on the sofa next to him. "Please know I mean no offence, but you shouldn't be here."

"He bloody well should." Manny slumped back in the sofa next to Francine. "He's one of us. If you don't tell him about Shahab and Chabahar, I will. Or Doc or Frey."

"What about her?" Ivan looked at Bree, who had taken a seat next to Phillip. She'd been quiet on the way here, observing. Ivan rubbed his scar as he studied her. "Do you trust her?"

"Me? No." Manny shrugged. "But everyone else seems

to think she's on the up and up."

"Can one be hurt and flattered at the same time?" Bree pushed her palm against her chest.

Phillip was staring at her eye. "Are you okay?"

"This? It will give me a scar and a cool story, so I'm really okay." Even though her words were playful, her expression was sincere and gentle when she looked at Phillip.

"I spoke to your brother's supervisor." Manny's lips twitched when Bree gasped.

"No!" Her mouth dropped open and she slammed both hands over her mouth, then spoke through her fingers. "Oh, man. Why did you have to go and do that? Here I thought we were getting on so well. Please tell me you didn't speak to my brother."

"I did." He looked at me. "I phoned around while you were out and the hazmat guys were all over the house. Her brother's boss' supervisor was my partner for two years when I was in Scotland Yard. He told me Gareth is a good sort." He looked at Bree. "He also told me Gareth's sister has shown amazing strength of character. Helped them a lot in a case two years ago. Your brother, on the other hand, told me that you're never careful enough."

Bree put her hands on top of her hat, pressing it lower on her head. "I'm never, ever, ever going to hear the end of this."

"I don't care." Manny looked at Ivan. "Everyone here has been vetted by me. You've been vetted by Daniel. Now tell us what the bloody hell is going on."

Ivan rubbed his eyes, then looked at Manny. "For the record, my bosses ordered me not to tell you. Not even with everything going on and not even after the house episode."

"Oh, leave those snivelling milksops to me." Manny lifted his chin and waited.

Ivan inhaled deeply. "Seven years ago, there was a bombing in Iran."

"Chabahar," Colin said softly.

"Yes." Ivan rubbed his scar.

I narrowed my eyes as a suspicion took place in my mind. "Is this where you got your injury?"

He jerked his hands apart. He glanced again at Bree, then came to a decision as he looked at me. "No one knew we were there. My team had been in Turkey for a training exchange when we got the call. The US had received intelligence that a series of bombs were planned to go off in the Chabahar port. They were planning to destroy at least seven ships with their cargo—all from western countries."

"Who are 'they'?" Daniel asked.

"To this day we don't know. It could've been any of the extremist terrorist factions in the area, but the fact remains that we were too late for one of those bombs." He looked down at the scar on his hand, his eyes unfocused as if he was lost in a memory. "The US had only one SEAL team in the area to find and disarm the bombs. My team was closest of all the other allied teams, so we were deployed.

"We got eight bombs, more than originally thought, but

were too late for the one in the shopping mall. We only heard of that at the last minute. The SEALs and our team rushed to the shopping mall, found the bomb and took it out of the crowded shopping centre to the parking area. We managed to get it quite far away from the shoppers, but seventeen civilians were still injured, as well as three SEALS and two on my team. One SEAL was critical."

"Fatalities?" Manny asked.

"One woman."

"You're lying." I didn't understand why he would.

"Technically, I'm not." He rubbed his scar. "Sahar Hatami died that day."

"What the fuck!" Vinnie stormed over from the kitchenette. "Hatami as in Shahab Hatami?"

"Yes. She was Shahab's wife."

"No way!" Francine looked from her laptop to her tablet to Ivan. "We've been looking into Shahab for the last year and not once heard as much as a whisper that he was married."

"Because he'd requested it to be considered top-secret information."

"Why?"

"Because of the nature of his work in the Criminal Investigation Police of NAJA—the police force of Iran—Shahab requested all the information about his family be redacted in all documents. He didn't want anyone to ever be able to use them against him."

"Like he used Patrik against Doctor Jan?" Francine's voice rose a pitch. "That sack of… scum."

It was quiet for three seconds. Vinnie returned to the kitchenette to prepare lunch.

Then Manny swore. "She's here, isn't she?"

"Yes."

"That must be what Shahab saw in the travel documentary." Bree looked at Ivan. "Is that possible? Oh, wait. No. Before you answer that, first tell us what happened to her and why she's here."

"Sahar married Shahab just after he joined the police. He was determined to be an officer of integrity and help his country become better at dealing with the West. He was a devoted Muslim, but not radical at all. He wanted the West to know that most Muslims were people like everyone else. Not terrorists."

"He must've been psychologically very volatile to have lost his marbles when he didn't get promoted." Bree thought about this for a second. She jerked, her hands balling into fists. "He beat her, didn't he? That's why she escaped."

"Only one of the reasons." Ivan sat back in the sofa. "Shahab started his illegal dealings and yes, he was physically abusive. That went hand in hand with emotional abuse that had Sahar considering suicide many times. But then she read about an NGO that helped women like her."

"Helped them how?" Roxy was sitting on one of the barstools by the kitchenette counter.

"Escape, find refugee status in another country and try to live a normal life."

"Natálie." So many things were falling into place. I looked

at Francine. "I wonder if we could find out if Natálie worked with women from Iran."

"She did." Ivan sighed. "She helped Sahar resettle. After the Americans smuggled her out."

"After they 'killed' her." Bree bit down on her bottom lip. "You said being beaten by Shahab was only one reason she left. What are the other reasons?"

"Her father." His discomfort was increasing. "He's the reason the West bent over backwards to accommodate Sahar. Reza Alikhani."

"Holy bloody hellfire!"

"Who's he?" Roxy asked.

"One of the most notorious terrorists still at large," Ivan said. "He's known as the architect of at least eleven bombings that we know of. He's also wanted for conspiring to destroy the embassies of numerous Western countries and a lot more. He's the devil."

"Talk about jumping from the frying pan into the fire. From her dad to Shahab. Poor Sahar." Bree shuddered.

"The moment she contacted the NGO, the US got involved. The intel Sahar could give on her father was far too valuable to let slip through their fingers."

"Then how did she end up here?" Phillip asked.

"She wanted to be here. She had no interest in going to the US. Her father and then Shahab never allowed her to travel anywhere. But she'd had unlimited access to the internet, so she said she travelled to all the places in the world. And Prague was the city she fell in love with from the first photo she saw.

"Since we are allies, NATO partners and generally have a good relationship with the US, they agreed to let her settle here as long as one of theirs could sit in on debriefings." Ivan looked at me. "That's how Sahar Hatami died and Klára Bittová came to life."

"That's pretty much everything I discovered as well." Francine raised both eyebrows when Manny swore and Ivan looked at her, his mouth wide open. "What? You thought I was just joking about hacking your police database to find out what was happening?" She shrugged. "I got into it this morning and poked around. I found a few emails between your bosses, showing how worried they are that they will lose their precious asset. I must say I don't like the way they talk about Klára. It's like they think she's a nice little chess piece they can use to get the US to do just what they want. I wonder if she knows how she's being used." She turned to Ivan, her face tight with anger. "Did you know?"

He raised both hands, palms out. "Not these details. I swear. I knew about Sahar. I knew she became Klára. I knew who her father is, but that's it. I knew the basics of the agreement between the US and us, but the rest of these details I only learned since you guys joined. Most of Shahab's crimes I only learned of in the last few days." He pinched the bridge of his nose and glanced at Francine. "Please tell me no one will ever know you hacked our system."

"As if." She relaxed back into the sofa. "Your guys are good, but I'm much, much, much better."

"I'm a little lost here." Roxy looked around. "Did I miss some part of the story?"

"I'll bullet-point it for you." Bree counted on her fingers. "Shahab marries Sahar. Around ten years ago Shahab is passed over for promotion and loses his shit. He starts his narcotics import and export business. He also starts beating poor Sahar. Seven years ago, the bomb in Chabahar gives the US and Czech the chance to get Sahar here and pump her for intel on her terrorist dad. Then a few years later—I don't know how many—Shahab sees Sahar on a travel documentary about Prague. He loses his shit even more."

"Do you know if this is true?" Colin asked Ivan.

"Yes. We checked that documentary and Sahar was on Charles Bridge staring up at the tower." His expression softened. "She looked so happy."

"Do you know when this was?" Colin asked.

"About three and a half years ago."

Immediately I saw where Colin was going with his question. "Sirani's *Venus and Cupid* was stolen from the Zemans three years ago."

Colin nodded. "Somehow Shahab must've gotten intel that Natálie had helped Sahar here in Prague. And he wanted something to use against them or against her to make them tell him where Sahar was."

"They wouldn't have told him." Francine's hair glided over her shoulders as she shook her head. "Everything I've read about them told me they would rather have lost everything they owned than help a psychopath find his wife."

Bree raised another finger. "So three years ago, Shahab steals the Sirani, but his blackmail plan doesn't work, so he starts working on another plan. His opioid weapon."

"I'm guessing it was too expensive, so he waited a bit to make more money." Roxy drummed her fingers on the kitchenette counter. "I told you guys such research equipment is very expensive."

"This could be where Seppo-Tommi comes in." Francine tapped her index finger on her lips. "Shahab withdrew money from Seppo-Tommi in Finland as well as use his own income from his drug dealing."

"But last year, we upended his plans when we froze all his assets." Phillip nodded. "That might have... No, I don't have a plausible explanation for the opioid weapon."

I thought about it. "The people he'd killed in Strasbourg last year were a threat to his drug business. The people he's been killing here in Prague were all in some way connected to Sahar or shelters for women. This doesn't give us any indication of what he plans to do with this weapon."

"If I were to guess at his motivation"—Francine smiled at me—"I know you don't like it, but it seems very logical that Shahab would want to take revenge on Sahar for betraying him."

I looked at Roxy. "What did you learn from Doctor Novotný's journal?"

"That he's a genius." She closed her eyes and took a shuddering breath before looking at me. "He created a weapon from an opioid analogue that is insanely potent.

When Shahab tested the delivery system and the opioid, he'd used only one five hundred thousandth of its strength. At full strength, you can spray it into a crowd and be pretty sure that everyone within a hundred-and-fifty-metre radius will be dead within a minute. Not enough time for ambulances or to get to a hospital."

"Any antidote?" I asked.

"No." She hugged herself. "Naloxone won't work for this. The opioid analogue is too strong. You would have to up the Naloxone dosage many times for it to counter the effects of this drug. And I think there's not enough Naloxone in Europe to treat even a hundred people who have been exposed to it."

"Doc, you were going to read the last pages of that journal. Anything there?"

I swallowed and crossed my arms. I didn't want to recall those pages.

"Doctor Novotný's last two pages were the most difficult to read." Roxy nodded at me. "It's filled with regret. He's heartbroken that this will be his legacy. Not the work he's done helping people his whole life. Not the cure for opioid addiction he was about to finalise. This. Creating a weapon that will kill people and destroy families. And not being strong enough to kill himself before Shahab got him to successfully create this weapon. There's a lot of self-hate and sadness on those pages."

His words about his lack of courage to kill himself and remove the possibility of his skills being used had disturbed me greatly. The way he had phrased his emotions had revealed the conflicting logical and irrationally emotional sides of him I'd seen represented throughout the journal. I seldom made decisions based on emotions, rationality winning out almost always. It had to be great inner torment to be torn between two such strong motivators.

"There…" My voice was hoarse from the stress of remembering those pages. I cleared my throat. "There were a few things that weren't clear."

"Yeah, for me too." Roxy nodded, her curls bobbing over her shoulders. "Are you talking about the ramblings on last moments?"

I nodded and looked at the others. "It started on the second-last page, which was written thirteen days before his death. Doctor Novotný sounded incoherent, but he wrote that Shahab wouldn't last much longer. He hoped that the person who was reading his journal would see that in the end he had to do the one thing he never thought he would do—use his science against a human being."

"Was he talking about Shahab's opioid weapon?" Daniel asked.

"I don't know." And I didn't want to speculate. "I'd rather you read that section and decide for yourself."

"Good idea." Francine handed me the tablet I'd used to read Doctor Novotný's journal. "You can read it for us."

I looked at the tablet for a few seconds before I took it. I didn't know if I wanted to read Doctor Novotný's last thoughts again. I swiped the screen, found the right passage and cleared my throat. "'Shahab found out. I know this. He hasn't said anything, but he's changed completely towards me since last night. He knows about the cloud, but I don't think he knows what I've been uploading. I'm writing this because this might be my last opportunity to express my deep regret for everything I've done in the last months of my life.

"'Yes, I think these are my last days, my last moments. Shahab will return from his outing today and kill me. He hasn't said as much, but I'm sure he killed my Patrik. Every day Shahab would remind me that Patrik's life depended on me. He hasn't done that since the day before yesterday. The shame is becoming too much for me to bear. In my last honest moments, I'm awaiting the bliss of death, hoping for a reprieve from this burden of my sins. How low I've gone to destroy my life's work in only six months.

"'I hope you who are reading my words will make sure that Shahab will not do this terrorist deed. I tried to outsmart him, but that didn't work. I considered building a failsafe into the delivery system, but Shahab was testing all the time. So I did something else. Something not forced on me by a psychopathic terrorist, but something I decided to do. I only hope that it's not too late.

"'I wish I could tell you where the laboratory is. I don't know. I wish I could tell you how to counter the effects of this weapon. I can't, because there is no agent that will act fast enough against the power of this evil that I created.

"'I've seen what Shahab is capable of when he wants something. The way he broke my poor Patrik's body. I fear that is what's waiting for me. I will embrace that pain as the punishment I deserve. And I will wait for death to end not only my selfish guilt, but also my own abilities that I have now shown to be as evil as the man who plotted all this. May the world forgive me for what I have done.'"

It was quiet in our hotel living area. My throat hurt. Not from reading these words aloud, but from the anguish I felt on Doctor Novotný's behalf. I put the tablet down and forced my thoughts back to the case. There was a lot to consider. A lot of elements whose roles and importance in Shahab's plan still hadn't been completely identified. I agreed with Roxy. We knew the weapon Shahab planned to use, we knew the delivery system, but we didn't know the when or where.

We also didn't know the why. And more often than not the reason driving someone to such brutal acts was key to stopping him. I looked at Ivan. "I want to speak to Sahar. Klára."

"I think she would prefer being called Klára." Ivan looked at Manny. "My bosses won't allow it."

"Ninnies." Manny took his smartphone from his pocket. "Let's get the presidents involved. These petty bleeding fights are going to get people killed."

Chapter NINETEEN

"I'M GOING TO TELL my wife she has competition." Ivan rubbed his stomach and smiled at Vinnie. "This was delicious, thank you."

"There's more." Vinnie nodded towards the two large serving dishes, one with mushroom risotto and one with enough ravioli for a group twice our number. Vinnie had borrowed the dishes from the hotel's kitchen as well as pots large enough to prepare food for the nine of us. Everyone, including me, had dished up a second time. It pleased Vinnie.

After Manny had called President Godard, things had fallen into place very quickly. Within five minutes, Ivan had received a call from his bosses, giving him carte blanche on this case. Pressure from the French and Czech presidents and Interpol had been great enough for them to give Ivan access to all case files related to Shahab, Klára and her father Reza Alikhani.

"Oh, I wish I could fit more in." Ivan straightened, his hands resting on his torso. "But there's really no place in my stomach for another bite."

"Okay, people." Manny walked back from their bedroom, his smartphone in his hand. "President Godard has given us permission to share as little or as much as needed with Klára to get information from her." He looked at me. "He says he trusts you to determine how she will treat top-secret information."

"When will she be here?"

Ivan looked at his watch. "Maybe another ten minutes. My team is bringing her from the spa."

Klára had been receiving a spa treatment with a friend when we'd located her. Since we'd been about to eat lunch and her treatment was to take another twenty minutes, Manny had agreed for Ivan's team only to speak to her once she was finished. They were on their way here and I was impatient to glean information from her about Shahab.

"That paparazza is going to get herself locked out if she doesn't show up before them." Manny sat down next to Francine and took the tea he'd left on the coffee table when he'd taken the call from President Godard.

"She'll be here." Francine took her tablet and tapped the screen. "I gave her all our numbers in case she runs late."

Bree had left as soon as she could to meet her assistant for lunch. The guilt on her face had been sincere when she'd explained that she'd cancelled lunch with him or had simply not shown up every day since they'd arrived. She planned to stop at their hotel before going to the restaurant. Her brother Gareth had been phoning and sending her messages and she needed to speak to him. She'd looked resigned and unenthused about that call.

Colin had asked Ty to make sure she was safe. And not to lose her again.

"Hey, have any of you seen a photo of Sahar?" Roxy took Phillip's empty plate and stacked it on a few others. "How old is she?"

"Give me a sec." Francine tapped on her tablet screen. "Now that we have access to Ivan's bosses' files, I can tell you all her secrets. Hmm. She's now thirty-seven, as short as you and has the most beautiful chocolate-brown eyes."

"I'm not short!" Roxy rolled her eyes when the room filled with chuckles and comments. She was maybe two or three centimetres taller than Bree, but still at the shorter end of the average height for women. She walked to Francine and looked at the tablet screen. "What a beauty."

Francine waited for Roxy to walk to the kitchen with the plates and turned the tablet for us to see. "The metadata places this photo as taken just after she arrived in Prague."

The woman on the tablet screen was completely covered by a dark blue cloak. Iranian women often wore a *chadar* when they went out in public. Only her face was visible, her plump cheeks pale against the dark material. Her posture and body language were mostly hidden under the *chada*r, but the expression captured on her face showed a combination of fear, excitement and sadness.

Ivan's phone pinged and he looked at the screen. He frowned as he tapped the screen and held the phone to his ear. He spoke in rapid Czech before ending the call and looking at us. "We are getting results back. Which do you want to hear first? The ME's findings on the tests he ran or the intel my team got on the Iranian company that traded with Seppo-Tammi?"

"The ME findings first," Manny said.

"The ME is worried. The five victims Shahab killed when he tested his opioid weapon all tested positive for the opioid described in Doctor Novotný's journal." He looked at Roxy as she took the last plates to the kitchen. "He also asked to thank you for forwarding the information you found in the journal. It helped him identify the opioid. He's considering sending out a nationwide alert. If this drug hits the streets, it will kill a lot of people."

"Hmm." Roxy walked back from the kitchen and sat down. "Shahab doesn't need a delivery system to kill people. All he needs to do is sell this to drug dealers. And he has the contacts to do that. He's been selling drugs in Europe for a decade."

I thought about this. "That won't fit in with Shahab's behaviour. The people he's killed… Let me correct myself. The victims we've linked to Shahab all had some connection to him. There might be more victims, but we haven't found any more whose deaths shared any of the similarities. I can't see Shahab changing his manner of killing to kill without motivation."

"Doc is right." Manny rubbed his head. "His MO hasn't changed. In Strasbourg his motivation was to protect his business. Here, his motivation seems to be connected to Sahar or Klára or whatever her name is now." He shook his head. "No. The ME shouldn't worry about random victims. We should worry about his plan to avenge Sahar leaving him and becoming Klára."

"That's all I have from the ME. The intel on the Iranian company is not surprising." Ivan tapped his phone. "I'm forwarding this to everyone. This company was established in 1952 by Klára's maternal grandfather. As soon as Klára's mother married Reza Alikhani, her father gave the business to them."

"What kind of business?" Phillip asked.

"An extremely successful children's toys company. They cater for the ridiculously rich in Iran. I mean, we're talking about four-meter-high, five-meter-wide princess castles for a little girl's bedroom. And Italian designer clothes for toddlers who will grow out of them in a few months. That kind of crazy rich-people stuff."

"I'm on their website." Francine rolled her eyes. "Ivan is right. These toys are stupid expensive."

"But they supply to Tehran's bazaar, right?" Vinnie looked from Francine to Ivan who nodded. "Hmm. You see, there are some asswipes who took advantage of the economic sanctions against Iran and became extremely rich by controlling import channels. Is there any mention of Reza being one of the *bazaris*?"

"Hmm." Francine swiped her tablet screen a few times, then shook her index finger at it. "Yes, right here."

Vinnie nodded. "The *bazaris* are businessmen with regime connections in government who found a way to control what comes into the country. It created economic problems with the inflation rate and crap like that. An honest few in the government have been trying to get rid of these *bazaris*, but it's still ongoing."

"Do I want to know how you know this?" Ivan smiled when Vinnie shook his head. "Thought so."

"This is also interesting," Francine said. "The business is in Klára's mother's name, but intel shows that it's the father running it."

"Does the mother know about Alikhani's terrorist activities?" Manny asked.

"Oh, yes." Francine looked at her tablet. "It says here she's as radicalised as him, if not more. Toxic people, the lot of them."

"Rumour is that Alikhani has been more successful than his father-in-law in using the company to import weapons and finance many terrorist activities." Ivan's lips tightened, the corners of his mouth turning down. "If I'd had this information earlier, it would've helped a lot."

"If we'd had this last year, we might have been able to stop Shahab long before this." Colin looked at Manny. "Why didn't Interpol have any of this?"

"I checked." Manny scowled. "This company was on Interpol's radar. But there's no mention anywhere that the company or Alikhani is connected to Shahab. Why, I don't know."

Ivan's *buccinator* muscles pulled his mouth into a sneer. "I think my bosses and the US might've wanted to keep this one for themselves. I have no proof, just a feeling." He paused. "And then there is the fact that this is a completely legal company. Their reputation for providing toys and joy to children for more than seventy years makes them an unlikely suspect in any crime."

"Oh, dude. That's naïve." Vinnie crossed his arms. "That makes them the perfect suspect, because no one would suspect them."

"True, but as it is, not one of the Western allies has found anything on that company." Ivan looked at his smartphone for a moment, scanning down the screen. "As soon as Klára told us and the US about her dad's company, we all investigated, but found nothing illegal. We and the US tried to infiltrate the company, but it's not possible. It's a family operation and they don't employ any outsiders. They've managed to keep the company small despite their success."

"Small and controllable," Colin said.

Ivan nodded, then blinked when his phone pinged. He checked the screen and tapped it. Again he spoke in quick Czech, then ended the call. "My guys are in the elevator with Klára. Natálie Zemanová is with them."

"How… Huh. She was the friend at the spa with Klára." Manny got up and walked to the door.

"Bree is going to miss all of this." Francine looked at Colin. "Ask Ty where she is."

"Why don't you phone her?" I asked.

"I tried." Francine rested a hand on her hip. "She killed the call and sent me a message that she can't talk. She'll see us soon."

Colin swiped the screen of his phone and sent a message.

"Ty always has his phone on silent in case it rings at a bad time."

A knock on the hotel door prevented any more discussion about Bree. Ivan had joined Manny at the door. Manny opened it, his posture alert. A man was standing in the hallway, two women behind him and another man behind them. The men's postures, vigilance and hands hovering close to their holsters made it clear they were Ivan's team members.

"Jiří, come in." Ivan nodded towards us. "We've been waiting for you."

The tall man walked past Ivan and held out his fist for a fist bump. Their nonverbal cues communicated the same respect and comradery I saw in Daniel's team. Jiří nodded at us, but stopped by the kitchenette and watched the two women walking in.

Francine and Roxy both reacted when they saw Klára—their eyes wide, their mouths slightly agape. Klára was no longer the slightly overweight woman we'd seen on the photo, covered in layers of material. She was wearing light green cropped trousers, a fussy dark green sweater and ankle boots. Her hair was a rich brown with lighter streaks, cut very short. Tastefully applied makeup completed an image of a confident, successful woman. She looked far more European than Persian. Her fit shape and the way she moved made me wonder what type of sport she'd started with her new life here.

She glanced at Manny and Ivan at the door, but walked to us. Her head was held high, her shoulders back, her arms slightly away from her torso. This was not the posture of a scared woman. “Hi, I’m Klára Bittová and I would like to know why I’m here.”

The second woman followed her quietly and stopped next to her. There was no mistaking that this was Natálie Zemanová. Her hair was a bit shorter, the wide smile I’d seen on both photos replaced with concern pulling at her eyes and mouth. “I’m Natálie Zemanová.”

“She’s my friend.” Klára didn’t turn to look at Natálie, but lifted her fists to rest on her hips. “I go nowhere without her. At least nowhere if there are police involved.”

It was interesting to watch these two women. Two things occurred to me. They both spoke accentless English and they both appeared prepared for an interview with the police. I doubted they had any knowledge of Shahab’s activities in Europe and now in Prague. Looking at Natálie’s nonverbal cues, I was convinced she didn’t know her parents had been murdered.

This was not going to be an easy meeting.

Ivan spoke to his two team members and closed the door behind them. Manny walked past the women and quietly sat down next to Francine. He must have observed something in the two women not to use his usual acerbic tone or employ his vexingly indifferent body language. Ivan walked to us and gestured to the open seats on one of the sofas. “Please sit down. We’ll explain everything.”

Klára looked at Natálie, then shrugged and sat down where Ivan had indicated. Ivan sat down next to Daniel. “My name is Ivan Kemr and I’m with the Prague police.

These people are a special investigative team that is helping us at the moment."

"You aren't from Czech." Klára looked around the room. "Where are you from?"

Ivan introduced us, only giving our first names and not revealing our team's work. When he finished he turned to Daniel. "The next part I will leave to Daniel. He's always been much better at this than me."

The immediate regret was fleeting on Daniel's face, but I'd seen it. He shifted to the edge of the sofa and rested his elbows on his knees. He inhaled to speak, but then turned to me. "Tell me when I should be wary or should stop."

I understood his meaning. We'd discussed in detail who would speak to Klára and had decided Daniel would be most suited. I'd insisted. His astute observations and empathy made him ideal. I didn't envy him.

He turned to Klára. "I know you've been used as a pawn the moment you left Iran. I can't begin to understand what you've been through and won't pretend that I do. We aren't here to use you for our own gain. We need your help. Your trust. And for that, I will give you as much information as I can."

"Wow." Klára tilted her head back and stared at us through narrowed eyes. "This is different from all the other times the cops spoke to me."

"We're not cops." Francine's smile was warm. She pointed at Daniel and Ivan. "Only those two are." She raised her chin towards Manny next to her. "And he's a little bit."

Manny scowled, but didn't say anything.

Klára looked at us again, her emotions flowing across her face. She closed her eyes for a moment and pressed her fingertips against her temples. On a deep inhale, she opened her eyes, lowered her hands and looked at me. "This is about Shahab, isn't it?"

I blinked in surprise. Daniel was the person who connected with people. Not me. But Klára didn't look away. Instead she raised both eyebrows, waiting for my response.

I nodded. "Yes. We are looking for Shahab."

"Looking for him?" She deflated, her face losing colour. "Why? Isn't he in Ira… He's here." Her hand flew to her throat, covering her suprasternal notch. Women often touched or covered the hollow area above the breastbone in times of great distress or fear. Or both.

"He's been in Europe for some time," Daniel said.

She didn't look at him, her eyes still on me. "How long is 'some time'?"

"A year. That we know of." I watched her reaction and nodded to myself. I'd been correct in my initial observation. She hadn't known Shahab was here.

She rubbed her arms twice, then pulled her shoulders back like she'd done when she'd entered our hotel floor. "He's killed people, hasn't he?"

"Why do you ask that?" Manny's tone was gentle.

"I'm asking *you*." She didn't look away from me.

I sighed when Daniel sat back on the sofa and nodded to me. I didn't want to be the one speaking to these two vulnerable, neurotypical women. I took a moment to collect my thoughts. "Last year, he killed people in France. He has a specific way he does that. That is how Ivan knew he was here in Prague."

"Do…" She took a deep breath and slowly breathed out an attempt to calm down. "Do you know if he's here because of me?"

"Yes, we think he is."

She gasped and shuddered when Natálie took her hand. "He won't find you, Klára. He won't even recognise you."

"But does he know I'm here?" Her attempts at staying calm was failing. Her chest rose and fell with rapid breaths and she shrank back into the sofa. "How does he know I'm here?"

"He saw a video of you on Charles Bridge some years ago. You were still overweight and looked much the same as when you'd left Iran. You look better now."

"Genevieve." Francine widened her eyes in the look she always gave me when I'd said something inappropriate.

"No, she's right." Klára waved away Francine's concern. "I lost twenty kilograms, cut and coloured my hair and started wearing these clothes for two reasons. The first reason was because I wanted to find my own identity. I didn't want to be someone's nameless wife. I didn't want to be invisible in black garb. I want my clothes to represent who I am. An independent, intelligent, strong woman." She huffed a self-mocking laugh. "Not that I feel like that at the moment. The second reason I changed was so I could really be Klára. So Shahab would never recognise me and force me to go back."

"He will never take you back." Natálie leaned forward to grab Klára's attention. "I won't allow it and these people won't allow it." She looked at me. "Right?"

I balked. When had I become the person neurotypicals trusted? Colin took my hand and lightly squeezed. I nodded. "We want to find Shahab and stop him from ever hurting anyone else again."

"He likes it." A tremor shook Klára's body. "You hear so many times women tell stories about their husbands beating them and apologising, promising to never do it again. Yeah. That wasn't Shahab. When we first got married he was kind. And quiet. He was idealistic and dreamed of being in one of the top positions in the police. He wanted to make sure the police did what they were supposed to. Protect the innocent, catch criminals and live honest lives. But when he didn't receive a promotion and it was given to someone who had a reputation for the many bribes he received, Shahab changed. At first he didn't speak to me at all. Then one day he started ranting about the man who'd been promoted. How he was extorting families, small business owners, anyone who crossed his path or caught his attention. Shahab said that if a man like that was promoted and Shahab overlooked even after being the perfect officer, he would show them exactly how corrupt a police officer could become.

"I made the mistake of telling him not to throw away everything he'd work for. Not to dishonour his name and our family." She touched her cheek. "He broke my arm, my jaw and two ribs. And while he did that, I saw the sick pleasure it gave him. The more I begged, the more he enjoyed it. He never apologised. Not once."

"I'm so sorry you had to go through that." Roxy wiped tears from her cheeks. "No woman should ever experience that kind of terror."

Klára's smile was cynical. "That was only the physical side of it. I grew up in a home where psychological abuse was normal. Both my mom and dad enjoyed telling me how useless I was. Wait." She inhaled sharply and froze, her eyes wide. "Is my father here too? Is he also involved?"

"No." I looked at Ivan, who shook his head, and looked back at Klára. "We have no indication that your father is here."

Klára looked at Natálie, then wrapped her arms around herself in a full self-hug. "I don't know how you think I can help you find Shahab. I didn't even know he was here."

"You can tell us more about his victims." It would help to know if there were any connections between the victims other than what we'd found.

"Um, Genevieve." Daniel moved to the edge of his seat again, his expression cautious. "Maybe I could?"

I didn't know what he was implying, but trusted him to be much more equipped to tell these women about the people Shahab had killed. I nodded in relief.

"No." Klára shook her head. "You're a cop. I've had enough of you people. She's telling me the truth."

"This is not going to be an easy truth to hear, Klára."

Daniel's tone and expression were gentle.

"Tell me." She looked at me.

I sighed heavily and looked at Natálie. "Your parents are dead."

"What?" Natálie jerked and moved towards Klára. Further away from me. She looked at Daniel. "What is she talking about?"

Daniel's eyebrows pulled in and down in regret. "I'm so sorry to tell you this, Natálie, but we found your mother and father unresponsive in their bedroom this morning."

"It's not possible. I spoke to them this morning." She was in full denial, shaking her head, her arms crossed tightly. "They can't be dead."

"I'm sorry, Natálie." Daniel's quiet words broke through her denial and she uttered a sound so primal in its pain, I shuddered.

"No! No!" Sobs wracked her body as she folded into herself.

Klára put her hand on Natálie's arm, but pulled back when Natálie moved away. "Oh, Nat. I'm so sorry."

Natálie shook her head and shifted on the sofa, putting even more distance between them. "I can't. I just can't."

Klára looked at me, devastated. Her expression implored me to intervene. I had no idea what to do.

"Natálie." Roxy got up and knelt in front of the weeping woman. "Why don't you come with me for a moment of privacy? My room is just over there and we can close the door if you want."

Another loud sob escaped when Natálie nodded and

took Roxy's hand. She blindly followed Roxy to her and Vinnie's room, her shoulders shaking as she wept. Roxy led her in and turned back to us. "The hotel?"

Daniel closed his eyes, but quickly opened them and looked at Roxy. "Tell her."

Roxy nodded and closed the bedroom door behind her. I was glad Roxy would be the one to tell Natálie about her friend Jarda's death. She would know how to handle it.

"What about the hotel?" Klára asked me.

I didn't know how to do this, except by being honest. "Shahab killed Jarda Zonyga."

"Oh, no." Klára covered her face with both hands and uttered a long, low moan. When she looked at me again, her fear had been replaced by intense sadness as well as anger. "They were best friends. I'd met Jarda. He is… was such a nice guy. Kind. Real. Oh, Nat is never going to forgive me."

"You didn't do anything wrong." At first I didn't see why she would need forgiveness. I thought about this from a neurotypical perspective and almost sighed. "Natálie can't hold you responsible for the actions of another person."

"The actions of an evil monster." Francine put her tablet aside and waited until Klára looked at her. "I'm the one who gets all the dirty details about people for our investigations. Everything I found about Natálie tells me that she knows this is not your fault. She just needs a moment."

"But it *is* my fault." Klára pulled her knees up and hugged them to her chest. "If I hadn't come here, none of these people would be dead."

"That is true." I ignored Francine's angry hiss. "But if we use that argument, you should never get in a car in case there is an accident. You should also not eat any food because other people are starving. If you want to take indirect responsibility, there is a lot of guilt you can wallow in if you so choose."

"That's a bit harsh." Klára rested her forehead on her knees for a moment, then looked at me again. "But you are right." She lowered her feet to the floor and pulled her shoulders back. "So how do we stop Shahab?"

Chapter TWENTY

"TELL US ABOUT YOUR father and his relationship with Shahab." Francine picked up her tablet again. "And also your father's company."

"I told the cops everything." Klára looked at Ivan. "And they kept pushing me for more and treating me as if I was lying."

"I apologise for this behaviour." Ivan's downward gaze as he slowly shook his head communicated his shame. "This is not how a valuable asset should be treated." He gestured around the room. "We don't have any political agenda."

"We have no agenda," Manny said. "Aside from stopping Shahab."

Klára studied Manny and then Ivan for a few seconds. "Okay, I can get behind this agenda. Shahab needs to be stopped." She glanced at Roxy's closed door and took a deep breath. "Reza Alikhani is my biological father, but I stopped referring to him as anything but Reza the moment I left Iran. He and Maryam, my mother, did nothing for me as a child to nurture any kind of well-being—emotional or spiritual.

"Physically, they took very good care of me. Because of

their business, we were wealthy and I had the best of everything. I wanted for nothing. Except love." Her shoulders relaxed marginally. "I got that from my Aunt Fatemeh. She was the mother I should've had. Reza and Maryam were always very busy with the business, so I often stayed with Fatemeh. Even at weekends.

"She was an accountant and by the time I went to high school, she was the CFO of a small, but influential tech company. She was everything my mother was not, even though she was my mother's sister and they almost looked like twins. Fatemeh was strong in her faith, but didn't wear the full-body cloak—the *chadar*—like Maryam and sometimes didn't even wear her headscarf—the *hijab*. Her faith helped her lead a better, richer life and helped her be a better, kinder person."

"She's the reason you are as resilient and strong as you are today." I could see those traits and more in her as she spoke.

"Strong?" Her short laugh held no humour. "I try to be, but I'm terrified of my own shadow. No, really. The first moments when I wake up every morning, I can barely breathe I'm so scared. Then I remind myself that I'm the one who holds all the power in my life. I'm the one who decides what I wear, what I eat, what music I listen to. I'm the one who came to Prague with nothing, but fought my way through university to get my accounting degree. I'm the one who learned to be fluent in Czech and English. I'm the one who got a job and I'm the one who qualified for a mortgage so I can buy my small one-bedroom flat. I did all this. Only then can I breathe again and start my day. Strong? No, I don't feel strong even though I wish I did."

"Your father? Reza?" I asked.

"An extremist. There is no other way to describe him. Iran is this amazing country filled with people who are warm and open-hearted towards foreigners. Sure, some people are a bit more cautious, but most Iranians love to meet new people. We have an ancient culture, which is good and bad. Good because it gives us so much to draw from. Bad because it doesn't always move with the times. In some ways women are still oppressed, but in others women have a lot of freedom. One example is that there are more female engineering students in Iran than in any other country in the world. There are—like in any country—people who are on the extreme ends of this. Reza and Maryam are two of those. They hate everything that represents Western culture.

"Make no mistake, there are quite a few things I'm not crazy about. I still live a rather conservative life. I don't condone the Western loose morals and thinking that it's okay to try everything at least once. Some things should never be tried. But I respect others' choices if they want to try something. That's maybe the one thing I love most about Western culture—the possibility, the freedom to choose.

"Reza and then later Shahab didn't agree with that. They believed that the general population is too stupid to choose wisely." A sad look crossed her face. "When I mentioned this once to Jarda, he laughed and said that there is a bit of truth in that. I liked him." She rubbed her temples and sighed. "Reza believed only a select few should make the decisions and the rest of the world should follow them without question. That included decisions about interpreting the Koran and everything to do with Islam.

"He would take passages from the Koran and twist them to justify his sick ideologies. Shahab was exactly like that. After he lost the promotion, he would sit for hours with Reza and they would discuss such things."

"They got on well?" Colin asked.

"Like a house on fire." Her top lip curled in contempt. "Even better after Shahab lost his promotion. Ours wasn't an arranged marriage by any means. But Reza and Maryam did everything they could to encourage our union after they'd introduced us. In the beginning it was wonderful. It wasn't difficult to give in to their pressure. Shahab was one of the few people who'd shown me affection and that was what I fell for. It was all false."

She fell quiet, trapped in her memories. The pain of that time was clear to see on her face.

"What do you know about Sven and Anna?" I wanted to know how the octogenarian owners of Seppo-Tommi fitted into Reza Alikhani and Shahab's world.

"From Helsinki? Or wait, they now live in some small coastal village." Her *depressor anguli oris* muscles turned the corners of her lips down. "Reza had more affection for them than for me."

"What was their relationship?"

"Reza studied finance and commerce in Helsinki after he left school. It was before he met Maryam. He was a struggling student with no friends and didn't fit in with his classmates. He went to have his eyes tested one day and this couple who did the test felt sorry for him. They invited him for dinner and within a month, he was living in their house with them. He always said they took care of him when he needed it most and he would do the same." She jolted upright. "Did Shahab kill them too?"

"No."

"Uh. Okay." She sat back, but didn't relax. "Well, I never met them. Reza used to go once a year to Finland to visit them. I know that they met Maryam and she liked them too. She often went to visit them too."

That explained how Sven and Anna came to own the company that had provided Shahab with funds. "How much do you know about your parents' company?"

"They sell toys." She shrugged. "I always thought it was the biggest irony of life—these two unloving, horrid people selling products that bring so much joy to children. Reza and Maryam were the two least joyful people I'd ever met. Maybe with the exception of Shahab." She paused for a moment, looking up and left. She shook her head. "No. I can't think of anything about their business that I haven't told the police."

All the information she was giving us was important. It helped created a more rounded profile of Shahab. But it wasn't bringing us any nearer to locating him and preventing that opioid weapon from killing people.

Klára continued to talk about how much she loved Iran, the people, the culture, but not her family. While she talked about the psychological abuse she suffered, I thought of everything we'd learned so far.

Shahab did everything with calculated purpose. His victims had been strategically chosen. He had not shown a change in his behaviour significant enough to make me expect his choice of when and where to use the opioid weapon to be without meaning.

I waited for Klára to finish talking about the many successful Iranian businesswomen. It was obvious to me she was trying to calm herself by talking about things and people not related to Shahab or her parents.

"Did you and Shahab ever talk about Prague?" I asked when she inhaled to continue telling us about a woman who had started an online recruiting service in Iran that now had over half a million registered professionals.

She winced and nodded. "Once. Because of Shahab's job, we had really good internet at home. The government controls, censors and slows down the internet like crazy. Our internet was never throttled, so I was able to visit many websites I otherwise wouldn't have been able to. He walked into the kitchen one day while I was browsing through photos of Prague. He hated it." She glanced at the tall windows. "He said the historic buildings show just what kind of sick capitalist, money-grabbing mentality the West suffers from. I showed him Charles Bridge and asked him if he didn't think it was an artistic and architectural beauty. He laughed at me. He said the moment people strive towards beauty is the moment those people need to be eradicated."

"Was there any other building or place he specifically hated?"

She thought about this. "No. He just went on and on about Charles Bridge. He said all the people in the photo who were on that bridge were infidels and didn't deserve to ever see paradise. He said the women in the photo wearing summer shirts, baring their arms and necks, were whores and should be severely punished."

That was probably the reason Klára had stood out on the video footage. The tourists had likely been dressed in light summer clothes. A dark blue cloak that had covered her from head to toe would have been in stark contrast.

I thought about Klára and the information we'd now been given access to. "I didn't see the date when you left Iran. Do you remember?"

"Remember the day my life truly started? Of course." She glanced again at Roxy's closed door. "That is why I took the day off work and Nat and I went to the spa to celebrate. It's seven years ago today."

"Bloody hell." Manny's words came out as a whisper, but everyone heard. He looked at me. "Doc?"

"This would fit in with his profile. If he were to do something, today would give it much more symbolism." I stared at Klára. "What else happened on this day?"

"How do you know something happened?"

"I saw it on your face."

"Oh. Huh. Well, you are right about Shahab being into

symbolism. We got married on the same date we met, three years later. And I left him on that day. This day."

"That's definitely one way of flipping him the bird." Francine's expression held approval.

"Holy mother of all the saints." Manny rubbed both hands over his face. "He's doing it today. Right, Doc?"

"It would fit." I looked at Francine.

She swiped her tablet screen and tapped it a few times. Her face lost all colour. "Um. Guys?"

The shot of adrenaline racing through my system felt cold. My grip on Colin's hand strengthened.

"What?" Manny twisted his torso to look at her tablet. "Oh, hell no."

"Millard?"

"It's Bree." Francine stared at her screen. "I tapped into the security cameras on Charles Bridge just to see if there's anything off." She turned her tablet for us to see. "This is live."

The camera was aimed towards the Lesser Town Bridge Towers serving as an entrance from the bridge to one of the streets leading to the castle. It wasn't surprising to see a crowd of people on the bridge on this beautiful sunny spring afternoon. Most people were still wearing coats, but a few tourists were in t-shirts. Almost everyone was taking photos.

Bree was standing in the centre of the bridge looking straight at the camera. People were streaming around her, no one taking particular note of a woman standing frozen in one place. That they did not notice her nonverbal cues amazed me. Her rapid breathing, stretched and drawn-back lips and widened eyes behind the lightly-coloured sunglasses shouted her fear louder than words could.

"What are you looking at?" Klára asked. "The woman standing in the middle?"

"Bree." Phillip pressed his fist against his chest. "Why isn't she moving?"

"I don't think she can." Daniel looked at Ivan. "We need to evacuate the bridge."

Ivan jumped up, his phone already against his ear.

"Where is the weapon?" I studied the image on Francine's screen. "Bree is without her coat. I can't see where a canister can be hidden."

"She's right." Vinnie walked closer and soon everyone was crowding around Francine's tablet.

"Wait a sec." Francine turned her tablet back and tapped a few times. She shook her head. "This is the camera from Bree's back. Look."

Bree's long braid hung straight down her back, the light breeze lifting a few strands that had worked their way out. Her muscle tension was immense. She was still wearing the same skinny plaid trousers she had on this morning, but her cream shirt and olive jacket had been replaced by a tight short-sleeve black t-shirt. There was no sign of a canister or any other way to deliver the opioid weapon.

"Go back to the previous view." My voice sounded gravelly from the distress of watching Bree. Francine changed the image and the others stood back to give me a better view of the tablet. "This is too far away."

"Give me a se… There." Francine had zoomed in on Bree, her face now clearly visible.

I waited for the third person to pass her to confirm my suspicion. "She doesn't want anyone to touch her."

"Why?" Manny's frown pulled his brow low over his eyes.

"I don't know." I had seen Bree's comfort with physical closeness to others. She wasn't like me.

Manny turned to Colin. "Where the bloody hell is your guy?"

"I don't know." Colin looked up from his phone. "I've sent him three messages and he hasn't read them yet. I'm beginning to worry about him."

"You damn well should." Manny's lips were in a thin line. "He was supposed to keep Bree safe."

"My team is there." Ivan walked over to us and pointed at the tablet. I looked back and saw people jerking to the side and then starting to move off the bridge as police officers came closer.

"Tell them to stay far away from Bree." The words rushed out of my mouth as I saw the increased fear on Bree's face. "No one should touch her."

Ivan spoke into his phone and the officers moved away from Bree. One officer turned back to Bree and held out one hand as if to calm her. He spoke to her, but she didn't respond. She didn't speak, didn't nod, didn't shake her head. She didn't move.

"She won't talk." I had no doubt about this, even though I didn't know the reason for it.

"Holy hell." Manny rubbed his hand over his head. "What's going on there?"

Francine handed her tablet to Manny and got up to get her laptop. Soon she had the same footage on the larger screen and handed the laptop to Colin, but looked at me. "You'll see her better there to keep an eye on everything."

Colin put the laptop on his knees and turned it towards me. I leaned in and studied Bree's face. Behind the amber-coloured lenses, her blinking was erratic and it held my attention. The lenses were transparent enough to see her eyes, the frame a smart distraction hiding her swollen eye. Her eyelids were the only parts of her body moving. She had not moved at all since I'd first seen her on the bridge. She was staring at the camera aimed at her.

At first I thought her blinking might be her attempt to communicate, possibly using something like Morse code, but it wasn't. It was to contain her tears. She was not successful. One tear ran down her left cheek and her fear intensified. Why was she scared to cry?

Men in hazmat suits came onto the bridge and spoke to Bree, but she didn't respond. Ivan kept repeating the same words into his phone and I hoped he was telling them to stay away from her. They did. In the twenty minutes it took for the hazmat team to clear the bridge and Bree from any traces of opioid, she did not move once.

I saw how her muscles started trembling and how she immediately forced herself to relax so there would be no movement. Curious.

"The bridge is clear. There are no bombs, no opioids,

nothing." Ivan looked at me. "What should we do?"

"Don't touch Bree and don't move her." I got up. "I want to speak to her."

Chapter TWENTY-ONE

"THIS IS NOT GOING bloody anywhere." Manny opened the SUV's back passenger door and got out. "It will be faster if we run."

I agreed. We'd rushed down to Colin's SUV to reach the bridge as fast as possible, but the traffic had now slowed down to a standstill. Most likely because the area around the bridge had been evacuated and cordoned off.

No one waited another second. Colin pulled to the side of the road and double-parked. All of us got out and ran. I estimated the distance to be another kilometre to the bridge. I wasn't a sprinter, but I jogged often enough not to feel winded as we veered around tourists gawking at the police presence on and around the bridge.

"Make way!" Manny shouted as we neared a group of tourists, all of them aiming their smartphones at the bridge. I felt like flinching when the phones turned towards us. But Bree's life was more important than my need to demand respect for my privacy.

Vinnie and Manny ran two metres ahead of us and soon Daniel and Ivan passed us as well, their fitness level clear in their ease as they pushed for speed. They reached the police cordon before us, Colin and me only half a minute behind them. An officer was holding the yellow tape high and we slowed down just enough to lower ourselves under it.

I didn't stop running when I got to the bridge. Ivan, Daniel and Vinnie were talking to Ivan's team, standing by a tall statue. Manny was already standing in front of Bree, a five-metre distance between then. His hands were held out in a placating manner.

I stopped next to Manny, my eyes not leaving Bree. Not even when Colin and Manny exchanged a quiet greeting. I stepped away from them, closer to Bree. "I won't touch you. I know you don't want that. I also know you can't or don't want to talk or move."

A tear ran down her cheek and she swallowed—even that movement controlled and minimised.

"We need to communicate and I recommend we keep it simple. I will ask questions and you can answer by blinking once for 'yes' and twice for 'no'."

She blinked once.

"Good." I stopped when her eyes widened and she looked behind me. I turned around to see Manny and Colin coming closer. I turned back to her. "Everyone here knows not to touch you. Understand?"

She blinked once.

"Will Shahab's weapon disperse that opioid if you move?"

She blinked once.

"Is there any camera connected to your sunglasses?"

She blinked twice.

"Are the glasses to hide your swollen eye only?"

She blinked once.

"I know you can't tell me, so I'm going to start guessing how he determines your movement."

Her eyes widened, then she looked down without moving her head. She was staring hard at her torso. The footage I'd seen of her wasn't clear, but even now I couldn't see anything under her black t-shirt. "There is something on your torso?"

She blinked once. Again her eyes widened and she looked to my side. Colin was standing next to me and held out his phone towards us. "Bree, I have Francine on the phone. She's on speaker and wants to ask you a few questions."

"Hey, girl." Francine's tone was gentle. "You're doing great. Now tell me if Shahab placed sensors on your body."

She blinked once.

"She's saying yes," Colin said.

"I saw that. I can see you guys on the security camera." Francine cleared her throat. "Bree, do you know how many Shahab placed on your body?"

She blinked once.

"Okay, now please count out how many by blinking. Five blinks for five sensors. Okay, start."

Bree blinked. Again. And again. And again. By the time she blinked twelve times another tear rolled down her cheek.

She stopped at fourteen.

"Bloody hell." Manny stepped forward and leaned

towards Colin's phone. "Can we stop these things?"

"Give me a sec. I want to speak to Ivan's team and his IT guys." The call ended.

Only now did I take the time to observe the rest of Bree's nonverbal cues. There wasn't much to assess since she didn't move at all, the tension in her muscles unmistakable. Yet there could be small cues that might prove important. I looked at her feet. She was resting her weight on the sides and the heels of her feet, avoiding any pressure on her toes. Her legs appeared normal under the cover of her plaid trousers, as did her torso. Even this scrutiny didn't enable me to see the sensors Shahab had placed on her body.

I looked at her chest and noticed her erratic breathing. At first I had thought it was due to the immense stress she was currently experiencing, but this seemed more. "Are you injured?"

She blinked once.

"Are your ribs broken?" That would explain why she was taking such shallow breaths.

She blinked once. Another tear rolled down her cheek. Then she closed her eyes for a few seconds, her attempt to regain her composure obvious. She opened her eyes and looked over my shoulder.

Jiří was walking towards us, an unfamiliar device in his hand. "Hello. I'm Jiří. I won't touch. I test for sensor." His broken English was softly spoken and his approach careful as if he didn't want to startle Bree. He held the device towards her and walked around her. He nodded. "There is transmission. We need to block."

Colin's phone vibrated and he swiped the screen. "Francine, you're on speaker."

"Jiří, is it transmitting?"

"Yes. I go get jammer from truck." Jiří ran full-out to the opposite side of the bridge.

"Hang in there, girl." Francine's voice had that slightly distracted tone it had when she was simultaneously working on her computer. "We're going to jam every signal even thinking of transmitting and you'll be good to go."

I studied Bree's face. When I'd seen her after she'd saved our lives in the Zeman's house, she hadn't given the impression that she was particularly concerned about the injury above her eyebrow. Yet now it was completely hidden under badly applied make-up.

"Did you put make-up on your injury?" I pointedly looked at her eyebrow.

She blinked twice.

"Did Shahab do this?"

She blinked once.

I considered this. The make-up and sunglasses could be because Shahab didn't want to attract unwanted attention to her. But if that was his reasoning, why place her in an unmoving position in the middle of a famous tourist attraction?

Bree looked over my shoulder and narrowed her eyes. Then her uninjured eye shot wide open. She stared at me.

"You just saw something that scared you."

She blinked once.

"Look at it again."

She looked past me towards a deserted artist stall. When the police had evacuated the area, they hadn't allowed the local artists and hawkers to take their wares with them. The informal stand held three easels with notebook-sized, colourful paintings of Prague—the castle, Charles Bridge and the Dancing House. Smaller paintings were displayed on the ground and a fourth paint-stained easel held an incomplete painting. There were no paintbrushes or tubes of paint, only spray cans.

I looked back at Bree. "Did Shahab leave something by the art?"

She blinked once.

"I have jammer." Jiří ran closer and put the square device on the ground a metre from Bree. "Francine, I turn jammer on."

"Okey-dokey. See you soon, Bree." Francine's voice was cut off.

"Now you speak." Jiří looked at Bree.

She blinked twice.

"Do you think the sensor will still transmit?" Manny asked.

She blinked once.

"Bloody hell." Manny rubbed his hands over his face. "Doc?"

"She's being truthful." I took a moment, then looked back at the artist's paintings. "Bree, is Shahab's weapon by the art?"

She blinked once.

Immediate panic tightened around my chest like a pressure belt. The artist had set up a mere six metres from where we were standing. If Shahab was indeed using the weapon Doctor Novotný had developed, six metres would still give us an immediate lethal dose of that opioid. The breeze was blowing in our direction. We had no chance.

Colin took my hand in a warm and firm grip. "We're okay, love. Just breathe."

I gasped when I realised I'd been holding my breath. I mentally started playing Mozart's Violin Sonata No. 36 in F major and took three slow breaths. "Ivan, the hazmat team need to remove everything that is there. Or wait a moment." I turned to Bree. "Is it safe to move or should they put it in a containment case? Blink once for moving it and twice for containing it."

She blinked twice.

"Get that done." Manny turned to Ivan. "And later I hope you shout at the bloody hazmat techs. They should've found it first time around."

Ivan's lips were in a thin line when he nodded. "There will be hell to pay."

Bree's eyes followed him as he walked away, the fear on her face intensifying. I needed her attention back to me. "Is this the only device Shahab had?"

She looked back at me and blinked twice.

"How many? Blink out the number."

She blinked three times.

"Holy mother of all the saints."

Bree's eyes strayed again to the artist's area. Three men dressed in their protective suits, complete with helmets, walked awkwardly towards the artist area. The little I could see of their faces showed their doubt. Two of the men were carrying what looked like a large crate. They reached the art and opened the crate to reveal a thick lining inside and seals that would prevent whatever contaminant they put in there from leaking.

They first placed the eight painted canvasses in the case, then carefully placed the spray paint cans on top of that. The third man paused when he picked up a can with a dark blue sticker around its side, but no lid. He spoke in Czech and the others turned to first look at him, then the can. One of the others took out a device and held it close to the can. He jerked and spoke in Czech.

"There's opioid in that can." Ivan put his fists on his hips and spoke in Czech before he turned back to us. "They're locking that in and it will be tested."

The relief on Bree's face was unmistakable. Yet she didn't move. I thought about this. "Do you know where Shahab placed the other cans?"

She blinked once.

I trusted her judgement whether it was safe for her to move or not. I'd rather she acted in an abundance of caution than dismiss whatever knowledge she had, resulting in numerous deaths. "I just want to confirm that you still don't feel safe to speak or move. Correct?"

She blinked once.

"Then we need to find out where Shahab placed the

other cans." I waited until she blinked once. "Is it in a public place?"

She blinked once.

"A tourist attraction?"

She blinked twice.

"A government building?"

She hesitated, then blinked twice.

"A building?"

She blinked once.

I took a moment to reconsider what I'd learned in this case. "Is it an organisation that helps women?"

She blinked once. And stared at me, hopeful.

I looked at Ivan. "What is the name of the organisation that employs Natálie? The one that helped Klára?"

"The Free Women's Council." Ivan waved at Jiří to come closer. "The FWC is the largest NGO in Czech as far as I know."

Bree watched him as he spoke in rapid Czech to Jiří. He turned back when Jiří sprinted away from us. "We'll deploy a team there now. It's close to one of our fire departments, which is equipped to deal with hazardous agents like this."

"You're doing great, Bree." Colin's tone was gentle. "We only need one more device."

She looked over our shoulders in the direction we'd come from. Her eyebrows pulled up and in, her face losing colour. Her fear was escalating. I didn't know how to calm her. I wasn't good at this.

Colin shifted a bit closer and spoke to Bree in a low

tone. He reassured her that Ivan's team was the best in Prague and our team the best in Europe. As he continued talking to her, I considered his statement. I didn't have other teams to compare our successes to and decided Colin's claim could not be proven and was therefore moot.

"They found the device." Ivan walked closer and stopped next to Manny. "Shahab didn't try to hide it at all. He just left it in the reception area." He leaned a bit closer to Bree. "My team made sure there's nothing transmitting from here. You can speak now. It's really safe."

"I don't know if it's safe." She whispered through her teeth, barely moving her lips. Bree closed her eyes and swallowed. When she opened her eyes, she looked at me. "He said the smallest movement, even speaking would set them off. He said the sensors could not be stopped from transmitting. I believe him. I don't want to set off the last one. I'm not moving."

"Then don't move." Manny's tone and expression was calming, but the tension in his body high. "Just tell us if you know where that last bloody device is."

"I don't know. He only told me how he's going to enjoy seeing me kill all these capitalist infidels on the bridge." Her eyes filled with tears. "He said I deserved to be punished for being a deviant. That it will be my fault that so many women in the FWC will die. That's how I know about the Free Women's Council."

"Oh, Bree." Colin sighed. "None of what he said against you or anyone else is true."

"I know." She swallowed. "But he's sick. Really sick."

"Do you mean physically or psychologically?" I didn't always know to which neurotypicals referred.

"He's definitely sick in his head." Her eyebrows pulled together. "But he looked ill. He was sweating a lot and lost his balance a few times. There's something very wrong with him."

"How did that bastard get you?" Manny asked.

Bree closed her eyes again for two seconds. "My fault. I followed up on the medical equipment Roxy mentioned. I have a friend who sells these expensive machines and I asked her to find out if someone ordered specific equipment. She found a name and a delivery address. I thought I would just drive by in my new rental car and check it out." She looked at Manny. "I was going to phone you as soon as I knew it was something worth looking into."

"Daft woman." Manny's expression was not as unkind as his words. "What happened?"

"He must've seen me sitting in my car. One moment I was still checking out the building, thinking about calling you, and the next the window next to me exploded. At least that's what it sounded and felt like. He'd broken my rental's window and pulled me out through it." She looked at Colin. "That guy following me was slumped in his car. I recognised him from before and thought I would be even safer since he was there. I don't know if he's okay."

"Where was this?" Ivan was standing with his smartphone in his hand.

Bree gave the address and exhaled in relief when Ivan

glanced at his phone, then ran to where his team was standing. Not having access to phones or even two-way radios was slowing us down. But it was possibly also keeping us and others safe from being poisoned with a lethal dose of an opioid analogue.

"Tell me exactly what Shahab said to you." If I knew, I might deduce his current location from that. "Especially about the third device."

"He has that with him." She swallowed. "After he dragged me from the car, he took me into that building. He pushed a gun into my ribs. I couldn't fight."

"You did everything right," Colin said. "You stayed alive."

She gave Colin a grateful look and forced herself to slow her breathing. "All the equipment is standing in the building. It looks like a lab. But everything is turned off. Shahab taunted me about the footage from the police station that had been deleted and that I was a suspect. He said it was fun to play with me. He tied me on top of one of the long lab desks and…" She took a few shallow breaths and looked at me, tears in her eyes. "He asked me what you know about him. I didn't tell him anything."

"He tortured you." I tightened my grip on Colin's hand and forced more Mozart into my mind.

"He broke my ribs. Then he decided it would be fun to break my toes." This time the tears spilled down her cheeks. "I didn't know toes are so difficult to break." She blinked a few times, her gaze watery. "I don't know for how much longer I'll be able to stand like this."

I didn't know what to say. How did one console a person while they were still suffering from horrendous torture? And how did one ask for more information when that would only cause more emotional and psychological distress? But we needed to know. "What else did he say?"

"He asked how many of your team was here. He named everyone. He knows who you are. And he wanted to know if everyone is here. I didn't tell him anything. It was strange. He asked me if you guys liked me. He said that it was as if Allah sent me to him so his job would be easier." She paused for a second. "He sounded crazy, as if he wasn't in his right mind. He said he didn't know how he was going to get to them, but if you liked me, it would be perfect. He said you would come for me. Then he said you took everything from him, so he will take everything from you."

Adrenaline sent cold fear through my system. Standing in front of this woman who'd been tortured because she'd protected us—me—humbled me. It also motivated me to push the darkness in my peripheral vision back and focus on what she'd said.

I turned to Manny, too scared to verbalise my conclusion.

"Doc?"

I shook my head.

"Spit it out, missy! I don't have time for your little problems."

"Your attempt to calm me by insulting me is weak. I can see the contrasting concern on your face." But his method had worked. I inhaled deeply. "Shahab wants to avenge the death of Sahar and the humiliation of being deceived. The bridge and the FWC is the perfect revenge on Czech's involvement and the city that took Sahar from him."

"But?" Manny's expression led me to believe he knew what I was about to say. He was already turning his torso, ready to move.

"We took a lot from Shahab." I counted on my fingers. "His job, his reputation, all his assets, everything he'd saved up to get back at his own country and later Sahar and Czech."

"Holy bloody hell!" Manny ran.

"Motherfucker!" Vinnie's face first went white, then red with the realisation and he immediately ran after Manny. "Roxy!"

I gave Bree one glance, took my hand from Colin's and ran faster than I'd ever run in my life.

Shahab was in our hotel room. With Roxy, Francine, Phillip, Natálie and Klára.

Chapter TWENTY-TWO

I LEANED FORWARD and put my hands on my knees, trying to catch my breath. We were in the elevator going up to our hotel floor. Vinnie was shifting from one foot to the other. Manny was swearing nonstop, glowering at the panel displaying the floor numbers as we moved up. Colin stood next to me, also breathing heavily after our sprint here.

"Vin, we have to do this right." Colin put his hand on Vinnie's shoulder.

"She didn't answer her phone. She always answers her phone when I call. Always." Vinnie swung around and glared at Colin. "He's got Rox, dude. My Roxy. And Franny."

"And Phillip." My throat closed as I tried to push the words past it.

"He's not going to fucking live to see another day."

"We have to do this right, big guy." Manny pressed his fists against his eyes. "Dan and Ivan are taking the URNA team up the stairs. We need to give them time to do their job."

"I can do that job." Vinnie punched one fist into his open palm.

"Vin." Colin tightened his grip on Vinnie's shoulder. "We need to keep everyone alive."

"Not that motherfucker."

"Stop." Manny straightened and turned to look at Vinnie. "Get your bloody head on straight or you're going to get Roxanne and Francine killed."

"And Phillip." My voice was hoarse.

Manny nodded at me. "And Phillip and the two other women." He looked back at Vinnie. "We need to contain the situation until the trained URNA guys can do their jobs. Can I trust you?"

Vinnie's nostrils flared, but he nodded once.

Manny jerked when his phone vibrated in his hand. He swiped the screen and put the phone to his ear. "Ivan?"

I knew it was physically impossible, but it felt like my stomach dropped to my feet when I saw Manny's expression. I straightened and wrapped my arms tightly around my torso.

"How many?" Manny pressed the heel of his hand against one eye, nodded and ended the call. He looked at us. "Gabriella was wrong. There are more than three devices. One exploded prematurely in a delivery van and killed the driver. The young mother who ran to help him when he crashed into a street light was also killed by the opioid weapon. As well as three of the five first responders."

"Fuck!" Vinnie lifted his fist as if to punch the metal wall of the elevator, but held back and slowly lowered his arm. "What else did Ivan say?"

"Another device was delivered, but went off too early. There was no one in the women's clinic except the cleaning lady." Manny rubbed his hands hard over his face. "Two paramedics also died."

"When did this happen?" Colin asked.

"A few hours ago. The bloody bastard has been at it before we found Gabriella on that bridge."

I stared at the electronic numbers showing the slow ascend to our floor. How many more people was Shahab going to kill before we found him? Before we stopped him? Darkness pushed into my peripheral vision as I thought of the possible danger Phillip, Francine and Roxy were in. Manny had phoned Francine while we'd rushed here. She also hadn't answered.

I was terrified.

Manny turned to me. "Doc, I need you and Frey to stay back. We can't protect you if you're all over the place."

"I'm never all over the place." I swallowed the rest of my argument when the elevator stopped and the doors pinged. As if in slow motion, the doors slid open to reveal an empty hallway.

Manny pressed a button on the elevator and the lights inside dimmed. The porter who had brought our luggage up had explained that it locked the elevator in place to allow guests to load or unload the elevator with suitcases or shopping.

Manny and Vinnie both had their weapons in their hands as they entered the hallway. Colin took a step closer to me and placed himself partly in front of me. All I could do was push more Mozart into my mind to prevent a shutdown from taking me.

"Genevieve!" Shahab's deep voice reached into the elevator and the tightness around my chest increased. "I know you are here. I heard the elevator. The door is open. Come on in."

"She's not here." Manny took a careful step away from the elevator, out of my line of sight.

"Then this one will die first."

Francine's scream lasted three seconds. The intense agony was unmistakable in that sound and darkness rushed into my vision. "Stay away, Genevieve!" She screamed again and I could hear Roxy sobbing in the background.

"If anyone other than Genevieve walks in here, they will both die. Slowly." Shahab sounded out of breath. "Are you coming, Genevieve?"

I didn't know what to do. Would my mind be able to handle the incredible stress awaiting me in there or would my mind shut down and cause the deaths of two women and a man who'd come to mean everything to me? I felt paralysed when I considered the options. My brain didn't want to function.

I shook my head in an irrational attempt to clear it. And came to a decision. Instead of micro-analysing the situation like I did in almost every aspect of my life, I acted.

I stepped around Colin and walked into the hallway.

"Doc, get back!" Manny's hiss accompanied his furious expression.

I shook my head. I might not have the tools to be a

good friend, but I did have tools. Fear was scratching at my brain and my voice was hoarse, but I was determined. "I can keep Shahab calm and contained until Ivan's team is in place. Until they end this."

"Bloody hell, Doc." Manny rubbed his one hand hard over his face.

The conflict on Vinnie's face was most distressing. When he looked towards the open door leading to our hotel area, I could clearly see his desperate concern for Roxy. But when he looked at me, I saw the same for me.

I took a step closer to them and pulled my shoulders back like Bree had done so many times in the last few days. "I can do this. I hate it, but I know how to manipulate. I know how to get into Shahab's head. Just make sure Ivan, Daniel and the team make haste."

"Jenny." Colin put his hand on my forearm. He didn't have to speak. I could see all his emotions on his face. His love, his dread at letting me do this and his respect.

"I know." I turned away from him before his emotions became too overwhelming for me. I shook out my hands and held them loosely at my side to be as non-threatening as possible and walked to the door. "I'm coming in, Shahab."

"At last." He was standing in the centre of the sofas, his feet apart, a handgun in one hand and a spray can in the other. He waved the weapon at me as I stepped deeper into the room. "That's far enough. Stand right there."

I stopped half a metre before I reached the sofa where Roxy and Francine were sitting. One glance at them and the darkness I was fighting returned. Francine was curled into herself, cradling her hand. Roxy had pulled Francine against her and was glaring at Shahab through her tears. Her curly hair was a complete mess and her mascara left black streaks under her eyes and down her cheeks.

I looked back at Shahab. "Let them go."

"No." His smile was without any emotion. "I'm enjoying this."

"What is 'this'?" Not only did I need to stall for time, I was actually interested in his answer.

"Their suffering." His smile turned into a sneer. "That makes me a psychopath. But you already know this. You've studied me for the last year. And you've ruined my life for the last year."

"I did no such thing." I shrugged, knowing how to make my indifference believable. "You're the criminal. You're the one who ruined your own life." I sighed as if I was bored. "Why am I here? What do you need from me?"

He blinked in surprise, but quickly recovered. "Where is Sahar?"

"Sahar is dead."

"Don't lie to me!" He put the can in his trouser pocket and reached out for Francine. She flinched back, but he grabbed her by the hair and pulled her to stand next to him. The whimper that came from her tested the hold I had over the looming shutdown.

It took every bit of focus I had not to look at Francine, not to make sure she was okay. I turned up the volume of Mozart's Violin Sonata playing in my mind. I shrugged again. "I'm not lying. Sahar Hatami is dead. You know that. You received the death certificate."

This time he stepped towards me, his posture threatening. "Don't play games with me."

"I'm only telling you the truth."

"And that is why I want you here." He glanced up to the left, recalling a memory. "You impressed me with your honesty when we worked together in Strasbourg. It's hard to think if there's ever been anyone else who has been this honest with me."

"You've been deceitful for a long time. I can't imagine too many of your acquaintances are known for their honesty." This was exhausting. I had indeed lied to him when I'd said I wasn't playing games. I was using my skills in a manner I loathed. But this was important.

I needed to do this if I wanted to keep Francine and Roxy safe. Alive.

"Tell me where the woman I married is." He pulled Francine's hair until her head was completely tilted back. Tears flowed out of the corners of her eyes into her hair. "Or this one's neck will be snapped."

I looked towards Roxy's room. The door was open and the room empty as far as I could see. There was no sign of Natálie or Klára. Or Phillip. "I don't know where she is. When I left here, she was sitting on that sofa." I pointed to the sofa behind him. "I don't see her here and I don't know where she is."

"They do." He shook Francine's head. More tears flowed from her eyes.

I looked away. "That is possible."

"Ask them."

I'd learned a lot watching Manny and Daniel in situations such as this. I tilted my head in an obvious thinking pose. "Only if you'll first answer a question for me."

Shahab studied me for two seconds. "Okay, I'll play your game."

"Are you ill?" I pointed at his sweaty face. Bree had been right. He looked physically ill. I remembered his healthy skin and clear eyes from our first meeting in Strasbourg. Now his eyes were bloodshot and his skin had a gray sheen to it. The way he braced his legs made me think he wasn't feeling stable on his feet.

He snorted. "Yes, I am. Jan killed me."

"You're still alive."

"But as good as dead. I had myself tested and the doctor said I have maybe one more week to live." He held out his hand holding the weapon. "See how I'm shaking? And sweating? Jan poisoned me."

"How is that possible?" I now understood the passage in the last pages of Doctor Novotný's book. "You controlled his days, his movement, his everything."

"Not as well as I thought." He trained the weapon on Roxy. "She told me the other doctor was wrong. I don't even have three days."

I glanced at Roxy and she nodded. Her chin wobbled with suppressed emotion. "I'm surprised he's still standing."

"And while I'm still standing, I want to see my wife."

I looked at Roxy, but changed my mind and made

myself look at Francine. Her left hand was pressed against her side, her thumb and middle finger in unnatural positions. Shahab had broken her fingers. I forced my eyes away and looked at her face. Her head was still uncomfortably tilted, but she was looking at me. Anger was predominant on her face. Overwhelming relief flooded me, but I only raised one eyebrow as I continued studying her. "Do you know where she is?"

Her lips twitched. I knew she understood I was trying to stall for time. She whimpered. "Yes."

"Where is she?" Shahab shouted into Francine's ear. She turned her head and spat in his face. He threw her on the floor and kicked out at her, but she was too fast. She rolled away from him, bumping her hand in the process. The agony on her face made me gasp.

Roxy got down on the floor and helped Francine back on the sofa.

"Get her to tell me!" Shahab aimed his weapon at the two women, his trembling hand worrying me. "Or they'll both die like that scum-of-the-earth journalist." He frowned and looked at me, a smile replacing his frown. "Did she die with all those infidel tourists?"

"No." I took a step to the right to force him away from looking at Francine and Roxy. "She's still alive."

"Impossible!" He shook his weapon at me. "What did you do?"

"What you wanted. Your plan was to get us away from here so you could find Sahar." I didn't want to bring his focus back to Roxy and Francine by mentioning the part of his plan to get us away from the hotel so he could hurt them. "You didn't succeed completely. We left, but we also managed to disable the opioid weapon on Charles Bridge and in the Free Women's Council."

He took a step back. "How did you know?"

"Really?" I used the word, tone and facial expression Nikki so often used to communicate her disbelief. "You are smart enough to know that I've built a complete profile on you and can predict your every move."

"Then you're not as smart as you think you are." For a moment, his tongue pushed between his lips—a sign of triumph. "You think I only created three weapons? Jan made many more for me. Everyone who played a role in taking Sahar away from me will suffer."

I rolled my eyes like Nikki did. "We also got your device before it was delivered to the women's clinic." My mind raced to use everything I'd learned against Shahab. "And we've already cleared the US embassy as well as the police headquarters and the offices of the Movement for Women's Equal Rights." His micro-expressions confirmed each guess I took. I only hoped Ivan was listening and sending his people to evacuate these buildings immediately. And that Bree was still able to remain standing. "Tell me this, if Doctor Novotný made the perfect weapon for you so you could exact your revenge, why did you torture him?"

"He betrayed me!" Shahab swayed on his feet, but took a step to the side and braced himself, his focus now completely on me. "He started feeding me this poison and then he stole all my data and stored it somewhere."

"We know." I made sure my smile was smug. "We have all that information."

"You think you know everything. You don't!" He reached for the can in his pocket, but stopped when I took a step closer.

My heart was racing, my breathing hard to control. I knew Manny, Vinnie and Colin would do everything in their power to ensure Daniel, Ivan and the team could come in here to neutralise Shahab. But I didn't know if I would be able to maintain this for much longer.

Shahab was sweating more, his blinking had increased and his eyes were constantly shifting around the room. He was escalating. I had to keep him engaged. "You are right. I don't know everything. I know why you tortured and killed all your other victims. But Antonin Korn? The fentanyl you put on his briefcase would've killed him quickly and painlessly. Why?"

"He was a friend." Confusion flittered across his face. "He didn't betray me. Not like everyone else. He was a friend. He helped me a lot over the years when others turned their backs on me. He wasn't like Sahar." He jerked his gaze from left to right. "Where is she? I need to speak to her. Where is Sahar?"

His hand was shaking out of control now, the weapon rattling in his hand. He pointed the gun at me and I froze. Even with the shaking, it would be easy to injure me fatally at this distance. "Where is Sahar?"

Everything happened at once. A familiar-looking device

rolled into the room. I didn't have time to warn Roxy and Francine. I slapped my hands over my ears, closed my eyes and dropped to the floor.

A terrifying bang sounded in the room, the blinding light penetrating my eyelids. A gunshot went off, followed by three more shots. Roxy screamed.

I couldn't move.

But the need to see if my friends were unharmed was immense. Strong enough to fight the looming shutdown. I couldn't get my hands to move, but managed to open my eyes.

Roxy was in Vinnie's arms, weeping against his chest. Francine was standing next to Manny, looking down at Shahab.

He was lying in front of me, his eyes wide open in death. Blood flowed freely from a perfectly round hole in the centre of his forehead. I scrambled back and hugged my knees to my chest.

Manny put his arm around Francine's shoulders and she sagged against him.

"Jenny." Colin kneeled in front of me, in my personal space, his body less than ten centimetres from mine. He put his hands lightly over mine—still against my ears. "Look at me. Focus on me."

I couldn't. Even though I was looking at him, I was still seeing the fear on Francine's face, the terror on Roxy's. If I'd been able to speak, I would've asked Colin to take me away from this carnage. I would've told him to first make sure Francine got the best medical care for her fingers, that Roxy had her favourite sneakers and that Bree was transported to the closest hospital.

I couldn't speak. I couldn't move. I could only stare at Colin as he moved even closer. The moment his arms closed around me and he gently pushed my head into his shoulder, I surrendered myself to the shutdown.

Chapter TWENTY-THREE

"I'M HERE! I'M HERE!" Roxy ran into my apartment, her curls bouncing around her head. She rushed to the kitchen holding a plastic bag out in front of her. "I've got your parmesan cheese."

Vinnie turned away from the stove where he was preparing dinner for us and took the bag. He opened it and staggered back. The look of horror on his face was genuine when he looked at Roxy. "This is cheap Grana Padano. Not the Parmigiano-Reggiano I asked you to buy. Oh, Roxy."

She burst out in giggles. "Oh, the look on your face. Oh, honey." She reached into her handbag and brought out a brown paper bag. "Here's your fancy cheese. Oh, man. You'd think I gave you a bag full of coal."

"It would be better than that plastic cheese you threatened me with." Vinnie threw the first bag on the counter. "If you truly love me, you'll never do that again."

I settled deeper into one of the two sofas in my sitting area and sipped my camomile tea. Colin was next to me, reading an article on his tablet about a new art exhibition. We were expecting Phillip, Nikki, Eric, Pink and Daniel to join us soon. The bantering in the kitchen settled my tumultuous emotions.

It had been a difficult four days since we'd returned from Prague. As soon as Ivan's team had killed Shahab, Phillip and the two women had returned from where he had hidden them on the small balcony off his hotel room. Shahab had been through all our hotel rooms including Phillip's, but had not seen the door leading to the balcony off Phillip's room. It had been Klára's clear thinking to partly close the curtain that had kept them hidden.

The memory of the fear I had experienced was still with me and I'd been fighting shutdowns every day since. The one that had followed the confrontation with Shahab had been one of my longer shutdowns. Colin had managed to take me to our room and had waited with me. In that time, Ivan's crime scene investigators had processed our hotel area and had mostly cleaned up. The moment my mind had allowed me to return, I'd insisted we return to Strasbourg.

Roxy was still giggling as she walked from the kitchen past Francine and held out her left fist. "Got him good, didn't I?"

Francine bumped Roxy's fist with her uninjured hand. "I couldn't have done that better myself. But I am wearing better shoes than you."

"Pah!" Roxy sat down next to Francine at the dining room table and lifted her foot. Today she was wearing canvas sneakers printed with abstract colours. "My shoes are gorgeous."

"It's all your fault, Franny." Vinnie shook a wooden spoon at Francine. "You're pulling my pure, innocent Rox to your dark side."

Francine slowly lifted her injured hand and turned it around. Her hand was wrapped in bandages, her middle finger and thumb in splints to immobilise them. The way she was holding her hand to Vinnie was giving him a rude gesture. "Welcome to my dark side, Vin."

He chuckled and shook his head. "I can't be angry with you when you're banged up like that."

"Someone make them stop." Manny slouched on the other sofa and put a news magazine down next to him. "Or make her stop." He turned to glare at Francine. "Do you know how many times I've been given the finger in the last two days? At least once an hour. Once every bloody hour."

Francine's smile became even more mischievous as she once again lifted her hand and turned it, this time towards Manny. "I don't think I've done it in the last hour."

He muttered an expletive as she blew him a kiss. He picked up his magazine again. "You're bloody annoying."

"You love me!" Francine bumped fists with Roxy again. "But not as much as Ivan's bosses love him."

"Hmm." Manny looked at me. "Did I tell you Ivan phoned me?"

"No."

"He said his bosses are saying *they* were the ones who pushed to investigate Shahab and stop the opioid weapon. They are taking full credit for finding and securing fifteen devices."

"That isn't what happened." I remembered the stress on Ivan's features as he'd navigated between our investigation and his bosses' demands. I also remembered his—and our—relief when we'd received confirmation that fifteen devices had been disarmed. Roxy had used Doctor Novotný's journal and other data to calculate that the weaponised opioid analogue Doctor Novotný had made would have filled no more than fifteen canisters similar to the one on Charles' Bridge. Ivan had slumped on the sofa when his old team had phoned him with the good news. "Ivan's bosses didn't even want us there."

"That's politics, Doc." He shrugged. "But at least Shahab is out of the picture."

"Did Ivan say anything about Klára's screwed-up parents?" Vinnie opened the oven and a mouth-watering smell filled the apartment.

"Reza and Maryam are both under arrest and are being held in Finland." The approval was clear on Manny's face. "Klára helped the Finnish police, Interpol and the Czech police set this up. She phoned her parents and said now that Shahab was dead, she wanted to come home. That she's in Helsinki, but too scared to travel to Iran. She asked that they both come get her. They were on the first plane out of Iran."

"What about the Iranian government?" Colin asked. "I can't imagine they are happy about such a sting."

"They completely distanced themselves from Klára's parents. As soon as they found out about Shahab's plan to kill hundreds or thousands of people in Prague in what would've been a terrorist attack, they wanted nothing to do with them any more."

"Makes sense," Colin said. "Iran is trying hard to maintain good relations with Europe to continue trading. This would've destroyed everything they'd negotiated in the last year."

The front door opened. "Ding-dong! We're here." Nikki and Pink walked in, Eric already wiggling to get down from Pink's hip. Phillip and Daniel followed, Daniel closing the door behind them. The moment Pink put Eric down, he ran towards me.

Colin caught him a moment before he reached me and lifted him high in the air. Eric squealed with laughter and kicked his legs. Colin lowered him and put him between us on the sofa. Eric immediately scuttled over to me and climbed on my lap, facing me.

"Hello, Eric." I loved looking at the unadulterated joy on his face. Pure emotions, as yet untouched by life.

"Dohgee." He leaned forward to kiss me and I pulled back. His smile dimmed and a small frown wrinkled his forehead. Then he threw his arms around my neck and hugged me so tight, I felt panic starting to rise.

"Easy there, tiger." Colin lifted Eric's one arm and tickled his ribs until he giggled. It was enough distraction for Eric to lose interest in kissing and hugging me. He turned on my lap and sat down facing everyone else.

"Look at him. Like a king on his throne." Nikki walked to the dining room table. "Spoiled brat."

"Genevieve." Phillip sat down next to Manny. "How are you?"

"I'm well." I studied him. "You look better. More relaxed."

"Well, that's what happens when I'm safe in my own home and I can sleep without worrying about a daughter I never had and a madman's revenge."

"True dat." Nikki sat down with Roxy and Francine. "Hey, ladies. How's the hand, Francine?"

Francine slowly raised her hand and gave Nikki the now familiar gesture. Nikki's laughter made us all smile. Francine lowered her hand and sighed. "It hurts, but the doctors said I'll be as good as new in a few weeks. Until then, I can't move the two fingers Shahab broke."

"Motherfucker." Vinnie brought the oven dish to the table and put it on a wrought-iron trivet. "He got what he deserved."

"Totes." Nikki stared at Francine's hand, her concern real. "So it's really going to be okay?"

"I hope so." Francine lifted her hand and turned it. "The doctors said there's no damage to any nerves or tendons. I just have to keep it still. Which means I can now only hack with one hand. And I'm getting quite good at that."

"Bloody hell." Manny shook his head, but there was no malice in his expression.

"Talking about hacking"—Roxy twirled a curl around her finger—"did you find any more of Shahab's hacking?"

"I did." Francine straightened and pulled her tablet closer. "I found his signature in a few places. He'd hacked the Czech immigration department and a few more Czech government departments."

"Looking for Sahar." Nikki had insisted on hearing the

whole story when we'd returned. I hadn't wanted to relive it verbally, so Colin and Vinnie had regaled her with the outcome of our latest case. "Poor woman."

"I looked through my logs and saw that he'd tried a few times to get past my firewalls to get into our system." Francine flicked her hair over her shoulder. "And of course he didn't get in. But most of his hacking was done in the Czech Republic."

"Thank all the saints we're out of that hell-hole." Manny picked up his magazine.

Nikki's eyes were wide. "Why? Prague is beautiful. The whole country is gorgeous. Why don't you like it?"

"Ooh, now we're in for it." Francine lowered herself as if hiding from Manny.

"Bugger off, the lot of you." Manny got up. "Is dinner ready yet? I'm hungry."

"Yup." Vinnie put the last dish on the table and stood back. "I hope this will be enough."

"This is enough to feed an army." Daniel slapped Pink on his back. "You're lucky that you get to eat here so often."

We went to the table and the teasing and joking continued. There was a higher level of relief than usual at the end of our cases. It took only one look at Francine's hand to bring back the debilitating horror I'd experienced while speaking to Shahab. Controlling that fear, my expressions and the conversation had been one of the hardest things I'd done.

It had affected all of us. Vinnie had always been physically affectionate towards Roxy. But since Prague, it seemed like he always needed to touch her. Even if it was playing with her hair or just sitting shoulder to shoulder.

Manny and Francine appeared emotionally closer than before. They would often share looks, and it was clear there was deep emotion behind those gazes. It was hard to explain, but what I saw in their nonverbal communication made me think this had made them stronger as a couple.

Colin was the same as before—supportive, quiet, present. But I was dealing with my inability to have stopped Shahab in time, to have prevented Francine from being injured and to have supported my friends when they'd needed me. No matter how much I wanted to learn how to do this or how much they needed me, when my brain was overwhelmed it would shut down. At the most crucial of times. I loathed being unreliable, yet unable to do anything about it.

"Bree phoned me." Phillip leaned a bit closer to me. "Her toes have been set and the doctors say she'll be fine."

"Yeah, she phoned me too." Francine took a large serving of the butternut lasagne Vinnie had prepared. "She's seriously peeved that she can't wear her hipster boots for six weeks. I found the best cupcake place in Düsseldorf and had them deliver a dozen cupcakes to her. She loves me."

Phillip smiled. "Her article will be published next week. She sent it to me to read." He nodded in approval. "It's exceptionally well-written. The research that went into it and the amount of information she has is impressive."

"She had some help." Francine elbowed Manny, which caused him to drop a spoon of beetroot salad on his plate. Some of it spilled on the table cloth. It would take careful cleaning to get that stain completely out.

"I just gave her a bloody email address."

"Oh, pah!" Francine leaned back in her chair to give Manny space to cut her lasagne into bite-size pieces. "You spent an hour talking to her on the phone. Don't think I didn't hear all your suggestions and advice. You like her."

"Hmph." Manny pushed her plate back to her and focused on his food.

"I'm still trying to wrap my mind around her dude-woman situation." Vinnie jerked, then looked at Roxy. "Don't kick me under the table. I know she's a woman. But she…" He jerked again. "Okay, fine. I'll just shut up."

"You better. Or next time I'll buy that grated special parmesan."

"Roxy. No." Vinnie's whisper was filled with horror. "They put wood pulp in that cheese. And Swiss and cheddar and some other stuff. Did you know that?"

"Wait. What?" Nikki put her knife and fork down. "Wood pulp? For reals?"

"Yup." Vinnie put a large forkful of lasagne in his mouth and nodded.

"That's just gross." She looked at Eric in his high chair. "From now on, you're only eating cheese Uncle Vinnie buys."

"Do we know what happened to Antonin?" Phillip

dabbed his mouth with a white napkin. "I phoned him, but that number was no longer in use."

Daniel put his fork back on his plate and cleared his throat. "Ivan told me Antonin, his wife and his lover went into the Czech version of a witness protection programme. He'll stay there until all the other arrests have been made and those people are in jail."

"How many arrests have been made?" Pink asked.

"Seventeen so far." Daniel looked at Manny. "Another thing his bosses are very happy about."

"It's been a good week for them."

"And Tomas Broz?" Nikki asked.

"Hmm." Daniel frowned. "I forgot to ask. I had the impression that his expensive lawyer was going to get him a deal that would not include any jail time."

"That thief will land behind bars sooner or later." Manny stretched to get more salad. He paused and looked at Colin as he put the salad bowl next to his plate. "Any word from your friend?"

"Ty?" Colin raised one eyebrow. "He's pissed off."

"And how." Vinnie snorted. "The dude almost bled out in that car."

"Bled out?" Pink asked. "What happened?"

"Shahab shot him, but missed his heart by less than a centimetre." Colin was still troubled about this. "Ty is pissed off because he underestimated Shahab and almost got killed."

"Didn't you tell him about Shahab's training?" Nikki asked.

"I did." Colin shifted in his chair. "And I thought he was smart enough to listen to me. I'm just glad he pulled through."

"Maybe his bestest bestie will also give him a fab gift voucher." Francine winked at me.

"Not again." Manny sighed.

"What voucher?" Nikki leaned closer to Francine.

"Doc made the bloody mistake of giving this one—" Manny gestured with his fork towards Francine"—a stupid spa voucher. If she's not giving me the finger, I have to hear about how she's going to love spending four hours being pampered. Who spends four hours in such a place?"

"I do." Francine leaned back in her chair, her dreamy expression exaggerated. "Oh, I do."

"Um, Manny?" Nikki's innocent expression warned me. "Why don't you like Prague?"

"Oh, for the love of…" Manny put his knife down with a clunk. "It's a bloody horrible place."

"Tell them." Francine's smile was both mischievous and understanding.

"No."

"Then I will." Francine rubbed her palms together and inhaled.

"Oh, hell no. You'll just add all kind of ridiculous details." He sighed and glared at Nikki. "If you laugh, I'm disowning you."

"Ooh! I'm in your will?" Nikki bounced in her seat and clapped her hands. That made Eric clap his hands and laugh, which made everyone either laugh or smile. Nikki settled down and leaned towards Manny. "I promise to try not to laugh. Please tell us."

"I was arrested in Prague once." Manny's lips tightened and he closed his eyes as reactions exploded around the table. Vinnie's booming laughter, Colin's vengeful smile, Roxy's giggles and Francine's faux-sympathetic noises made him even more uncomfortable. "If you're finished having your fun?"

"Ooh, we're finished." Nikki tried to control her expression, but a smile kept tugging at the corners of her mouth. "Why were you arrested?"

"Yes, Millard." Colin's tone and expression were filled with satire. "Why?"

"Mistaken identity." Manny waited again for everyone's comments to die down. "I was there on an Interpol investigation and rented a car. But the damn rental company—which was recommended by a colleague, by the way—had a few stolen vehicles on their lot. And I so happened to be driving one when the police stopped me."

"Oh, this is beautiful." Colin rested his hands over his heart and leaned back in his chair. "Millard. You are giving me a gift worth more than money could ever buy."

"They had him in cuffs and everything." Francine raised her uninjured hand when Manny swung around to glare at her. "What? You're not telling the whole story." She looked back at us. "He resisted arrest and they wrestled him to the ground. He tore one of those horrid brown trousers he likes so much. He should've been arrested for wearing those."

"Bloody hell." Manny rubbed his hand over his face. "I might've insulted the officer and he unfortunately spoke fluent English." He looked at Colin. "They cuffed me, threw me in the back of their car and locked me up. I spent the night in a dingy little cell. Happy?"

"As a pig in mud." Colin bowed his head. "Thank you."

And so it went on. I took another helping of the butternut lasagne and watched the people around my table. Eric was making a mess on his high chair tray and Nikki kept cleaning up while glancing and smiling at me. The others were chatting, laughing and teasing each other.

Observing them, I realised this was the reason I was willing to continue working on these cases. The last extremely distressing days had resulted in saving hundreds if not thousands of lives. There were families around a table similar to mine tonight that didn't even know their lives had been in danger a few days ago when they were taking selfies on Charles Bridge.

I took the last bite of lasagne and hoped that for as long as I could and as long as my autistic mind would allow, I would continue working with these people in my apartment to make a small difference in the world.

~ ~ ~ ~ ~

Look at Sirani's Venus and Cupid*, learn more about Elisabetta Sirani, Artificial Intelligence, Machine Learning, Deep Leaning and Opioids at:*

http://estelleryan.com/the-sirani-connection.html

~ ~ ~ ~ ~

Be first to find out when Genevieve's next adventure will be published. Sign up for the newsletter at

http://estelleryan.com/contact.html

~ ~ ~ ~ ~

Other books in the Genevieve Lenard Series:

Book 1: The Gauguin Connection

Book 2: The Dante Connection

Book 3: The Braque Connection

Book 4: The Flinck Connection

Book 5: The Courbet Connection

Book 6: The Pucelle Connection

Book 7: The Léger Connection

Book 8: The Morisot Connection

Book 9: The Vecellio Connection

and more…

For more books in this series, go to
http://estelleryan.com/books.html

Please visit me on my **Facebook Page** *to become part of the process as I'm writing Genevieve's next adventure.*

and

Explore my **website** *to find out more about me and Genevieve.*

Made in the USA
Monee, IL
21 August 2024

64240677R00204